"It sounds like fun." But then, everything did when Sunny and Piper were involved.

"It is fun. We usually have two or three residents with us—whoever has nowhere else to go—but this year, everyone I've talked with has other plans, so it was just going to be Piper and me. We'd love to have you join us. And don't feel like you have to stay for the whole board game and Christmas light part of the day unless you want to."

"I want to." Maybe it wasn't wise, but Adam wanted to spend as much time with Sunny and Piper as possible before he left for good. Maybe memories of a Thanksgiving celebration together would brighten some evenings when he was alone. "What can I bring?"

"Just yourself. You're all I need." Her eyes widened slightly, as though she hadn't intended to say the last part. Their eyes met and held.

"Sunny..." he whispered and took a step closer.

Dear Reader,

This story is all about family. Sunny Galloway has no relatives except for her daughter, Piper, but her job as activities director at the Easy Living Senior Apartments in Palmer, Alaska, puts her and Piper at the center of the Easy Living family. So when a new real estate management company buys the apartment building and it looks like they might be shut down, she and the residents jump into action to save this special place.

If you've read *Alaskan Dreams* or *An Alaskan Homecoming*, you'll be familiar with the Mat Mates, six octogenarians who share a yoga class and a penchant for creative problem-solving. If you haven't, don't worry, you'll get to know Bonnie and her friends as they dive in to rescue their community and maybe give Sunny's romantic life a little nudge while they're at it.

I hope you enjoy this, my tenth book in the Northern Lights series. If you'd like to receive news about books, giveaways and recipes, you can sign up for my newsletter at bethcarpenterbooks.blogspot.com. Just go to the Newsletter tab. You can find my Facebook, Instagram and Twitter contacts there, as well. I'd love to hear from you.

Happy reading!

Beth Carpenter

HEARTWARMING

An Alaskan Family Thanksgiving

—

Beth Carpenter

⬙HARLEQUIN
HEARTWARMING

H HARLEQUIN®
HEARTWARMING™

ISBN-13: 978-1-335-58473-1

An Alaskan Family Thanksgiving

Copyright © 2022 by Lisa Deckert

Harlequin Enterprises ULC
22 Adelaide St. West, 41st Floor
Toronto, Ontario M5H 4E3, Canada
www.Harlequin.com

Printed in U.S.A.

Beth Carpenter is thankful for good books, a good dog, a good man and a dream job creating happily-ever-afters. She and her husband now split their time between Alaska and Arizona, where she occasionally encounters a moose in the yard or a scorpion in the basement. She prefers the moose.

Books by Beth Carpenter

Harlequin Heartwarming

A Northern Lights Novel

The Alaskan Catch
A Gift for Santa
Alaskan Hideaway
An Alaskan Proposal
Sweet Home Alaska
Alaskan Dreams
An Alaskan Family Christmas
An Alaskan Homecoming
An Alaskan Family Found

Visit the Author Profile page
at Harlequin.com for more titles.

This book is dedicated to the cooks, the shoppers, the table setters, the flower arrangers, the dishwashers and everyone else who pitches in to create wonderful Thanksgiving meals for friends and family. And especially to the memory of my mother, who hosted so many of them. I'll be forever grateful for her unwavering love and support throughout my life.

Also thanks to my editor, Kathryn Lye, and my agent, Barbara Rosenberg, for all you've done to make this book the best it can be.

CHAPTER ONE

FRAMED AGAINST A backdrop of snowcapped mountains, the old-fashioned water tower read Palmer, which meant Adam Lloyd had arrived in the right place after following Highway 1 from Anchorage. He wasn't sure he'd ever been on a Highway 1 before. Not a lot of roads in Alaska, apparently. Now he just needed to locate the seniors' apartment complex in Palmer that he'd been assigned to evaluate. Following the GPS instructions, he passed the public library and turned right onto the next street.

"Halt!"

Adam hit the brakes as a woman wearing a neon-orange top stepped into his path and held a broomstick horizontally in front of her. Matching orange streaks formed a starburst in her white hair, like the orange-and-vanilla ice cream treats Adam had loved as a child. Behind her, a Canada goose stepped off the curb, followed closely by the rest of the flock. Most of the geese seemed a little smaller than the first, probably this year's goslings, almost grown and ready to fly south.

Seemingly in no hurry, they meandered between the pavement and the curb, but eventually they all crossed and moved on toward the grassy area behind the library. A second full-size goose examined Adam's rental car with a beady eye as he brought up the rear guard. Once the geese were all safely across the road, the orange-haired lady nodded her thanks at him and returned to the sidewalk to sweep up a few fallen leaves. Apparently, goose crossing guard wasn't her primary occupation.

Mindful of more possible hazards, Adam eased forward beside the two-story building surrounded by wide lawns and gardens and spotted the Easy Living Apartments Parking sign. Only someone had added *SL* in red paint before the *E*. Graffiti was never a good omen. He made a mental note to take care of that, first thing.

The parking lot was almost full, but he located a space in the back and got out to stretch his stiff muscles. After putting in a full workday yesterday wrapping up loose ends, he'd caught a late flight from Boise to Seattle, laid over for three hours, and then flown overnight on to Anchorage. He claimed his luggage and rental car and driven to Palmer, arriving at what should have been morning rush hour. In Palmer, Alaska, however, the only traffic holdups seemed to be the lines at the brightly painted drive-through coffee carts.

If you didn't count the geese.

Despite his best efforts, a yawn escaped. It might be better to head straight for the extended-stay hotel the office staff had reserved in nearby Wasilla rather than check out the apartment complex. After all, no one was expecting him for another three days. But the sooner he got a handle on the situation here, the sooner he could get the job done and return to headquarters. No use wasting a weekend sitting around.

A small blue car pulled into a spot not far from him. A woman hopped out, her red-blond ponytail bobbing as she lifted the hatchback, held it open with one hand while she reached inside for what looked like a broken ski pole and propped the trunk open. She leaned in to pick up something big and furry, staggered back a few feet, and gently set what turned out to be an elderly golden retriever on his feet.

As Adam drew nearer, the white-faced dog turned soft brown eyes in his direction and wandered over. Adam reached to pet him, and the woman said, "Hi. That's Bob you're petting, and I'm Sunny Galloway." She flashed a smile, and the brilliance of it almost made

Adam blink. "Linda told me you'd be coming by this morning. We really appreciate your help. This thing just seems to get bigger every year, and we're running short of space." She reached inside the car and hefted out a large cardboard carton. "Here, could you take this one, please? I'll show you where we're setting up and get you started on the project."

Before Adam could ask who Linda was, the woman had deposited a surprisingly heavy box in his arms. She then balanced a slightly smaller box on her own hip, and in a well-practiced move, pulled out the stick and tossed it inside while the hatchback closed itself. After throwing another dazzling smile over her shoulder, she started toward the building.

The dog ambled after her and Adam followed. "You need new lift supports."

"What's that?"

"Your car. The hatchback needs new lift supports."

"Oh, I know. It's on the list, believe me. Right after new snow tires."

As they approached the building, an older man held the door open. "Here, Sunny. Let me take that."

"I've got it, Ralph, but thanks for getting the door. Where's Alice?" She led Adam and the dog into a spacious lobby. Several healthy-looking potted plants lined the front atrium-style window, and a few café tables and chairs had been arranged, as well.

"Alice is already in with the others, setting up." The man eyed Adam. "Looks like you've got yourself a better helper, anyhow. Is this your boyfriend?"

She laughed. "I told you, Ralph. Once I found Alice had already scooped you off the market, I swore off dating. This is Linda's grand-nephew, who volunteered to build the new bookcases for the reading room." She looked toward Adam. "I'm sorry, I don't think she told me your name."

"Adam, but I'm—"

Before he could explain that he wasn't any relation to this Linda person, the woman with the orange-streaked hair came rushing inside, still carrying her broom. "Those skateboarders are back. I'll bet they're the ones who vandalized the sign. Sleazy Living, indeed. If we can't scrub the paint off, we'll have to take down the sign and put up a new one. We can't have people thinking we've got something disreputable going on here. Especially not now, with the new manager coming. It's posted—no skateboarding. But if I run them off, they'll probably paint more graffiti just to spite me."

Sunny spoke up. "Bea, were they actually

skateboarding or were they just carrying their boards toward the park?" She moved toward the elevator at the back of the lobby and pushed the up button with her elbow.

"Carrying their boards," Bea admitted, frowning. Then her face brightened. "I know. I'll grab my Rollerblades and ask if I can skate with them. That will scare them off for sure."

Ralph grinned. "You get 'em, Bea."

As the woman dashed down a hallway, the elevator doors opened. Sunny stepped in, moving aside to make room for Adam and the dog. "Bea used to be a teacher," she explained. After leaning her box on the rail, Sunny pushed the button for the second floor. As the door closed, she wrinkled her nose. It was a nice nose, with a sprinkling of freckles on the bridge. "She's not usually such a fusspot about kids and their skateboards. She's just keyed up because we're expecting a new manager on Monday, and she wants everything to look its best. She's on a mission to find out who messed up the sign out front."

"I saw that. Is vandalism an ongoing problem here?"

Sunny chuckled. "Not at all. The closest thing to vandalism I've seen in the three years I've been here is the occasional dog walker taking a shortcut through a flower bed. I have a feeling one of the other residents changed the sign just to yank Bea's chain. I haven't had a chance to examine the sign yet, but it looked to me like someone used poster paint. If so, it will wash right off."

That was good news anyway. "So, you work here?"

"Yes. Sorry, I guess I didn't tell you that. I'm the activities director. At least for now. Hopefully, I'll still have a job come Monday after the new guy shows up. He's from an out-of-state real estate investment outfit that somehow ended up buying this place, and nobody knows exactly what's going to happen." A shadow crossed her face briefly, but then the smile returned. "Lou—he's the manager now, but he's retiring so he and his wife can move to Oregon to be near the grandkids—he says he'll put in a good word for me, so, fingers crossed."

Adam knew he should, in good conscience, identify himself immediately as the dreaded new manager. In fact, he might be doing her a favor to hint that while nothing was decided yet, it wouldn't be a bad idea for her to start checking online job sites. But he wasn't officially on the clock yet, and he just couldn't summon the will to wipe that beautiful smile off her face this early in the morning. Especially since he was running on practically no sleep. Instead, he gave a noncommittal "Mmm."

Sunny seemed to find that answer enough. "I don't know if Linda has talked to you about it, but the residents are really worried about this new ownership. Everybody loves Lou, and nobody knows what this new guy might have in mind. Bea's theory is that if everything is spit-shined, he'll take one look, decide we're doing something right, and keep it all the same. She's been following the cleaning crew around with a white glove, looking for specks they might have missed.

"Alice says it's not about appearance, it's about the bottom line. Phil, our resident pessimist, is sure the new company is either raising rents or tearing the place down to put in a giant box store, although there are less than seven thousand people in Palmer and it's only about fifteen minutes to shop in Wasilla, so I can't see why they'd want to do that. But change is always scary."

Bob leaned against her leg, and she shifted so she could free a hand to stroke his head. "Anyway, I guess we'll just have to wait and see. Maybe the new manager will turn out to be great and make this place even better. Who knows?"

"Right." Adam, deciding a change of topic was in order, nodded at the dog. "So, this is Bob?"

"Yes. Bob Cratchit."

Adam chuckled. "You named him after a Dickens character?"

"Bob's original owner was a retired literature professor. About two years ago, he had a health issue and decided to move to an assisted living place near his son in Colorado." The elevator door opened, and she hefted her box and started down the hall, still chatting. "He was able to take his chihuahua, Tiny Tim, along with him, but they didn't accept big dogs like Bob, so Bob came to live with us."

Us presumably being Sunny and her husband, although Ralph, downstairs, had teased her about a boyfriend, so maybe not. It didn't matter, one way or the other. Adam never dated people he worked with, and her marital status had no bearing on her job performance. Still, he wondered.

Adam followed her toward a set of open double doors at the end of the hall, still toting the larger box, which was growing heavier by the minute.

What was in there, gold bars?

The room, with a bank of windows overlooking the park across the street, buzzed with activity. Several people were unpacking boxes of books. Others were arranging chairs and pillows into conversational groupings or hanging motivational posters on the wall. One woman in silver-framed glasses taped a laminated sign labeled Mystery to a bookcase next to the door. Near the windows, a man about Adam's age was operating a miter saw. No doubt Linda's grandnephew, the bookcase builder, which meant it was time for Adam to disappear before Sunny put two and two together.

A woman with a long gray braid tapped his arm. "If those are the donated books Sunny picked up, you can just set them here."

Gratefully, he placed the box on a folding table. The woman opened the lid and pulled out a few slim volumes. The top one, entitled *A is for Australia*, had a cartoon kangaroo on the cover. "Oh good. We needed more picture books."

"Are picture books popular here?" It was hard to imagine, but then Adam had never worked with a group of seniors before. Maybe the ABC books were for visiting grandkids.

"Oh yes. We get a lot of first and second graders, and some even bring their preschool siblings."

"Preschool? I thought this was a seniors' housing development."

"Yes, of course, but we've been sponsoring the library's after-school reading program for several years now. Isn't that why you're here?"

"No. I, uh, was just passing by," Adam said, hedging, as he eased out the doors into the hall. If he wasn't gone soon, he was going to be forced to come clean about his real identity to Sunny, and he preferred that not happen in a room full of people.

He could already tell this assignment wasn't going to be as straightforward as he'd hoped. Generally, an underperforming apartment complex in a good market was a simple fix with minor remodeling and better management. But it was obvious the residents here took pride in the place and if Sunny was to be believed, management was competent, or at least well-liked. So why was it losing money? He found the door to the stairway and stepped inside.

"Adam?" It was Sunny's voice. For an instant, he was tempted to turn back and offer to haul up more books just to see that bright smile again. His better judgment prevailed, however, and he continued down the stairs and out to his car.

Better check into that hotel and get some sleep, after all, because it was obvious he wasn't thinking clearly.

"SUNNY, MY GRANDNEPHEW, Travis, says he can get all three bookcases done today." Linda pushed her silver glasses back up her nose. "He wanted to ask you about paint."

"If your nephew is Travis, then who is Adam?" Sunny looked around, but the man who had carried up the box of books for her was nowhere in sight. "Adam?"

"Is that the name of the handsome man who was carrying your books?" Molly, a member of Linda's yoga group, the Mat Mates, asked with a smile. "I think he left already. Is he a friend of yours? Or more than a friend?"

"I never met him before," Sunny replied truthfully. But she felt her cheeks growing warm under Molly's amused gaze, even though she had nothing to be embarrassed about.

The Mat Mates, six women who had been in the same yoga class for something like thirty years, all currently lived in the Easy Living Apartments. Despite being a decade or two older than most of the other residents, the Mat Mates were indisputably the most active participants in the activities Sunny organized.

Linda, a former librarian, had started the read-ins before Sunny had begun working there, but she had welcomed Sunny's ideas for expanding the program. Molly taught art classes. Rosemary, an octogenarian flower child, freely shared her gardening expertise. Bonnie, Bea, Alice, and Ralph, Alice's husband, who wasn't technically a Mat Mate but was often roped into their projects, were always generous with their time, energy and opinions. And they paid attention to the details—even when Sunny wished they wouldn't.

Bonnie, a former dairy farmer, was grinning at Sunny now. "Aw, honey, you're blushing redder than an Oklahoma sunset after a dust storm."

Sunny swiped her hands over her cheeks, willing the color to subside. Okay, she couldn't help but notice the man was good-looking. And maybe she'd babbled a little, which she tended to do when she was nervous, but that didn't mean she had a thing for the guy. She shouldn't let their teasing get to her. "I saw him in the parking lot, looking around, and I thought he was Linda's nephew."

"No, Travis got here an hour ago." Linda gestured toward the man sawing boards in the back of the room. "He wanted to get an early start. This Adam must be here to visit someone."

"I don't think he's been here before," Molly mused, "or at least I've never seen him. With those bright blue eyes, I'm sure I'd remember."

"Are we talking about that hunk that came

in with Sunny?" Bea had breezed into the activities room and made a beeline toward them. "What a hottie!"

"What happened with the skateboarders?" Sunny asked her, attempting to redirect the conversation.

Bea shrugged. "They were already gone by the time I found my skates and made it back. So, was that a new boyfriend with you in the lobby?"

"No." Sunny allowed a little note of irritation into her voice. "Why does everyone keep asking me that?"

"Because they care about you," Molly said gently. "They want to see you happy."

"I am happy," Sunny insisted. "I have Piper, and I have all of you. My plate is full."

"That doesn't mean there's no room for dessert," Bea replied. She tilted her head and openly checked out the carpenter as he positioned another board in his saw. "If you're not interested in the handsome man you came in with, how about Linda's grandnephew? He's cute, too."

"His wife would agree," Linda informed her. "But I do want Sunny to meet him." She linked her arm through Sunny's and drew her away from the others. "Bea means well, you know."

"I suppose." One of the few downsides to working with the residents at Easy Living was their tendency to bulldoze through normal professional boundaries. It was like having sixty beloved but outspoken grandparents hanging around with her at work all day. Sunny looked around the room at the posters on the wall and the rapidly filling bookcases. "This reading program is really coming together. You've done a great job." Linda had retired many years ago, but that didn't keep her from putting in hours of volunteer work for the library.

"Mostly thanks to you and your organization skills. The first two years, we just had a one-day event giving away donated books. It wasn't until you came that we started the weekly read-ins and prizes. The library staff is excited. They say they've already had a record number of children sign up for the reading program, even though they haven't sent home flyers in the school packets yet."

"Piper signed up Saturday."

"I know." Linda laughed. "Nikki, the children's librarian, told me Piper not only signed up, she recruited two other kids who were only there to use the computers, telling them all about our read-ins and the prizes. We should give Piper an official title, something like Library Ambassador."

Sunny smiled. "She's pretty enthusiastic. Oh,

that reminds me. I sent Lou the request for funds to buy prizes, but I haven't heard back."

"Tilly said she put it in his in-box, but he's been swamped, trying to get everything done before they go. You may have to wait until next week and get approval from the new manager."

"That seems like a lot of fuss. The prizes are just stickers and pencils, stuff like that."

"I know. But Lou and Tilly have been preparing for the big move out of their house as well as the office. They're expecting their first great-grandbaby in three weeks, you know."

"I know. Tilly says it's a girl. She's thrilled. And since Lou has been managing this place since it was built twenty-five years ago, I'm sure there's a ton of stuff to go through." Sunny sighed. "It won't be the same without them. Lou's always been great about finding money for special projects. I hope the new guy won't be a pain about that sort of thing. Molly offered to teach a class in oils next month if we can supply canvases, paints and brushes, but she sent me an initial supply list, and the stuff isn't cheap."

"If he balks, point out that it would normally cost a fortune to get a teacher as good as Molly. After taking her calligraphy class, I hand-lettered the wedding invitations to Travis and Gayle's wedding." They paused the conversation while the carpenter finished cutting a board. "Travis, I wanted you to meet Sunny. She's in charge of activities here."

"Nice to meet you." He offered a hand and Sunny shook it. Bea was right. With his blond hair and friendly grin, Travis was cute. But even if Sunny hadn't known he was married, he wouldn't have given her that butterflies-in-the-stomach, jabber-inducing thrill she'd felt when she first saw Adam. Which was fortunate. It was much easier to work with someone when she wasn't reduced to a babbling bundle of nerves.

"Thank you so much for volunteering. We were really running short of shelf space," she told the carpenter.

"Glad to help. Aunt Linda said you bought paint already. Did you get primer?" Travis asked.

"Yes, but I want you to see it and make sure I bought the right kind. I'll run down and get it out of my car."

Sunny took the stairs. At the front door, she met Ralph coming in, carrying a rag and a spray bottle. "I got the sign cleaned up," he told Sunny, "so let Bea know she can relax. The new manager won't be scandalized."

"That's good news." Sunny had noticed Ralph and a couple of the other men snickering in the corner of the lobby yesterday. "I don't suppose you have any inside information about the possible perpetrators?"

Ralph gave a little smirk. "I'll take the Fifth on that."

"Uh-huh. Well, since you got it all cleaned up, I suppose there's no harm done. Thanks, Ralph."

She got the bookcase paint and primer out of her car, but before she headed upstairs, she noticed that the spot where Adam had parked was now empty. It must have been a short visit. Maybe he was just dropping something off, which likely meant he'd never have any reason to return to the Easy Living Apartments. After the way she'd embarrassed herself, assuming he was Linda's nephew and babbling on about the new manager and other stuff he likely had no interest in, she should be relieved about that.

But the thought of never running into him again left her feeling strangely disappointed. Like she might have missed out on something good.

CHAPTER TWO

THAT AFTERNOON, ADAM once again made his way to the Easy Living Apartments, this time without encountering geese or being drafted into carrying boxes. With four hours of sleep and a meal under his belt, he felt more like himself again, ready to focus on the job. But he did note that the little blue hatchback was still parked in the lot.

Several residents seemed to be milling around some raised garden beds on the far edge of the property. Another couple walked briskly along the sidewalk that circled the building. Adam made his way inside, this time noticing a signboard on the wall indicating the way to the manager's office. A vase of sunflowers rested on the table below. Adam made a mental note to check the floral budget as a possible cost-cutting measure. He headed down the hallway.

In the glass-walled manager's office, a woman with purplish-red hair permed into tiny curls typed on a computer out front. A door stood open behind her. She didn't look up when Adam stepped into the office, but she held up a finger. "One sec, hon. Just let me get this last number in." After a moment, she turned toward him. "Hello. May I help you?"

"Yes. I'm Adam Lloyd from Western Real Estate Investment headquarters. I wondered if Lou Sanchez had a few minutes to talk with me."

She blinked. "You're from headquarters?"

"Yes."

"But you're not supposed to be here until Monday."

"I know, but I got on an earlier flight, so I thought we might as well get started."

"Huh." Instead of using an intercom, she raised her voice. "Lou! The guy from headquarters is here."

"He's here now?" a gravelly voice called back. A few seconds later, a man with a gray-streaked beard and glasses stepped out. He wore a plaid shirt and jeans. "Hi. We weren't expecting you until Monday. Adam, right? Come in, come in."

Lou waved him toward one of the padded chairs in front of his desk and shut the door behind them. The office was oddly bare, other than a bunch of small potted plants in front of the window. Lou chose his desk chair. "You're from headquarters."

"Yes, Adam Lloyd." He reached across the desk to offer his hand, which Lou shook.

"So how do we do this?" Lou asked. "We just change seats or what?"

Adam laughed. "Well, first, maybe you could give me a little information about the place." He reached into his leather case and pulled out a file folder. "You're at about seventy percent occupancy rate."

"What? No. We're full."

"Full? All your units are rented?"

"Yes, and we have a waiting list."

"Interesting." Adam glanced down at the analyst's report. "What do you think is the reason for your high delinquency rate?"

Lou shook his head. "I don't know where you're getting your figures, but every one of our tenants is paid up and current."

"Hmm." Adam hadn't personally worked these numbers, relying instead on the report. He turned to the last page to see who had run the report. Oh no. The figures had come from a former employee who they'd discovered had a bad habit of writing fiction instead of chasing down the facts.

He'd come with excellent references, but two months into his job, someone noticed he had posted pictures of himself at a concert in Vegas at the same time he was supposedly completing an on-site inspection of a building in Twin Falls. After a little investigation, HR had determined his references were as fake as his data.

Adam mentally kicked himself for trusting the figures without looking to see who had entered them. He returned his gaze to Lou. "I apologize. Apparently, my information is not reliable." Adam showed him the bottom-line figures. "This is what I have listed as income from this building for the past year."

"That looks about right," Lou replied.

"Hmm. What's the cost of maintenance for this building?"

Lou gave him a figure, which seemed right in line. Adam was puzzled. "So, you're fully occupied, your maintenance costs are in line with other similar units and your tenants generally pay promptly."

"Yes."

"But your income-to-expense ratio is barely breaking even, and if you include capital cost, you're losing money."

"Right," Lou agreed readily.

Adam met his eyes. "Why is that?"

A row of lines appeared between Lou's eyebrows. "You don't know?"

"No." Adam bit back a flash of impatience. "Why don't you tell me?"

"This place was never intended to make

money. It was built by Oscar Ravenwood, from Ravenwood Property Company, twenty-five years ago."

"Yes. We acquired a package of properties from them. The other properties—five medical facilities, a shopping center and three apartment buildings in Anchorage—are all profitable."

"Yeah, but Mr. Ravenwood—I'm talking the old man now, Oscar, the one who passed on last year—it was his special project for his wife. See, Mrs. Ravenwood, Jill, her mom and dad were not so well off, but they were too proud to take any help from their daughter. The Ravenwoods decided to build this apartment building for seniors. The rent the tenants pay is based on their income."

"So, some renters qualify for subsidies?"

"Sort of. When a potential renter applies, we check their income, of course, just like any other apartment. But the rent we quote is based on that. As far as the tenant knows, they're paying the same rent as everyone else, because Mrs. Ravenwood's parents would never have moved in here if they thought they weren't paying their own way. They're gone now, the parents as well as Oscar and Jill, but there are plenty of other seniors in the same situation."

"So you charge—"

"A little over the going rate for the people who can afford to pay it, since we offer certain extras. The activities are a big draw, and we allow people from outside the complex to join in for a small fee, which is one of the reasons we have that waiting list I told you about."

"I have trouble believing the tenants haven't figured out that they're not all paying the same amount."

"Well, I can't vouch for what people know, but if they've figured it out, they haven't complained to me about it."

"What percentage of the renters pay full price?"

"Around half. It's on a sliding scale after that, down to thirty-five percent of full price."

"These contracts are month-to-month or—"

"Six-month leases. So, as they expire, you're legally free to raise the rent." He caught Adam's eye. "But I'm hoping you won't."

Adam frowned at the figures in his lap. "When my employer bought this property as part of the package, it was valued as an asset, not a nonprofit enterprise."

"Well, you'd have to take that up with the Ravenwood sons who inherited from their father and sold you the package. I'm just telling you how it's been done in the past."

"Okay. Well, maybe on Monday, we can go over the books—"

"About that. Since you're here, I'm thinking maybe I'll just go ahead and resign today."

"What?"

"You see, we've got a granddaughter down in Oregon pregnant with our first great-grandbaby, and we got word this morning that she's gone into labor early. The wife and I would like to be there to lend a hand." He opened the desk drawer and pulled out a folder and a set of keys. "Here's a list of where to find everything, and phone numbers for the bookkeeper, suppliers and such. My cell number's on there, too, if you have any questions. We're driving the Alaska highway, though, so I can't swear we'll always have a cell signal."

"But what about—"

"You look to be a competent man. I'm sure you can handle whatever comes up." Lou picked up a box piled high with books, framed photos and other assorted items from behind his desk and carried it to the door. He turned so that he could shake Adam's hand. "Best of luck, son. I hope you'll do the right thing. The residents here are good people."

He opened the door to expose the assistant standing behind it, where she'd obviously been eavesdropping. She stepped back as a familiar face appeared at the entrance from the hallway.

"Tilly, just wanted to see if Lou—" Sunny looked through the door to Lou's office. "Oh, sorry. I didn't realize you were in the middle of something." She took a step back.

"Wait, Sunny." Lou motioned Adam forward. "I wanted to introduce you to Adam Lloyd from Western Real Estate Investment headquarters. He'll be the new manager here, effective immediately."

"The new manager?" Sunny squeaked. Those brown eyes grew even bigger, and the natural blush in her cheeks grew pinker.

"Adam, this is Sunny Galloway," Lou said, smiling, "the best darn activities director–cat herder in the forty-ninth state. She keeps everyone hopping around here."

"So I've noticed. A pleasure," Adam said, extending his hand.

After a moment's hesitation, Sunny took his hand and shook it. "Um, welcome to your new job?" It was more a question than a statement.

Adam chuckled. "Thank you. It promises to be…interesting."

BRIGHT AND EARLY on Monday morning, Adam buttoned his blazer—not his usual daily attire, but he liked to make a good first impression— and marched toward his new office at the Easy Living Apartments. He'd spent the weekend going over the information he had and making lists of the records he needed. Now he just had to locate them. He'd planned to spend the first few days working alongside Lou, but since Lou had pulled the plug, Adam was going to have to get up to speed quickly. It shouldn't be too difficult. In his experience it was the assistant who knew all the wheres and whens, anyhow, and Lou's assistant had a settled look, as if she'd been in the position a long time.

Unfortunately, Adam had somehow neglected to get her name on Friday. That wasn't like him. He'd long ago learned the value of getting to know all the support staff. He blamed his oversight on Sunny Galloway stumbling into the office and sending everything else fleeing from his mind. Sunny—was that her real name? If so, her parents must have been clairvoyant, because he'd never seen a name more well-suited to a person. That easy smile, the sparkle in her brown eyes, the bounce in her step, even her hair seemed to have a joyful energy. He didn't doubt that she was an excellent activities director. The question was, could they afford an activities director at all?

Adam's stepfather had taught him early on that the people who invested with their real estate company weren't just numbers on a page. The money was someone's retirement savings, their child's college fund, the deposit they hoped to use to buy their first house. People entrusted Western Real Estate Investment with their dreams. And it was Adam's job, along with the other employees, to make sure the properties were well-managed and yielded a reasonable return on their investment. They couldn't keep running the Easy Living Apartments at a loss, even if it caused problems for the people who lived here. It wasn't that Dad was averse to charitable causes. In fact, he gave generously of his time and money and encouraged his employees to do the same. But the investors' money wasn't theirs to give away.

No one was at the assistant's desk when Adam arrived, but it was early still. In the meantime, he unpacked his laptop, his favorite travel mug—currently empty because he'd skipped the long line in front of the hotel's coffee urn this morning—and two framed photos, which he set up on Lou's old desk.

Of all the photos he'd ever taken, these two were his favorites. The one of his mom, taken when Adam was still in high school, caught her expression as she'd just finished taking a bow on an outdoor stage. Adam couldn't even remember the play, but he loved the joy and pride on her face as she accepted the applause for a particularly good performance. She may have never hit the big time, but she took her craft seriously. The second photo, taken about five years ago, also featured his mother, but this one was a shot of her and Adam's stepfather in an unguarded moment. Dad must have made a joke, because he was grinning and Mom's head was thrown back in laughter, her hand on his arm.

On the surface, they were complete opposites. Mom was an actor, who liked to live in the moment. Dad was a planner. He researched all the details, ran the numbers and made sure the columns added up. But their differences complemented each other, and they were the happiest couple Adam knew. His stepfather had been a great dad to Adam, too.

The assistant still hadn't arrived by the time Adam had finished setting up, so he decided to make coffee. A brewing machine and a few mugs rested on a tray on a credenza under the window in the assistant's office. He opened the doors underneath and found filters, but no coffee. The small refrigerator in the corner held two bottles of water and a lonely can of strawberry soda, which, according to the label, was caffeine-free. Great. Had he known, he could have made coffee in his hotel suite or picked up a cup at one of many coffee carts, but he'd been in a hurry to get to the office. He made a note to buy coffee.

Once his assistant arrived, he'd get the lay of the land and ask her the best time to schedule a meet and greet with the residents. It needed to happen soon, before there was too much speculation. Ideally, it should have happened when Lou was still there to introduce him, but that couldn't be helped now. Adam had just opened the can of soda and sat down at the battered pine desk in his new office when his cell phone rang. He should have expected it. It was two hours later in Boise, and Dad would be chomping at the bit for a report.

"Good morning."

"Hi, Adam. How's it going up in the frozen north?"

Adam glanced out the window, where a dozen or so residents seemed to be doing something around several raised planting beds. He thought he spotted a red-blond ponytail among them. "Chilly, but not frozen, although the trees are changing colors."

"Hmm." The obligatory weather comment complete, Dad dove right into business. "So, what's your take so far?"

"Well, I found out why they're losing money." Adam explained about the differential rents they were charging.

"Not good. We could sue the seller for failing to disclose the relevant facts about this business, but I don't want to do that. It could jeopardize the entire deal, and the other properties in the package appear to be solid earners."

"I don't think we'd stand a chance, anyway. Turns out the report we based the purchase on was run by Chad."

"What! I thought I told the department to rerun anything he'd done."

"Well, apparently, they overlooked this one, and so did I until I was talking with the old manager here. Turns out Chad used the correct gross income, but the rest of the report is pretty much fiction."

"Ugh. Fired that guy four months ago, and he's still coming back to haunt us. So, what do you think we should do?"

"The way I see it, we have three options. The first choice is to keep the property, and as the leases expire, inform the tenants they will be required to pay full price. The downside of that, of course, is that according to the outgoing manager, about half of the residents here wouldn't be able to afford that."

"Mmm." Adam could picture Dad's face frowning over that one.

Outside, one of the gardeners seemed to be telling a story. A humorous one, judging by the grins on the other faces around him. The residents here did seem to have a good time together. "Throwing a bunch of retirees out into the cold also wouldn't generate much goodwill in the community," Adam pointed out.

"True. What else have you got?"

"Option two is to somehow raise revenues and/or cut expenses. It will take some digging to find out if either of those avenues is possible."

"Okay."

"And option three, obviously, is to cut our losses and sell. But of course, any new owners would be in the same dilemma."

"Right. Well, it sounds like you have your work cut out for you."

"Yes."

"And speaking of work, your mom has a new radio commercial out."

"Oh yeah?" Adam smiled. During his childhood, his mom had paid the rent with waitress and retail gigs, but her passion was acting. She'd always been a stalwart in local community theater, and would occasionally snag a role in a local commercial or a company training film. She'd even gotten four lines in a movie shot in Boise once, but only one of the lines made the final cut. After she married Dad, he'd encouraged her to quit her day job, which had opened up new opportunities, and her name appeared among the credits of a dozen or so prime-time television episodes. Now in her sixties, she kept her hand in working as a voice actor for a local marketing firm. "Can you send me a clip?"

"Will do. It's for a travel agency, and they've offered her a discount on a cruise through the Panama Canal. It's next week. We're thinking about it."

"That's exciting. How long is this cruise, though? I've never known you to take off more than a week at a time."

"Eighteen days. I was a little hesitant to step out for that long, but Fallon assures me she can handle things at the office."

"I'm sure she can." Fallon Wright, Senior Analyst, was highly competent. And ambitious.

"Okay, well, I'll let you get back to it, then. Bye, son."

"Bye, Dad. Take care."

Adam returned his phone to his pocket. So Fallon was encouraging Dad to take a long vacation during the time Adam would be off in Alaska. Dad had dropped a hint or two that retirement might be in his near future, and the obvious candidates for his replacement were Adam and Fallon. The board would make its decision based on job performance, not nepotism, but Adam knew his stepfather had high hopes that he would be the one to fill his shoes when the time came. If Fallon did well while she was in charge, that would be a point in her favor. It was a clever move; Adam had to give her that. On the other hand, Fallon was fond of his parents. Maybe she just wanted them to have some fun.

CHAPTER THREE

"HERE, TAKE MY folding basket if you need it."
Sunny handed it to one of the newer residents
who was standing at the edges of the group.
"Next spring you can have your own gardening space to grow whatever you want, but in
the meantime, you're allowed to pick from the
common bed here. There's a nice crop of leaf
lettuce and the Brussels sprouts are good. Do
you like zucchini? We need to pick it all today
because there's a slight chance of frost tonight.
Bonnie has a great recipe for zucchini bread
she'll share with you."

"That sounds good. I do like baking," the
woman admitted, "but I've never gardened before. How do I pick a zucchini?"

"We'll ask Rosemary the proper procedure."
Sunny beckoned Rosemary closer. "She's a
master gardener."

"Our gardens are all organic," Rosemary
explained, flipping her gray braid behind her
shoulder before picking up a pair of pruners.
"So you don't need to worry about eating any-

thing harmful. If you're sauteing or grilling, I'd choose one or two of these smaller zucchinis, but if you plan to grate it for baking, you might want to take this bigger one. Just clip the stem an inch or two above the squash."

The woman harvested the squash and held it like a trophy. "I did it!"

"You sure did." Bonnie patted the lady's shoulder. "I'll bring the recipe by later. It's from my granddaughter, Rowan. She came in second on a television cook-off once."

"Wow."

"Take a couple of these carrots, too," Rosemary added some to the woman's basket and looked around. "Sunny, didn't we have some chives seedlings we were going to pot up for the indoor herb garden today?"

"I thought so. Oh, I believe Tilly said she was moving them to Lou's office window. I'll go get them." Sunny dusted the dirt from her hands as she walked toward the building and made her way to the manager's office. The bare desk looked lonely without Tilly and her usual collection of sticky note reminders, pens in several ink colors and empty strawberry soda cans scattered across the surface. She crossed the outer office. Through the open door she could see Adam pawing through a file drawer with his back to her.

She hadn't encountered him since their formal introduction on Friday. That would have been the time to apologize, but she'd been too mortified to react properly. She'd spent much of the weekend debating whether to bring it up again, but had finally concluded that her best response was to carry on as though everything was normal. Which it was, really. It was just a simple mistake, and she never would have babbled on like that if Adam hadn't thrown off her equilibrium by looking at her with those incredible blue eyes. Really, it was his fault for being so, so…okay, enough of that. He was her boss. It was time to show him she was a professional.

Or at least that she could act like one.

She knocked on the doorframe. "Excuse me. I just need to get those seedlings out of your window. The residents will be repotting them today."

Adam turned to face her. "Oh, that's good news. I was just wondering if I should give them a quick and painless death or let them linger on for a week or two first."

She laughed. "Not a gardener, I take it."

"I've never tried gardening, but I've killed every houseplant I've ever owned, including one that I'm pretty sure was fake."

"Well, if you stick around, Rosemary will

probably convert you. She's amazing. In the meantime, I'll get these out of your hair." She picked up the tray and started for the door, but that felt wrong, like she was running away. She stopped and turned. "How are you settling in?"

"Slowly. Say, is the assistant part-time or something?" He looked at his watch. "It's nine thirty and I haven't seen any sign of her."

"You mean Tilly?"

"If she's the assistant who was here on Friday, then yes."

"Tilly's gone. She and Lou are probably driving through Canada as we speak."

"Oh." The office chair creaked as Adam sunk into it, a dazed look on his face. "Lou said he was leaving immediately, but I didn't realize that went for the assistant, too."

"Lou and Tilly celebrated their fortieth anniversary last September."

Adam nodded absently.

"Was there something you needed to ask Tilly? I've filled in at the office a time or two, so I might be able to help you. At least until you can hire someone new."

"Do you happen to know where the coffee is kept?"

"Did Tilly hide it again?" Sunny laughed. "Every so often, she'd threaten Lou that if he didn't cut down on his caffeine, she'd put it where he couldn't find it. Sometimes, she even carried through."

"Do you have any idea where she would have put it?"

"No, but someone might. I'll ask." Sunny smiled as she left the office. She delivered the tray of chive seedlings to Rosemary and crossed to the other side of the garden, where Linda and Alice were looking at a book and debating whether some plant was a wildflower or a weed. "Linda, Tilly apparently hid the coffee again. Do you know where I should look for it?"

Linda shook her head. "Sorry, she didn't tell me. Bonnie!" she called. "Do you know where Tilly hid the office coffee?"

Bonnie, who was holding her little dachshund, Wilson, came closer and laughed. "Was Tilly stealing Lou's coffee again? Didn't she know that when she did that, he just mooched off Ralph and Alice's pot? No, I don't know where she hid it, but we always keep a couple of welcome baskets in the storeroom, and they have coffee in them." She winked. "Can't let that handsome new manager suffer from caffeine withdrawal. You'd better collect that welcome basket and go save the day."

Sunny decided to ignore the "handsome" comment. "I'll do that." Why were they so eager to push her toward Adam? They'd never even met him. Sunny was just glad Bea wasn't into gardening, because if she were there, she would have certainly had something to say.

Sunny did find a welcome basket in the first-floor storeroom on a shelf between a cornhole set and some Valentine's Day decorations. She carried it to the office.

"I didn't find Tilly's hiding place, but here." She set the basket in front of Adam on his desk. "Coffee, tea, a few coupons for local restaurants and shops, Bonnie's raspberry jam and Rosemary's honey."

"Wow, thank you. You didn't have to go to all this trouble."

"Oh, I didn't—I mean it's a standard welcome basket we give to new residents. I brought it because it has coffee in it, not as a welcome for you. Not to say you're not welcome, but—" Sunny shut her mouth, about three sentences too late, and took a breath. She smiled weakly. "Want me to show you how to work the coffee maker? It's a little tricky."

The corners of Adam's mouth tugged upward, but at least he didn't laugh. "I'd appreciate that."

She showed him how to position the basket a certain way and push a tab into place so the filter wouldn't fold over and let the grounds escape into the coffeepot. "Then it's just like any other machine. Turn it on, add water and wait."

"Okay." He did as she instructed. "Did you say the basket contains rosemary honey? I've never heard of that."

"No, Rosemary's honey. Rosemary is a resident here, and our gardening expert. She was also helping prepare for the read-in on Friday. You know, the woman with the long braid? Wearing the embroidered long-sleeve top?"

"Yes, I remember."

"She's also a beekeeper."

"Interesting. She doesn't, um, keep her bees here by any chance?"

"No." Sunny grinned. "Lou convinced her the bees would be happier at Bonnie's old farm. Bonnie's grandson and his wife raise goats there now, and there's plenty of clover and wildflowers for the bees."

"That's a relief." Adam poured a cup of coffee and took his first sip. "That hits the spot."

"Glad I could be of help."

He took another swallow. "Seriously, that's outstanding coffee."

"It's local. You can buy it fresh from the roaster. I think there's a coupon in your basket."

"Excellent." He set the cup on the assistant's desk. "So, you're the activities director. When would be the best time to get all the residents together and meet them?"

"Are you talking a formal presentation or just saying hello?"

He hesitated. "Which do you think would be better?"

"You want my opinion?" She was surprised. He was the one with the experience.

"Yes. You know the people here. Will they want a slides-and-handouts presentation on me and the company, or an informal meeting, so they'll know who to complain to if something goes wrong?"

"Informal. They'll want a chance to ask questions and feel you out."

"Trouble is, I don't have the answers yet. That's why I'm here, to get a handle on the place and decide where to go from here."

"Oh, so you're not permanent?" She wasn't sure whether to be relieved or disappointed.

"No. I doubt I'll be here more than a month or so. Depending on the direction we go, we'll most likely be hiring a new manager. You could apply."

"No thanks. I'd never trade my position as activities director for a boring office job. Not to say your job is boring," she hurried to assure him, "just—"

"Not your cup of tea. I understand."

"Exactly. This afternoon several of the residents will be working upstairs on the book drive again. If you're free, I could spread the word that you'll be there to meet people around two thirty."

"Sounds good. Is there enough time to get the word out?"

"Oh, sure. Unless someone has a previous engagement, they'll be there—especially if I let it be known there will be treats. I could pick up a couple boxes of cookies from the local bakery on my lunch hour if you like."

"Excellent." He pulled out his wallet.

"Don't you want me to fill out an expense form and submit it first?" Sunny asked. That's how Lou always handled things like this.

"No, this one's on me." Adam handed her a fifty. "Is that enough?"

"Plenty, but—" She started to ask why he wouldn't take money from the entertainment and recreation fund, but thought better of it. He was the boss, after all. "Thanks. I'll see you upstairs at two thirty."

"See you then, Sunny. Thank you for going by the bakery, and for the coffee." He raised his mug as if toasting her. "And for the advice."

"So, THAT'S A little bit about Western Real Estate Investment, and who I am." Adam looked toward the wall, where Sunny was setting out platters of cookies beside a coffee urn. "Help yourself to refreshments, and I'll be circulating around to meet all of you and answer any of your questions." Looking around the room, Adam was glad he'd followed Sunny's advice to keep things informal. He'd been prepared with a standard introductory slideshow, but this was better. It was easy to spot one or two mutinous faces among the crowd, and in his experience, detractors loved an audience. If he could deal with them one-on-one instead of in front of a crowd, they were usually easier to handle. Especially since he really didn't have any of the answers to their questions yet.

One of the men who had worn a scowl from the moment Adam stepped into the room was headed in his direction, but a woman with tightly curled white hair got there first and smiled at him. "So, you're from Boise."

"Yes, ma'am."

"Ah, nice manners, too. I'm Margaret Schelling. I used to visit Boise on special occasions when I was a girl. I grew up in a little town you've never heard of not too far from Twin Falls."

"You might be surprised. We have some properties in Twin Falls, and I've gotten to know the area."

"It's a little town called Dinkley."

"Dinkley." Adam thought back. "Don't you have a water tower painted to look like a baseball?"

"We do!" She beamed. "We won the state championship back in 1953, and the town council decided to commemorate it by painting the water tower. Imagine you knowing that."

"Move along, Margaret. There's other people that need to talk to the fella." The scowler had arrived.

"You'll get your turn, Phil. Adam and I are having a conversation." She turned back to him. "Sounds like you know Idaho, all right. How are you finding Alaska?"

"So far, so good." Adam hadn't had much time for sightseeing, but he had to admit the drive between Palmer and Wasilla, where his hotel was located, was quite scenic. "The people I've met here have been more than kind."

"Most are. Don't let a few bad apples," she paused and threw a pointed look in Phil's direction, "spoil your impression of Alaskans. You take care, and we'll talk more another time." She patted his arm before drifting off.

Phil stepped forward. "How much did your outfit pay for this building?" There was a clear challenge in the man's eyes. He was setting a trap, but Adam just wasn't sure what it was yet.

"I don't have that figure memorized, but I'm

sure you'll be able to look up the value in the tax records soon if it's not already there. And you are?"

"Phil Smith. The value is there, and it's high. Will you be raising rents to cover your costs?"

"Honestly, Phil, I don't know. I've only been here a day, and it's going to take some time to go over the books."

"But you're not ruling it out." Phil wasn't cutting him any slack.

"I'm not, no," Adam admitted.

"I looked it up. In Alaska you've legally got to give thirty days' notice to raise the rent. And you can't raise it until the lease expires."

Adam hadn't looked up state requirements yet. "That sounds reasonable. But as I said, no decision has been made."

"Yeah, sure." And with a grunt, Phil stomped to the back of the room, snatched up a cookie and stood by himself in the corner, glaring out at the crowd.

Another woman approached Adam. "I wanted to ask about the pet policy. Are you still limiting residents to two pets? Because my son—"

"Francine, you are not going to keep that hog in this apartment building!" a lady wearing a Seawolves sweatshirt exclaimed.

"It's not a hog. It's a potbelly pig. And besides—"

"I've seen that pig. What does it weigh, two hundred pounds?"

"One seventy-five. And he's very loving. Ray says he's a great pet."

"Livestock," one of the men muttered, "doesn't belong in an apartment."

"Just because an animal is livestock, doesn't mean it can't be a pet. Bonnie, you have goats at your farm. They're funny and affectionate, right?"

The woman she'd addressed chuckled. "Yes, but we don't keep them in the house. Don't drag me into this, Francine."

Adam held up his hands. "I'm going to have to check the rules, but I don't think a pig—"

"But I'm not talking about the pig," Francine interjected while making a face at the Seawolves fan. "I am trying to explain, my son runs an animal shelter, and he recently took in a mama cat with a litter of kittens. They're almost ready to be weaned, but they'd been feral, and they'll need fostering before they're ready for adoption. I wanted to ask if you'd make an exception to the two-pet rule for a short time so that I can take them in and socialize them."

Sunny had drifted over from the refreshment table at the back of the room. "How many kittens and for how long?" she asked Francine.

"Five. At least a month, but it could be two or three months before they're all adopted."

Adam exchanged a look with Sunny. She gave a little shrug. "We could put it up for a vote."

"Good idea." Adam cleared his throat. "Everyone, could I have your attention please? Everyone?" It took several minutes and some nudging, but eventually they all quieted down and looked in his direction. "Thank you. One of our residents—"

"Francine Lopez," Sunny whispered.

"Francine Lopez would like a waiver of policy to foster five kittens in her apartment for no more than three months. This is only a waiver. It doesn't change the existing pet policy. I think you should be the ones to decide. Discussion?"

"Would they be running in and out, bothering the birds at the feeder?" someone asked.

"No, they're indoor cats," Francine assured them. "They would stay in my apartment."

"Then what's it to us?" a man said. "I vote yes." A general murmur followed this pronouncement.

"All right. All in favor of granting the waiver?" Adam asked. A chorus of yays rang out. "Opposed?"

"Nay." The only voice was from Phil Smith, who was still scowling. There were a few annoyed glances in his direction, but no one seemed surprised.

"Very well. The waiver is granted. Thank you, Ms. Lopez."

"Francine." She beamed at Adam. "Thank you!"

More residents came to introduce themselves and ask questions. Many seemed doubtful of his intentions, but other than Phil, no one challenged him directly. After about an hour, once the cookies were gone, some of the people went back to sorting and shelving books. This seemed to be the signal for a general exodus of anyone who wasn't involved in the project.

As most of the group streamed out of the door, the woman with orange hair who had stopped his car for the geese pushed her way inside. Only today, her hair was dyed to match the pink-and-purple tie-dyed top she wore. "Drat, I missed the cookies. The farrier ran long."

"I saved you one, Bea." The woman who Francine had identified as Bonnie, with some connection to a goat farm, pulled two napkin-wrapped packages from her pocket and handed one to Bea and the other to Adam. "I also saved one for you. I figured you wouldn't have time to eat."

"Thank you." Adam accepted the cookie.

"You did good." Bonnie patted him on the shoulder as if he were six and had just finished reciting a poem. "Don't worry too much about Phil. He's never found anything he couldn't complain about."

"Sunny mentioned you're only staying temporarily," Bonnie commented. "Will you be hiring a new assistant in the meantime?"

"I'm not sure yet." Adam needed more information about the state of finances before he made any budget decisions like hiring. "But anyone is welcome to drop by and fill out an application. Better not send them too soon, though," he confided, "because I still don't know my way around the office."

"I've filled in for Tilly now and then." The lady with the silver glasses who seemed to be heading up the reading project handed him a sticky note. "Here's my cell. Call me if you need help finding anything. I'm Linda."

"Thank you. I may take you up on that, Linda."

"You should," Sunny told him. "Linda is a retired librarian. She knows everything, and anything that she doesn't know, she can find out."

"Great. Thank you, Linda. And thank you, Sunny, for putting this together on such short notice."

"Of course. I'm always happy to help out,"

Sunny replied. And she was, even if it did mean all the matchmakers in the room were silently patting themselves on the back.

CHAPTER FOUR

"I THINK THAT went well." Sunny folded in the legs of the table where she'd set up cookies and coffee. With Bonnie's help, she stowed the table in the closet.

"Good call, serving refreshments." Bonnie shut the closet door. "A dose of sugar and butter does wonders for people's moods, or at least mine. Phil was being a pill as usual, but he had a point. Do you think he's right, that they'll be raising rents?"

"I think Adam is being honest when he says they haven't made a decision."

"I hope they don't." Bonnie lowered her voice. "I'm in good shape, financially, but not everyone here is. Linda, for instance, used up most of her savings during her mother's final illness. She gets her retirement pension, but since she was a public employee, Linda doesn't qualify for social security."

"I didn't realize that."

"Margaret's on a tight budget, too. She invested a bunch in a relative's start-up business, and I understand things aren't going so well for him."

"That's a shame."

"Sunny!" Linda called. "Come give me your opinion on something."

Sunny crossed the room to where Linda was hanging a poster showing the number of points the children could earn for each book read. She stopped to admire the bookcases Linda's nephew had built. She and Linda had added a couple of coats of teal blue paint, and they'd come out looking quite nice. "What can I help with?"

"Do you think we should set up the prize center in here like we did last year or use the closet in the hallway like we did the year before?"

"I liked having it in the same room as the readers." Sunny remembered how the kids would debate for what seemed like hours over whether to trade in their points for a fancy pencil now or save up to get something bigger, like a mini soccer ball or stuffed animal.

"Yes, but sometimes they disturb the others who are trying to read."

"Maybe if we put the prizes in a bookshelf over in the corner away from the rest of the room?"

"Good idea."

"I'll give you a hand to move the bookcase." Sunny tipped it far enough to let Linda slip some sliders under the corners. Together, they scooted the shelves across the room to the far corner.

Alice came to inspect their work. "I like this here. Ralph said he'd attach all the bookcases to the walls with safety cables once we've got everything where we want it. We don't need any bookcases falling over in an earthquake, or because someone tries to climb up to see a prize on the top shelf."

"Tell him thanks." Sunny checked her watch. "And speaking of prizes, I have just enough time to drop by the office to see if Adam has approved that funding request before I pick up Piper at school."

Sunny grabbed her purse and trotted down the stairs. She found Adam in the outer office, fetching paper clips from the desk drawer. "Hi."

"Hello, Sunny." He seemed pleased to see her. "Thanks for your advice today."

"No problem. Say, I wondered if you'd had a chance to look through your in-box." She realized he was just getting on his feet, but she needed to get those prizes in place before the kids showed up.

"I have an in-box?" Adam looked around.

"Actually, it's an in-folder, and Lou kept it in his left desk drawer. That's where Tilly dropped everything that needed his immediate attention."

"And I gather you have something that falls into that category? Let's take a look." Adam went into the inner office, opened the drawer and pulled out the front folder. It contained three slips of paper. "Let's see what we have here. 'Schedule a plumber. Francine Lopez thinks she dropped her engagement ring down the disposal.' Oops, this is dated last Thursday. Francine was the woman with the kittens, right? I wonder why she didn't mention anything about this?" He checked the second slip. "Oh, here we go. 'Never mind, Francine found the ring in her bread dough.'" He chuckled. "I love it when problems solve themselves."

"Too bad it doesn't always work out that way."

"Yes." The third item was Sunny's funding request for prizes. He read it over and frowned. "I don't understand. Prizes for what?"

"For an after-school reading program. We partner with the local library, which is just across the park from us. The residents here host a read-in for the elementary school kids every Thursday afternoon throughout the fall. The first meeting is this week. They give a book to every kid who joins in, and the kids can earn points for reading. Once they've gathered enough points, they can trade them in for various additional books and prizes. They're nothing extravagant, but the kids love them."

He drew his eyebrows together. "Sunny, I can't approve this."

"What? Why not? It's only enough to buy pencils, stickers, bookmarks, maybe a few small toys and stuffed animals."

"But it's not for the use of the residents here."

"The residents are sponsors. Lou has approved it for the past two years."

"When Lou ran the apartments, they were privately owned. Now they're under the management of an investment company, and we have a responsibility to the investors."

"But what about your responsibility to the residents?"

"Exactly. These prizes aren't for the residents. Besides, I can't approve any further expenses until I've got a handle on cash flow."

"But the program starts next week. We were counting on that money. Kids have already started to sign up, and we've promised prizes."

"I'm sorry, but the answer is no."

"Fine."

How could he pull the rug out from under her like that? She turned quickly and headed for the exit to hide the tears of frustration welling up in her eyes. Tears were always near the surface for Sunny, much to her embarrassment. She was not going to be seen crying over a rejected funding proposal. She'd figure out another way to make this happen.

"Sunny, wait."

She stopped but didn't turn toward him. Instead, she blinked away the tears and managed to make her voice sound normal. "What?"

"Here. Take this." When she looked back, he was pulling some bills from his wallet and setting them on the desk.

"What are you doing?"

"You needed two hundred, right?" He added a fifty to the stack.

"I don't need it in cash. The local toy store here gives me a discount and sends the bill to Easy Living."

"Just take it."

"All right." Slowly, she picked up the money. "I'll bring you a receipt so you can get reimbursed from bookkeeping."

"That's not necessary."

What was he doing?

"You can't fund this out of your own pocket."

He shook his head, but he chuckled. "Sunny, there's a saying in business. 'Never sell past sold.' Just take the money."

The kids really did love this program. "Thank you."

"You're welcome. Now, was there anything else you needed?"

"Not today."

"Fine. Have a good afternoon." He closed the desk drawer and opened his laptop computer. Obviously, she was dismissed.

She tucked the cash into the outer pocket of her purse, went downstairs and drove to the elementary school. Piper stood with a few of the other children in her fourth-grade class, looking animated as she talked. When Sunny made it to the front of the pickup line, her daughter waved goodbye to her friends and skipped toward the car.

"Hi, Mommy. Can I try out for Book Battles?"

"What's that?"

"It's a competition. You all read the same books and you answer questions about them. If I make the team, we get to compete against teams from other schools."

"That sounds terrific. What do I need to do?"

"You have to sign a form saying it's okay, and that I can come in early on Fridays to practice if I make the team. Okay?"

"Of course. Did you get your stars today?" Piper's teacher had implemented a reward system in which Piper had the opportunity to earn star stickers for staying quietly in her seat during lessons. She could earn up to four each day.

"I got three. I lost the one this morning because I had to tell Marnie about the read-in," Piper admitted.

"I appreciate you spreading the word, but you know you're supposed to wait for recess to talk with your friends."

"I know, but I was afraid I'd forget, and it was important. Can I help Miss Linda and the other Mat Mates get the room ready today?"

"Yes, but first we're going to stop by the toy store. I thought you might like to help me pick out the prizes."

"All right!" Piper bounced in her seat. "I love your job."

Sunny laughed. "I love it, too."

"Ms. Linda!" Piper rushed ahead into the room where five of the Mat Mates were still sorting and shelving boxes of children's books. She dumped out one of the bags and picked up a strip of stickers. "We got the prizes, and look! When you look at the stickers this way, they look like a tiger, but when you move them like this, they change into a bear. Isn't that cool?"

"It is cool." Linda duly admired the stickers. The other women in the room stopped what they were doing to gather around Piper. Wilson, Bonnie's dachshund, came to sniff noses with Bob.

"Fancy," Bonnie commented as Piper demonstrated the holographic stickers. "What else have you got there?"

"Pencils, sidewalk chalk, bubbles, bookmarks, stuffed animals and a bunch of other stuff."

"These stencils are cute," Molly said. "And I like the little rulers."

"Watch this." Piper slapped the ruler against her wrist, and it curled into a bracelet. "Ta-da!"

Molly beamed as though she'd done a magic trick. "How clever."

"Ooh, temporary tattoos." Bea held up a picture of a rainbow to her cheek. "I wonder how many books I'd have to read to earn one of these?"

"You have to be in kindergarten through sixth grade to be in the reading program," Piper explained solemnly. "Sorry."

"Oh, well," Bea answered. "Guess I'll just have to stick to rainbows in my hair."

Sunny carried two more overflowing tote bags full of goodies to the table. "Here, take these and I'll bring up the rest." She pointed to a dolly parked beside the table. "May I borrow that?"

"Sure." Bonnie rolled it around the table. "How much more do you have?"

"Three more boxes," Sunny said. "For the bigger prizes we got craft items, games, building kits and stuffed animals. Piper, you want to come to the car with me to bring up the big surprise?"

"Yeah!" She turned to the others. "It's for the person who reads the most books by the end of the year. It's something big. Guess what it is."

"An African elephant," Molly ventured.

"No!" Piper giggled.

"A castle?" Linda suggested.

"A cow?"

"A Clydesdale?" the others guessed.

"You can't fit a castle or a cow or a horse in a car."

"Oh, good point," Bonnie said.

"I think it's a book," Rosemary suggested. "Because a book can open up whole new worlds, but still fit in a car."

"Part of it is a book," Piper told them.

Alice and Ralph came into the room, Ralph carrying a toolbox. "What are we meeting about here?"

"Piper and Sunny brought the prizes for the read-ins," Linda told them, "but Piper says there's a special grand prize downstairs in the car, and she's making us guess what it is."

"It's real big," Piper told the newcomers.

"Hmm, is it a trip around the world?" Alice asked.

"A ride in a rocket ship," Ralph suggested.

Piper giggled. "No. You'll see. I'll be right back." She ran ahead to push the elevator button so that Sunny could roll the dolly aboard. "Do you think everybody will like it?"

"Of course," Sunny answered, although she secretly hoped Piper wouldn't be the winner. A bed, desk and chest of drawers already filled most of her bedroom.

Sunny loaded the boxes onto the dolly and helped Piper drape the emergency blanket they always carried in the car over the mystery prize, and then they headed upstairs once again. Piper carried her bundle—which was almost as large as she was—across the room and waited until everyone was looking at her before she unveiled it. "Ta-da!"

"It's a bear! I should have guessed," Molly said.

The teddy bear wore wire-rimmed glasses and held a book in his paws. His lap was big enough for a small child to crawl into.

"Wow, impressive. How much was your prize budget?" Alice whispered to Sunny.

"The bear was a donation from the owner of the toy store," Sunny answered. "She's rearranging her children's book section and doesn't want it anymore. And the rest was from the new manager here."

Sunny spoke quietly, but Bonnie had made her way to stand with them and was listening.

"So, the new guy didn't give you any grief about the funding?" Bonnie asked.

"That's the weird thing. He did. First he said no, he couldn't approve any expenditures that weren't directly for the residents, but then he turned around and donated the money himself."

"Interesting."

"I know. He seems to be a real stickler for the rules." Sunny bit her lip as she watched her daughter tell Ralph a knock-knock joke. "Do you think he'll give me a hard time about Piper?"

If Sunny had to start paying childcare, her already stretched paycheck just might snap. And even worse, Piper wouldn't get to spend time with the people here who meant so much to her. But Adam would be well within his rights to tell her she couldn't bring her daughter to work anymore.

"If he does, we'll figure something out," Alice told her. "After all, you have an entire building full of potential babysitters here."

"If we need to, we can even take turns picking her up from school," Bonnie affirmed. "Don't go borrowing trouble."

She was right. "I won't. So, how are we doing on those book donations?"

"We were almost caught up, but someone dropped off another box a little while ago."

"Then let's get them sorted. We'll let Linda and Rosemary set up the prize display."

The new box of books must have come from someone's attic, because there wasn't one in there that was younger than Sunny. Most were in surprisingly good condition, though. She loved the old-fashioned artwork, but she wasn't sure whether books this old should go to the children.

"Maybe we should set these aside until Linda takes a look."

"All right," Alice said, "but let's at least take an inventory and see what we have here. Oh look! *Treasure Island.*" Bonnie and Alice exclaimed happily over many of the stories they'd read as children, or to their own children.

Piper wandered over and picked up a worn copy of *The Velveteen Rabbit*. "This book smells weird."

"It's been in a box for a long time," Sunny told her.

"My mother read this story to me when I was a little girl," Alice told Piper.

"Wow, that's really old!" the nine-year-old exclaimed.

Bonnie and Alice laughed.

"Why don't you read it to us while we work?" Bonnie suggested.

"Be careful, though," Sunny warned. "The pages might be brittle."

Piper sat down and gently opened the book. She read aloud, the words coming faster as she got caught up in the story. The three adults emptied the box and sorted the books as they listened. Piper was about halfway through the book when steps from the hallway made Sunny look up. Adam came in, gave a general greeting and started in her direction.

Wilson got to him first, so he bent down to pet the little dog. "Hello there."

"That's Wilson. He's Bonnie's dog," Piper volunteered.

"Hello, Wilson." He nodded to everyone and then turned his gaze to Piper and smiled. "I'm Adam. Are you visiting Bonnie today?"

"I'm visiting everybody. I come every day, after school," Piper told him. "Are you visiting somebody?"

"Me? No." Adam chuckled. "I work here."

"Oh. Do you ride on the mower?" she asked eagerly. "I wish I could, but Mommy says it's not safe."

"Uh, no. I work in the office."

"Oh." Piper shrugged, and her eyes dropped back to her book, clearly unimpressed.

Sunny briefly considered letting Adam believe Piper was a relative of one of the residents, but he'd find out the truth eventually. "Adam, this is my daughter, Piper. Piper, this is Mr. Lloyd, my new boss."

"I thought Mr. Lou was your boss," Piper said.

"You remember, Lou and Tilly are moving to Oregon. We had their retirement party last week."

"Oh, yeah. With chocolate cake. I forgot."

"Mr. Lloyd is my new boss."

"Adam," he corrected.

"Hello, Mr. Adam." Piper looked him in the eyes and thrust her hand toward him. "It's nice to meet you." Then she glanced at Alice for confirmation. "Is that right?" she whispered.

"Well done," Alice whispered back. "Once you master the curtsy, you'll be ready to meet a queen."

Adam chuckled and shook Piper's hand. "A pleasure to meet you as well, Miss Piper. Sunny, I wonder if I could see you in my office for just a few minutes."

"Oh, um, sure. Piper, you stay here with Alice and Bonnie. I'll be back soon."

With a sinking heart, she followed Adam

down the stairs to his office. As soon as he closed the door, she opened her mouth to ask for a few days to arrange for alternate child-care.

Before she could say anything, though, he unlocked the desk drawer and pulled out a folder. "I called the bookkeeper, and she said she'd forward me some information I asked for. Unfortunately, she sent it to the general office email account." He pulled out a sheet torn from a yellow legal pad covered with Lou's hand-writing. A few drops of some liquid had been spilled on it, most likely from one of Tilly's strawberry sodas, smudging the ink. "Can you make out that computer password?"

Sunny leaned closer. "It looks like it starts with a *P* or a *D*, but I can't make out the rest. Let me check something." She opened the top desk drawer and felt around underneath. Sure enough, she found a piece of paper taped there. "Here it is—Pioneer1991."

Adam shook his head. "Does everyone in the building know where the passwords are hidden?"

"Probably not. Most of them were right out in the open, attached to Tilly's computer on sticky notes."

"Somehow, that doesn't make me feel better about security."

"Lou and Tilly were the trusting type. You might want to change the passwords."

"I'll do that." He typed the old one into the computer. "What do you know? It works." He smiled at her. "Thanks for your help."

She waited, but he just continued clicking on the keyboard.

"So, you don't want to talk about anything else?" she asked slowly.

"Like what?"

"Like me bringing my daughter to work with me?"

"Is this an every day thing?"

"Yes. But it only takes fifteen minutes to pick her up from school. It's officially my afternoon coffee break." She didn't want him to think she was using company time.

"I'm not worried about you putting in your hours. I've seen your car here after quitting time almost every day since I arrived. What about summer, though, when school is out?"

"Lou always let me bring Piper in all day. I guess I could look into a camp or something for her…" Assuming she still had a job next summer.

"Doesn't your daughter get bored with no other kids to play with all day?"

"Oh no. There's always something fun going on here. She loves spending time with the residents and joins in most of the activities. Ralph is currently teaching her to play chess."

"Seems to me that if she's well-behaved and the residents aren't complaining, it's really not my concern if Piper decides to visit her friends daily. As far as I know, we have no restrictions on age or frequency of visitors."

"Really? Wow. Thank you." She grinned. "I thought for sure you were going to say that if you let me bring my daughter, you'd have to let the next person bring their kids and soon the whole place would be one giant day care." Sunny slapped her hand over her mouth. She hadn't meant to say that last part aloud.

Adam just laughed. "You and I are the only full-time employees, and I don't have any kids, so unless you and your husband are planning—"

"I'm single." That sounded kind of weird and desperate. She tried again. "I mean, it's just Piper and me, so you don't have to worry about me bringing more kids to work."

"I shouldn't have said anything. As your employer, your marital and child status is none of my business."

"You really don't mind if Piper comes to work with me?"

"I really don't. Now, as I've mentioned, I'm

only here temporarily, but as long as I'm in charge, your daughter is welcome."

ADAM PRETENDED TO be engrossed in opening the email on the computer, but in truth, he was looking past the screen to watch the way Sunny's ponytail gave a happy bounce as she left the office. He'd hated that familiar flash of panic in her eyes when she thought she was going to have to arrange for outside childcare. Familiar because he'd seen it so many times as a child in his mother's eyes, when the car broke down or the rent went up or a utility bill came in higher than expected.

Adam had a lot of admiration for his mom. She'd managed to support herself and him while never giving up on her dream. In order to be available for auditions and rehearsals, she'd usually taken waitress or retail jobs with flexible hours. But that meant there was seldom money for any extras, like after-school programs or sports. Adam was a latchkey kid for much of his childhood, and it had been a good lesson in self-sufficiency. He'd learned to make his own snacks and to manage his time so that he'd finished his chores and homework, at least partly, before his mother got home.

All that had changed when Mom remarried. They'd moved into a home in a neighborhood with old trees, big yards and even a cockapoo named Toffee. Suddenly, his mother had been available to drive him to practices and activities, which Dad encouraged. His stepfather had even reviewed Adam's homework with him every evening and held him to a higher standard than he'd gotten away with before.

Adam's grades improved to the point where he'd eventually graduated both high school and college with honors. But all that time spent alone had taken a toll. Although he always tried to project an air of confidence, he still sometimes struggled to feel comfortable in social settings.

From what he could see of Sunny's daughter, she had no such issues. A miniature of her mother with the same strawberry-blond hair, dark eyes and friendly smile, she'd looked entirely at home reading to the group of older ladies, who clearly doted on her. Maybe he should have at least checked into possible liability issues before allowing Sunny to continue to bring her daughter to work, but at the end of the day, it was just the right thing to do. Especially now that he knew Sunny was a single parent.

Turning his mind back to the task at hand, he opened an email and downloaded the financial summaries the bookkeeper had sent him. It was clear to Adam that Sunny and her daughter were thriving at the Easy Living Apartments, and that Sunny's leadership kept the residents involved and happy. The people here had managed to form a successful community. Hopefully, Adam would be able to juggle the finances so that the community could stay together.

TWO AFTERNOONS LATER, Adam found himself nodding off as his eyes skimmed the revenue figures for the past several months. He decided a walk around the grounds would be a healthier alternative than yet another cup of coffee, although since stocking the office with a bag from the local roaster Sunny had mentioned, he'd been thoroughly enjoying his coffee breaks. He closed the spreadsheet, got up to stretch and started toward the lobby. Ralph and a few of his buddies had set up a table near the windows there, and seemed to be engrossed in a rousing game of backgammon. They waved at Adam as he walked by.

He waved back and stepped outside. It had rained that morning, leaving the sidewalk damp, but now the sun was trying to make an appearance between the clouds. A few of the residents seemed to have had the same idea as him, taking advantage of the break in the weather to do a few laps around the building.

He immediately recognized Bea, she of the multicolored hair, striding purposefully with two other women trailing in her wake. On a bench near the front entrance, Piper sat swinging her legs. She seemed to be frowning at something mechanical she was holding on her lap.

Adam moved closer. "Hi. What have you got there?"

Piper looked up and smiled. "Hi, Mr. Adam. Ms. Francine gave me a camera. It used to belong to her husband. She says she doesn't know how to use it, so I can have it if I want. But I don't know how to use it, either."

"May I see?" Adam had been in the photography club in high school and taken classes in college. He used to spend a fair amount of time on his hobby, but somehow as he grew busier in his work, he'd let that slip away.

Piper handed him the camera. It was a nice one, not as expensive as the one Adam had treated himself to about ten years ago, but a good quality single-lens reflex digital with an 18-55 mm lens. Probably too advanced for a child Piper's age, but then she seemed rather advanced herself. Not that Adam had much experience with children, but he'd noticed that

Piper seemed almost adult in her interactions with the seniors upstairs.

"Is it broken?" she asked him.

"I don't think so," he replied. "The battery probably needs charging." He checked the port. "It looks like a standard mini-A USB plug. I'm pretty sure I have an extra. I can go get it for you."

"Thank you! Will you show me how to use the camera, too? I want to take pictures of the people here."

"Sure, I can do that. Give me just a minute."

When Adam returned with the cord and a charger, Sunny was there, talking with her daughter. Yet another box was strapped to a dolly, parked next to the bench.

"More books?" he asked.

"Yes. Linda says we can never have too many. The first reading club meeting is tomorrow afternoon." Sunny smiled at him. "Piper was just telling me you were letting her borrow a cord to charge the camera. Thank you. We'll return it once we pick one up."

"Don't bother. I always carry a couple of spares. Here, Piper. Plug this in tonight, and tomorrow after your club meeting, I'll show you how to operate the camera."

"You don't have to do that," Sunny protested.

"I can probably find the operating manual online."

"No, I'm looking forward to it. I used to have a camera almost like this. It's probably still at my parents' house somewhere. That's if you still want to, Piper?"

She nodded, her face serious, as though making a promise.

"Okay then." Sunny rolled the dolly forward. "Piper, want to go upstairs with me? We can plug in the camera while we sort through these books."

"Okay." The girl got to her feet, carefully cradling the camera in her hands. "See you tomorrow, Mr. Adam."

"Tomorrow," he promised.

CHAPTER FIVE

TWO BOYS AND a girl raced out of the elevator and down the hall toward the open doors of the reading room. One of the boys cut in front of the girl, and she squealed in protest.

"Slow down and use your inside voice!" their mom hollered from the elevator, her voice adding to the general pandemonium, but not having much effect on the behavior of the kids. Fortunately, the three residents with apartments between the elevator and the reading room were quite tolerant of the children's noise. Still, Sunny waylaid the three and reminded them that they were guests of the residents and had to act accordingly.

"You understand?" she asked, looking each of the children in the eye and waiting until she'd received a nod. "Good," she said, smiling, "because we've got some great books and prizes for you this year, and I'd hate for you to miss out. Go on in and see the ladies at the first table to get started."

They ran on ahead, and the mom caught up

with Sunny. "Sorry. They're just so excited. Someone told them they have a chance of winning a giant bear."

"That's right. You'll need to sign a form to get them registered. After that, you can stay and read, or slip away for a little alone time."

"Sounds like heaven." The woman trailed after her kids, and Sunny swept her gaze over the room to make sure all was going smoothly.

Rosemary, Bea and Molly staffed the registration table, getting parents to sign the forms and kids to design their name tags. One of the children waiting in line stared in fascination at the hot pink hair Bea had chosen to display that day. Molly had to ask twice before the girl stepped up to the front of the line.

Once they were registered, the children were directed to Linda, Bonnie and Margaret, who helped them select a book of their own and paste their own bookplate inside the cover. Piper was "assisting" with a running commentary on the books and the program. Linda felt strongly that children should have some books of their very own.

Alice and Ralph were setting up for story time near the window, putting out props on the table next to a rocking chair. The book they'd chosen included several different animals, and Molly had created a set of animal masks for

Alice to hold in front of her face as she read each character. Bonnie was arranging a craft table where the kids could make their own animal masks from paper plates and elastic bands.

Everything looked to be running smoothly. Sunny waved at Linda and pointed to her phone to let her know to call if she needed her for anything. Linda nodded, and Sunny went downstairs to collect the snack Bonnie's granddaughter, Rowan, had donated. They'd agreed it would be best for the books if they waited until the end of the read-in to offer food. Once she had the cranberry mini muffins arranged on a tray and covered with foil, Sunny returned upstairs.

Twenty or so children had gathered on the rug at Alice's feet while she read the story. Bob was right in the middle of them, snoozing, even while two or three children stroked his fur. A few older kids who had chosen to skip story time lounged in chairs and beanbags around the room, immersed in their own books. Several parents seemed to be enjoying reading time as well. One boy was conferring with Linda, apparently still trying to choose his first book to take home.

Sunny set the tray on a table. Behind her the door opened, and when she turned, she saw Adam step in.

"Hi," he whispered. "Just thought I'd come and see how it's going."

"It's going well." Sunny pointed over to where the children sat, transfixed as Alice changed to a walrus mask and made her voice deep and husky. "The kids—"

"A spider!" One of the children jumped up off the rug.

"Where?" another child screamed, and within a few seconds, all the kids surrounding Alice were shrieking and hopping up and down. One backed into the table next to Alice, knocking it over and sending the masks and a lamp crashing to the floor, which elicited more squeals. Some of the older kids and parents had jumped up and joined the panic.

"Kill it!" one boy shouted.

Piper stepped in front of the spider. "Don't kill it! Spiders are good."

"I'm not scared of spiders," one of the children boasted. "My brother has a tarantula."

"Please calm down." Alice's words were lost in the general melee.

Sunny snagged one boy before he ran out the door. "Hang on. You're okay."

A shrill whistle pierced through the noise, bringing a sudden silence as everyone looked toward its source.

Adam gestured to an area away from the

rug. "If you'll please step over here, we'll move the spider to his normal habitat and return to the story already in progress." Something in his voice seemed to convince the children to remain calm, and they began to gather in the general area he had indicated.

Meanwhile, Rosemary had made her way to the rug, armed with an index card and a drinking glass. Skillfully, she slid the card under the spider and trapped it under the glass. "It's a daddy longlegs," she announced. "Technically, they're not spiders since they don't have waists and can't spin webs, but they are a close relative. We love having them in the garden because they eat slugs and soft-bodied insects that tend to damage our plants. Would anyone like to see him before I take him downstairs and set him loose?"

Many of the same kids who had been the first to panic were now the most eager to look at the spider, or rather, almost-spider.

Sunny turned to Adam. "Thanks for your help."

"No problem. Are your read-ins always this exciting?"

"Uh, no. But next week we're meeting in the garden and Bonnie's granddaughter-in-law is bringing goats for a visit, so you never know."

Adam laughed. The kids had finished inspecting the spider and settled down on the rug once again to hear the end of Alice's story while Rosemary carried it outside. Adam nodded toward them. "This is a nice thing you're doing for the community."

"Linda and the Mat Mates started it. I just facilitate."

"Well, your facilitation seems to be quite effective. Spider or no, the kids are having a good time."

"Thanks."

"See you later," he said as he pushed his way through the doors.

Sunny watched him go. Not much seemed to ruffle their new manager, and she found that reassuring. Maybe everything would be all right in the end.

"Mr. Adam? Are you busy?" An eager little face peered from the doorway into his office.

Sunny was a few steps behind, standing next to the desk where Linda was going through some files. "Piper's eager to learn, but it you're in the middle of something—"

"Nothing that can't wait, and I could use a break." Adam saved and closed the spreadsheet he'd been working on and motioned the girl inside. "Hi, Piper. Did your camera charge up okay?"

"I don't know." She came closer to the desk,

and after carefully removing the strap from her neck, handed him the camera. "Can you show me how to turn it on?"

"See this button right here? Press it."

She did. "Oh, the light comes on."

"Yep. That means it's charged. Looks like you have a flash card inserted. That's where the pictures are stored."

Sunny glanced at her watch. "I'm due at a salsa dance class in five minutes. It's such a nice day, we're meeting outside. You're sure you're okay with Piper here?"

"Definitely," Adam told her. "We'll come find you once we're done with the lesson."

Piper, engrossed in the camera, didn't even look up. "Bye, Mommy."

Sunny chuckled. "Bye. See you in a little while." She slipped out the door.

Adam checked the digital settings and changed them all to automatic for now. "This button is the shutter. That's what takes the picture. Here, hold the camera like this." He positioned her hands on it with her index finger above the shutter. "Now look through the viewfinder. That's this little hole right here. Hold it up to your eye."

Piper frowned. "On my mom's phone, you can see the picture on the back."

"You can do that on this camera, too, if you

want, but sometimes it's hard to see the screen in the sunshine. Try holding it up to your eye," he suggested again, guiding her hands so that she had the camera positioned correctly. "Can you see anything?"

"I can! I see the filing cabinet!"

He chuckled. "We can probably find you a better subject than that for your first picture. Come over to the window."

Looking out across the lawn, he spotted Sunny with a dozen or so women and two men gathered in a group. They all wore sweaters or jackets and seemed to enjoy being outdoors. Sunny's hair was down today, shining in the sunshine. Bob lay on the grass nearby with his head tilted, watching them.

"Look, there's your mom."

Piper came to join him at the window. Meanwhile, Sunny pressed a button on an old boom box and demonstrated a dance step. The double windows in the complex were soundproof, but watching her move, he could almost hear the beat of the music. Someone must have made a funny comment because Sunny laughed.

"You want to take a couple of pictures of the group?" Adam asked Piper.

"Yes!" Piper squeezed up to the window.

"Wait just a sec. Sometimes you get weird reflections if you try to photograph through glass." He opened the window and removed the screen to give her a clear shot of the activity. The catchy music streamed into the room, and Piper swayed in time to it even as she concentrated on the camera.

Linda walked in, returned the file to the cabinet in Adam's office, and walked out again but Piper was so engrossed, she didn't even notice.

Adam stood next to her. "Okay, look through the viewfinder until you see the picture you want to take. Then slowly press the shutter halfway down to focus. Once you like what you see, press it the rest of the way down, and you'll have your picture."

The shutter clicked. "Did I do it right?" Piper asked.

"Let's see." Adam showed her which buttons to press to pull up the last photo on the screen. She'd lowered the camera as she pressed the shutter, a common problem, which caused her to cut off the top of someone's head, but it wasn't a bad picture at all. "Look at that!"

"I did it!"

"You sure did. Do you want me to show you how to operate the zoom lens, so you can take a few close-ups?"

Piper nodded eagerly. Adam took a couple of pictures to demonstrate how to work the lens, and seconds later, she was snapping away.

Sunny was dancing with Ralph now, while the rest of the group looked on. Who knew the old guy could move like that? After another two spins, Sunny turned him back over to his wife and began dancing solo, encouraging all the others to join in.

As the song ended, Sunny applauded them all and then launched them into the next tune. It looked like good exercise, as well as a whole lot of fun. Adam found himself itching for his own camera. It had been a few years since he'd done any photography other than the occasional snapshot on his cell phone, and he missed it.

"Can we look at the pictures now?" Piper asked.

"Sure. Do you remember how to pull them up?" After a bit of fumbling, she managed to do it and scrolled through them. One or two shots were out of focus, and he showed her how to remove them from the camera's memory, but she was quite pleased overall.

Adam figured she would lose interest in the new toy before long, but maybe not. The girl's enthusiasm reminded him of his own when he was just starting to learn about photography. Maybe he'd ask his mother to ship him his favorite camera. He might as well record some of those amazing views he saw every day on his way to and from work.

"Are you ready to go join your mom in the class now?" he asked Piper.

Piper nodded and carefully replaced the lens cap before turning to smile at him. "Thank you for showing me how to take pictures."

"You're welcome. Come back after you've taken a bunch and I'll show you how to download them onto a computer, okay?"

"Okay!"

"MAIL CALL!" FRANCINE carried the bundle of envelopes and flyers through the door and set them on Adam's desk. Ever since the kitten vote, she'd been dropping by the office most days with baked treats or offers of assistance.

"Thanks." Even though this arrangement blurred the boundaries between resident and management, Adam was grateful for the help. From what he'd seen of the books so far, he probably wouldn't be hiring an assistant. Every expense they could cut would be needed if they were going to keep this place going. "Have the kittens moved in?"

"My son is bringing them later today. I'm all set up for them. Thank you for allowing this."

"It wasn't me. The whole group voted."

She smiled. "Yes, but you could have said 'rules are rules' and never allowed the vote, and nobody would have blamed you." She picked up Adam's wastepaper basket and emptied it into the one in the outer office. "Now, if you'd gone and told Sunny she couldn't bring Piper here anymore, you might have had a mutiny on your hands."

"You heard about that?"

"Of course. If you sneeze around here, you'll have chicken soup on your desk within the hour."

"I've noticed," he replied. "Do the residents like having Piper around?"

He'd already seen evidence that they did, but he wanted to hear what Francine had to say.

"Absolutely. That little girl is probably the most popular person in the building. I even saw Phil give her a silver dollar once, and that man hates everybody."

Piper must be a magician if she'd charmed that surly guy. Francine was obviously a fan, too. "Piper showed me the camera you gave her. A rather expensive one for a child, don't you think?"

"Piper's not your average child," Francine replied. "She's very responsible. And we tend to be especially protective of her and Sunny, since they don't have anyone else. Sunny's parents are both gone. And apparently, Piper's father left Sunny high and dry when she was pregnant." Francine shook her head in disapproval.

She returned Adam's trash can to its usual spot. "Besides, the camera wasn't doing any good sitting on the shelf in my closet. My husband was a photography buff, but I never slow down long enough to take pictures. He used to say he had to use fast shutter speeds with me, or I'd just be a blur."

Adam laughed. "I believe that."

"So, what else can I help you with today?"

It wasn't Francine's job to help him, but Adam had learned it was no use arguing with her. "I got a report of a dripping faucet in 223. If you'd call a plumber, I'd appreciate it."

She scoffed. "A plumber will charge a fortune just to show up. It probably needs a new washer. I've got spares in my apartment. I'll take care of it." She bustled toward the door.

"Francine, are you sure—" But it was too late. She was already halfway down the hall, completely focused on her mission. Adam could chase her down and insist on using a professional, but if she was anywhere near as competent as a repair person as she was as office assistant, she'd probably have that faucet fixed in the time it would have taken him to find the number for the plumber. He made a note to follow up and make sure the resident was pleased with the repair.

If only all the building's problems were so

easy to solve. But the deeper he dug into the finances, the worse the situation looked. He was still rearranging numbers, running models of various what-if scenarios, but so far, he hadn't figured out how to make the investment pay out.

He closed the laptop and picked up the mail. Mostly junk. An invoice from the cleaning contractor for the public areas, who seemed to be doing an excellent job at a reasonable price. There was also a letter addressed specifically to Western Real Estate Investment at this address. Adam picked up the souvenir Iditarod letter opener he'd inherited with the desk and slit the envelope. Inside, he found an offer from another real estate company to purchase the building.

Curious, he typed in a search for the company on his computer. It looked like they worked mostly in Anchorage, acquiring older residential properties and converting them either into office spaces to lease or upscale apartments, depending on the location. The zoning in this area would work for either, and the price they were offering was fair. If this were any other piece of real estate, he would probably recommend selling.

But this wasn't just any property, it was home for a very special group of people. They were a real community, and he wasn't going to sell to someone who would break it up until he'd exhausted every possibility to keep Easy Living Apartments viable. So far, though, it wasn't looking good.

"Excuse me." It was Margaret, the nice woman from Dinkley, Idaho, the tiny town with the baseball water tower. She was one of the tenants whose rental payments were well below the market rate, and based on the income estimate she'd submitted, she wouldn't be able to afford an increase.

She carried a can of mixed nuts. "I wondered if you could open this for me, please. I don't have the strength to pull the ring tops anymore."

"Of course." Adam took the can, peeled off the lid and handed it back.

"Thank you." Margaret beamed. "Such a help. Say, would you care to join me for lunch? You can tell me about the places you've visited in Idaho."

Adam had planned to order something delivered so he could eat at his desk while he worked. Margaret's eager face changed his mind even though he had a feeling her lunch would be something more along the lines of tea and tiny finger sandwiches.

A little pleasant conversation was the least

he could do for her, because someday soon, he might just be turning her life upside down.

"MORE CHILI?" MARGARET'S lunch had turned out to be more substantial than Adam had expected.

"No, I couldn't eat another bite. That was delicious. I've never had moose chili before."

"Glad you enjoyed it. An old friend keeps my freezer stocked." Margaret glanced at the clock on the mantel. Maybe he was keeping her from a favorite television show.

"Guess I'd better get back to work." Adam stood and started to gather his dishes, but Margaret protested.

"Oh, no. Sit. I've got oatmeal cookies."

"Thanks, but I really am full, and I've got a lot of work to do, so—"

"But wait. I need to show you…" She paused and swept her eyes across the room until they fell on a low bookshelf. "…some old Alaska photographs. I know you'll appreciate them, since you're into photography." She grabbed a leather-bound album from the shelf and brought it to the table.

"I'd love to see them sometime, but I should—"

Margaret opened the book. "Here I am with some friends at the Matanuska Glacier in 1979, right after I moved to Alaska." They were all dressed similarly in flare-legged jeans and color-blocked jackets, but Margaret's pretty face was easily recognizable among the five young women posed in front of a cave of deep blue ice.

"Great picture of you. How close is this glacier?" he asked. Maybe he'd go by one weekend once he had his camera.

"Not far. There's a trail over near Sutton, but it's on private land so you have to make arrangements with the owner." She turned the page to a mountain scene. "Now this picture—" Her phone chimed. She glanced at it and closed the book. "But I'm keeping you from your work. You can look at my photos another time."

"Uh, okay," he said, confused over the abrupt about-face. "Thanks for lunch."

"You're welcome." She crossed the room and put her hand on the doorknob.

She opened the door for him, but when he stepped into the hall, a group was waiting. "Surprise!" Francine called. "You're coming with us."

"Coming where?" Adam asked, even as he was being swept along the hall.

"Everywhere," Ralph answered and leaned in closer to whisper, "Don't bother protesting. With this group, it's best just to go with the flow."

"We're kidnapping you," Bea explained cheerfully. "You've hardly stepped foot out of that office. It's time you saw Palmer."

"All right." Adam figured he might as well humor them. Considering the size of the town, it shouldn't take long.

"Why were you so late?" Margaret hissed to Alice.

"The bus just got back," Alice explained. "The mushroom hunters were tardy."

"Sorry about that," Rosemary said. "We got into a good patch of winter chanterelles and lost track of time."

The twelve-passenger Easy Living bus waited at the curb. "Adam, you're young and active. Can you take the back seat?" Molly asked.

"Sure." He squeezed past the row in front of it, only to find Sunny already ensconced in one of the two rear seats. "What's going on?" he asked as he buckled his seatbelt.

"No idea," Sunny replied. "I was told to go sit in the back of the bus, so here I am."

He had a suspicion the residents might be doing a little matchmaking, but he couldn't say he minded sitting next to Sunny.

The residents all seated themselves. Bonnie's little dachshund, Wilson, peered over her shoulder at Adam from two seats ahead. Margaret set a cushion in the driver's seat before climbing in, but she still looked like she was barely taller than the steering wheel. He leaned close to Sunny. "Should we be trusting her to drive?"

"I don't see why not," she whispered back. "The school district trusted her to drive a school bus up until she retired a year ago with a perfect safety record. And that was her second career, after spending twenty years as an ice road trucker." Adam waited for the punchline, but Sunny appeared to be serious.

Margaret looked both ways and pulled smoothly out of the parking lot.

"We should pick up provisions at Salmonberry Bakery," Bonnie suggested.

"Adam just finished Margaret's moose chili," Alice said. "He won't be hungry yet."

"I wasn't thinking about Adam," Bonnie admitted.

"Their cranberry almond scones are legendary," Sunny told Adam.

"We'll stop by the bakery on the way back," Margaret said. "I'll take you to the best view of Pioneer Peak first, just to give you a clear look at the valley."

Five minutes later they were driving along a country road. As they approached a green building, Wilson began barking. "That's my granddaughter's husband's veterinary office,"

Bonnie explained over the noise. "Wilson hates it because that's where he gets his nails clipped."

"Zack runs a wildlife rehabilitation center in the woods behind it," Linda said, once Bonnie managed to shush the dog. "I saw in their newsletter that they have a lynx with a broken shoulder right now. They just released a young moose back into the wild last week."

"Fascinating." Adam hadn't realized they had anything like that in Palmer.

The road wound upward to higher ground. Eventually, they reached a pullout, where Margaret parked. "Here's the view I was telling you about."

They all piled out of the bus. They were overlooking a small lake, the blue water peaceful and still. Beyond, the valley was filled with shades of green and gold from the crops and native plants. A few black-and-white cows dotted a pasture to the east. Behind them, birches lined the foothills, all dwarfed by the majestic snowcapped mountain rising up against the sky. And then, just to complete the scene, a bald eagle soared past the mountain. Adam took a few photos with his phone, but he itched for his camera and zoom lens.

Margaret pointed toward the tree line. "You can't see it from here, but the Knik River runs between us and Pioneer Peak. That's the river you crossed coming from Anchorage." Once they'd duly admired the scenery and reboarded the bus, she drove them to the downtown area.

Alice pointed toward a white clapboard house with green window boxes. "There's one of the first homes in Palmer, restored. As part of the New Deal, the government sent more than two hundred families here to start an agricultural settlement in the thirties."

"You should be here in June when we celebrate the town's history," Bonnie told Adam. "We have a parade, a market, kid's events, all kinds of fun things. Or at Christmas, when we do pretty much the same thing but light up the water tower."

"Over there is the train depot." Francine waved toward an attractive blue building. "Margaret, isn't that where your boyfriend hung that huge sign asking you to marry him and you shot him down in front of the whole town?"

Margaret scoffed. "Well, he shouldn't have put me on the spot. I don't know why I even went out with him. He only talked about himself. Dull as a butter knife."

"Didn't he go on to become a state senator?" Ralph asked.

"Yep." Margaret tossed her head. "But he didn't get my vote."

"You didn't hear this from me," Alice said, "but his secretary claimed she listened to recordings of his speeches whenever she got insomnia. Three monotone sentences, and she was out like a light."

Bonnie laughed. "How about your current boyfriend, Margaret, the one who brings you moose meat. Ever thought of tying the knot with him?"

"Not happening. He loves that dilapidated backcountry cabin of his, and I need more social life than that." Margaret pulled the bus around so that they could see the other side of the railway station. Large planters flanked a pathway, but instead of holding flowers, they were filled with red and yellow-stemmed bushy plants.

"Rosemary," Adam asked, "what's that growing there?"

"Swiss chard," she answered. "It's part of the edible rail trail."

"What's that?"

"There are forty planters along this path, filled with zucchini, chard, dill, and other vegetables and herbs," she explained. "They're free for anyone who wants to pick them."

"And nobody just runs off with all the vegetables?" Adam wanted to know.

"On the contrary," Rosemary assured him.

"Generosity spawns more generosity. Some people, after enjoying the fresh produce, have started their own vegetable gardens and plant an extra row to donate to the local food bank."

"Speaking of vegetables, Adam, it's too bad you missed the Alaska State Fair," Ralph mentioned. "The winning cabbage weighed in at eighty-six pounds this year."

"He's kidding, right?" Adam asked Sunny.

She shook her head. "No, they really can grow cabbage that big here."

"That would be a lot of coleslaw."

"It's too late to see the real giant cabbages," Molly said, "but they do have a cabbage sculpture at the visitor's center."

"Let's take Adam by the showcase garden," Rosemary suggested. "There are still things growing, and it's a beautiful day for a walk."

Margaret pulled into a parking lot next to both a museum and visitor's center where there was indeed a sculpture of a giant cabbage, zucchini, and two other vegetables Adam didn't recognize.

Next to the museum was a large garden. Some of the beds had been cleared, but many still held plants with a few late blooms. Bonnie pointed toward a coffee cart in the corner of the parking lot painted with yellow daisies. "I'm just going to pick up something to drink."

"I want to see if that new variety of coreopsis is still in bloom." Rosemary headed toward the back of the garden. The rest of the group split and followed the two women, leaving Adam and Sunny alone.

Sunny tilted her face into the sun and stretched her arms wide, as if to give the whole world a hug. Between that dazzling smile and the sunlight sparkling off her hair, she almost appeared to be lit from within.

Adam felt an overwhelming urge to reach out and touch her, as if that joyful energy was something that could travel from one person to another physically, like an electrical current. If only they weren't coworkers—but they were.

Instead, he nodded toward the group gathered at the coffee cart. "They're really something, aren't they?"

"Indeed they are," Sunny replied. "I love it. Working at Easy Living is like having one huge extended family."

He thought about what Francine had told him. "You don't have any family of your own?"

"Just Piper," Sunny answered. "My parents are both gone. How about you? Lots of family?"

"Sure. Aunts, uncles, cousins, grandparents, but they're in Ohio, not Boise. I see them at family reunions every couple years. I'm close with my parents, though. Never really knew my birth father, but I have a fantastic stepfather."

"That's great."

"Yeah. I'm lucky."

"So am I." Sunny waved and shook her head no to Bonnie, who was calling to ask if she wanted anything from the coffee cart. She turned back to Adam. "I have Piper, and I have all the people at Easy Living. Life is good."

CHAPTER SIX

TUESDAY MORNING, SUNNY had just walked in the door with Bob and was heading for her office—well, technically a corner of a supply closet where she'd made room for a desk, bulletin board and Bob's bed—when a voice behind her called, "Sunny, wait!" She turned to see Molly waving a piece of paper. Molly wore yoga pants and a long tee in an abstract print. "I've got that revised list of what we'll need for the painting class that you asked for."

"Thanks. Looks like you're on your way to yoga." Sunny set down the tote bag carrying her laptop and the basket of fall leaves she'd collected for a craft project and took the page.

"Yes, the Mat Mates always meet early on Tuesday mornings." Molly gave her an innocent smile. "You're welcome to join us anytime."

"No, thanks." Sunny had only been to the Mat Mates yoga class once. The six members of that class might look like little old ladies, but every one of them could hold a plank or a tree pose for what seemed like hours, while after thirty seconds, Sunny's core muscles were composing a letter of resignation. "Besides, I'm leading balloon volleyball this morning. That plays more to my strengths."

Molly laughed. "All right, then. But don't forget, because of this amazing streak of warm weather, they've scheduled a special session of goat yoga at the farm this Saturday afternoon."

"Oh, I'm glad you reminded me. Piper would never forgive me if I didn't take her to see the goats one more time before winter." Sunny looked over the neat list of art supplies. "Thanks for getting this together."

"I talked to the manager at the art store, and she says they'll give us a ten percent discount. If you need to cut costs, we could switch to smaller canvases, but I like to give people room to express themselves if we can."

"Okay, I'll see if I can get Adam to approve it. When I asked about prizes for the read-in, he said he couldn't okay any expenditures until he'd gone through the books, but hopefully he's had time to work on that."

"Lou never had a problem funding classes. He knew the classes and activities are a big draw."

"I know, but Adam works for this new company. They may have a different philosophy than the old one."

"Well, if he balks, we'll just have to set him straight. We could sic Bea on him."

Sunny laughed. "That should scare him, all right. I'll try to get in to see him later this morning. Have fun at yoga."

Sunny tucked the list into her tote and carried it to her desk before heading over to set up the net for balloon volleyball. With the six Mat Mates out of the building, the turnout was lighter than usual, but she still had enough for two teams of seven each batting the balloon back-and-forth across the net with as much enthusiasm as if they were competing for a national title.

Afterward, she took Molly's list and was crossing the lobby on the way to Adam's office when she spotted a familiar brown truck pulling up outside. She detoured out the front door. "Hi, Dave."

"Oh hi, Sunny. I've got something for…" He looked at the label. "Adam Lloyd. New resident?" He scanned the label into the system and handed over the package.

"New manager."

"Oh. Did Lou finally retire?"

"Yes. He and Tilly moved to the lower forty-eight to spend time with their grandchildren. A new company bought the place."

"I hope they don't make a lot of changes.

My dad put his name on the waiting list for an apartment here a few weeks ago."

"That's great news! We'd love having Martin here." Dave's father, who currently lived in a rambling house on the other side of the library, could always be counted on to make up a fourth for bridge and liked to drop in for football-watching parties. Sunny knew Martin was finding it hard to keep up with all the household maintenance on his old place. "He and Margaret came this close to upsetting Alice and Ralph's perfect winning streak in the last bridge tournament."

"I know." Dave grinned. "I heard all about it. Gotta go. See you, Sunny."

"Bye, Dave." She looked at the package in her hands. The return address was Boise, Idaho. Good. Maybe a package from home would put Adam in a good mood. She carried the box to his office and stepped inside the reception area.

Adam sat at Lou's old desk, his eyebrows drawn together, staring at his computer screen. The man even managed to look good when he frowned. For the sake of the painting class budget, she hoped he was just concentrating and not annoyed. Maybe she should go away and come back later. But she did need to deliver his package.

The decision was taken out of her hands when

he looked up and smiled. "Sunny, hi. What can I do for you?"

"Hi. First of all, this came for you." She handed over the box.

"Oh, great." Adam reached for his letter opener to cut the tape, then carefully unwound layers and layers of Bubble Wrap until he revealed a camera. The wear on the leather strap and a few scratches on the black paint of the camera spoke of much use. "Working with Piper the other day made me lonely for my own camera."

"It was so nice of you to do that."

"My pleasure." Adam removed another bundle from the box which, when unwrapped, proved to be a telephoto lens.

"Piper's been prowling around here, taking pictures of everything and everyone. She says she wants to be a professional photographer when she grows up."

"I had the same dream once, but it's not an easy profession to break into. Life led me in another direction."

"Well, last week Piper wanted to be an elephant trainer, and a few months ago a stunt pilot, so I won't worry. But whether it's a profession or a hobby, I think she'll stick with photography. This Saturday afternoon I'm taking her to Now and Forever Farm's goat yoga, so she should find lots of photo ops there."

Adam blinked. "Did you say goat yoga?"

Sunny nodded. "Yeah, it's a real thing. You remember Bonnie? Well, she used to run a cow dairy farm, but her grandson and his wife have converted it into a goat dairy and cheese-making operation with a tasting room and everything. Anyway, during the summer they have these yoga classes on weekends where they let a bunch of baby goats in to play with the yoga people, and with such a nice forecast, they've decided to have one more session before the season changes. The Mat Mates always go. That's Bonnie, Alice, Molly, Rosemary, Linda and Bea. They've been in a yoga class together forever."

"Bea. She's the one with the colored streaks in her hair?"

"Right. Linda is the one running the read-in for the kids. Rosemary is kind of a flower child, Molly's an artist and Alice used to work for the governor's office. She knows everybody. Hey, you should come try it."

Adam just grinned, but said, "Before Piper heads out on a photography excursion, send her to me and I'll show her how to download her photos and clear her memory card."

"I will. Thanks." Adam set the camera and lens on his desk. "What was the second thing?"

"Second thing?"

"You said first of all, you had a package. What else did you need?"

"Oh, right. Molly has agreed to teach a class in oil painting, and I need you to approve the expense so that I can shop for supplies." She handed him Molly's list. At his frown, she added, "It looks like a lot, but it's the end of September, and I've spent less than fifty percent of the annual activities budget Lou gave me. I'm sure I can keep it below budget for the rest of the year."

"That's good, except…" He paused.

"Except what?"

"Sunny, I'm going to level with you. This place is bleeding money."

"What? But Lou said—"

"Lou was working under a different set of assumptions. From what I can tell, his budget for operating costs, activities and maintenance was based on the rent collected."

"Uh-huh." That sounded reasonable.

"But it didn't cover capital investment."

"Sorry, you've lost me."

"Okay. Based on what I've been able to uncover, Oscar Ravenwood built this place so that his wife's parents and people like them would be able to afford a comfortable place to live even though their income was limited. In effect, he gave them free use of the building, and continued that up until he died. Some of the people here pay full rent, but based on their income, others pay much less. The total amount of rent collected is enough to cover the costs of utilities, salaries and maintenance, but hasn't covered the building cost."

"Funny that we never knew that. I guess I understood that Ravenwood was the name of the company that owned the building, but I never met anyone from there. Lou seemed to handle everything."

"Yes, I gather Mr. Ravenwood gave Lou pretty much free rein to run the place as he saw fit."

"But when Mr. Ravenwood died—"

"His sons inherited his many properties, including this one, and sold them to my company."

"So, you're saying Oscar Ravenwood paid to have the apartments built as a gift to the seniors—"

"More of a loan, really, because he never gave up ownership of the building."

"Who were his wife's parents?"

"Their name was Maddox. Peter and Ruby."

"I don't know them, but the bench out front has a plaque in their memory."

"You and I would both have been teenagers when they passed away."

"But Mr. Ravenwood still let the place operate the same way, only charging people what they could afford, after his relations were gone."

"Apparently, yes."

Sunny thought about it. "Obviously, he cared about the seniors here. I wonder why he didn't leave the building to them, or to a trust of some sort."

"I wondered the same thing. But he and his wife died in a boating accident. They were both in their sixties. It's possible he just hadn't gotten around to setting anything up. I guess we'll never know."

"And your company can't give the people here the same deal?"

He turned his palms up in a helpless gesture. "We have a fiduciary responsibility to our investors. They paid for a building and expect to see a return."

"But what about the residents? Can't your company help them?"

"I wish we could, but we're an investment company. There are laws against diverting funds. Besides, people trust us to invest their savings in real estate. Imagine how you would feel if you put money in the bank, and when you went to get it out, the teller told you the bank had given it away to someone who they felt needed it more."

Sunny sighed. "I guess you're right, but a lot of the seniors here are on tight incomes. They're not going to be able to afford a sharp increase in rent."

"I know."

"So, you'd just turn them out? Where are they going to go? This is the only place like this in Palmer. They'll have to move to Wasilla, or maybe even Anchorage. And they'll probably need some sort of assistance, too."

"Yes." His face remained impassive.

"How can you stay so calm when you're talking about turning a bunch of old people out of their homes?" And then another thought struck her. "Do I need to be looking for another job?"

Adam grimaced. "I won't lie to you. It's possible, but as a favor, I'm asking you not to leave yet." He drew in a breath. "Sunny, I don't want to displace the people here any more than you do. We have an offer, but if we sell the building, the new company will most likely evict everyone and convert it to a different use. If we keep the building, we might have to raise rents more than most of the residents can afford in order to make it pay. I'm trying to figure out how to keep the building and allow everyone to stay. So far, I'm not having a lot of luck—"

"What if you eliminated my position?" Sunny would hate to leave, but if it meant people like Margaret could stay, it might be worth it. She could volunteer on her time off—maybe. "Would that be enough—"

"Not even close. But the fact that your first reaction was to look out for the residents tells me you're exactly right for this job. Yes, it would probably be a good idea for you to update your résumé and start looking around, but I am going to try my best to figure out a way to keep you in your job and the current residents in their apartments."

Sunny took a deep breath. "Okay. How can I help?"

"I don't think—"

"I need to do something. I'll talk to Molly and see what we can do to reduce expenses for this class. I know it's just a drop in the ocean, but every little bit helps, right?"

"Sure." He didn't look convinced, but he didn't argue.

"We can do this." Sunny was mostly trying to convince herself, but she wanted Adam to believe it, too. "I'll come up with ideas to reduce expenses and you can work on the numbers. We can make it happen."

He raised his eyebrows again. "Do you ever give up?"

"Give up?" Sunny shook her head. "We're just getting started."

THE MAT MATES must have decided to make a day of it, because Sunny had just returned from picking Piper up at school when she spotted the six women in front of the Salmonberry Bakery loading two big boxes into Bonnie's car.

Sunny parked behind them and got out. Linda waved and gestured toward the boxes. "More books!" The expression on her face made it clear she was really saying, "More treasure!"

"Crystal, our yoga instructor, clued us into her neighbor, who was turning her two sons' old room into a quilting retreat and had lots of books to get rid of," Bonnie explained. "So, we went to ask, and before you know it, Alice and I were emptying out the bookshelves and painting them, while Linda and Bea packed up all the books and Rosemary and Molly helped her go through her fat quarters and sort them into colors. It's going to be a real nice quilting room."

"Even better, these are mostly middle-grade

adventure stories and kid-appropriate sports stories, and historical biographies," Linda said. "I know of three or four kids in the program who are going to be thrilled to take some of these books home. Oh, and Piper, I saw one about photography."

"Really?" Piper helped Linda lift the box into the car. "I only have one more library book to read, and then I'll have enough points for a keeper book. Oh, and guess what? I'm on my school's team for Book Battles! I'm the only fourth grader on the whole team."

"That's awesome!" Linda, who was obviously familiar with the program, offered her a high five. "When is your first match?"

"Not until December," Piper answered. "Because we have to read all the books and practice first."

"Well, congratulations! I'm so proud of you. When it's time to compete, I'll be there to cheer you on."

Linda was so good with Piper. Good with all the kids. A true asset to the community. They needed people like her here. Someone had mentioned that Linda spent all her savings on medical bills before her mother died and was getting by on her state pension. She wouldn't be able to afford a significant bump in rent, but it would be a loss to her and to everyone at Easy Living if she had to move. Sunny had to think of a plan of action for her and all the others to stay here.

Sunny followed the Mat Mates back to Easy Living, and they all walked in together.

Piper skipped on ahead and then looked back over her shoulder. "Mommy, I'm going to get my camera and go see Mr. Adam, okay? He said he'd show me how to make my pictures go on a computer."

"All right. You can take my laptop, but be very careful, okay?"

"I will." Piper ducked down the hall toward Sunny's office, while the rest of the group headed for the elevator. This place was as much home for her daughter as it was for the residents, and they were her family, too. If Sunny had to find a new job, maybe move to another town, Piper would lose all this. There had to be a way to keep it all together.

While they waited for the elevator, Sunny moved over beside Molly. "I need to talk with you about the supplies for the painting class."

"By the look on your face, I gather the new manager didn't approve? As I said, we could switch to smaller canvases. That would knock about ten percent off the total." The elevator arrived, and Molly stepped inside along with the rest of the group.

Sunny followed. "Is there any way we could switch to a different sort of class? Maybe a drawing class?"

Molly looked skeptical. "That bad?"

Sunny decided there was no reason to sugar-coat it. "That bad."

"All right, then. Why don't I make it a char-coal drawing class? The cost will be minimal, just charcoal pencils and paper. In fact, I'll pay for the supplies. Then you don't need approval at all."

"What's this about changing the class?" Bea pushed between two other ladies to stand be-side Molly. "I was looking forward to learning to paint with oils."

"Budget cuts," Molly explained. The eleva-tor door opened, and they all stepped out into the hallway. The doors shut behind them.

"Budget cuts? Why?" Bea raised her chin. "If we're still paying the same rent, the new company has no business cutting the activities budget. I'm going to have a little talk with Mr. Adam Lloyd." While Linda pushed her load of books toward the double doors at the end of the hall, Bea marched toward the door to the staircase, apparently unwilling to wait for the elevator to return.

"Wait, Bea!" Sunny called. "Don't go yet."

"Why not?" Bea stopped with her hand on

the knob. Her hair, streaked with purple today, actually quivered with indignation. "If he's making changes we don't like, he needs to hear about it."

"Let's talk about it first," Sunny urged. "Come to the multipurpose room."

"What's to talk about?" Bea sputtered. "We need to nip this in the bud. Let him know we're not going to stand for this kind of treatment. Make our demands known."

Alice laid a hand on Bea's arm. "Before we go storming in there, let's hear what Sunny has to say. She may have more information than us, and it's always good to get all the facts before formulating a plan of attack."

Bea considered this. "Okay, I'll listen. But I'm not going to let this go." She followed the rest of the group to the room all set up for read-ins.

Sunny brought up the rear and closed the doors behind them. Linda was already unpacking the books, but a sharp glance in Sunny's direction revealed she was listening. The rest of the women looked at her expectantly.

How much to tell? Adam hadn't specifically asked her to keep the information to herself, but he hadn't said not to, either. Still, it wasn't fair to let Bea charge into his office and ream him over something that clearly wasn't his fault. She didn't want to start a panic among the residents, but she knew these six women, and she trusted them.

"Okay, um, this isn't official or anything yet, but Easy Living is in trouble."

"Financial trouble?" Alice asked.

Sunny nodded. "I didn't realize before, but apparently Oscar Ravenwood owned the building."

Molly said, "His company built it about twenty-five years ago. It was the first non-assisted-living senior housing unit in the Mat-Su Valley."

Linda set down the book she was holding. "When I moved in ten years ago, one of the older residents mentioned that the owner originally built it partly because his wife's parents needed someplace like this, and he didn't want them to have to move away to get it."

"I didn't realize this was one of the Ravenwood properties," Alice commented. "I worked with Oscar Ravenwood on a couple of low-income housing projects the state sponsored. He was a good builder. Kept the overhead low and the quality high. As I recall from his obituary, neither of his sons followed him into the business. One is a dentist in Juneau, and the other is a doctor in Badger—no, maybe it's Bethel. Anyway, when Oscar and his wife died in a boating accident, I assume the sons must have sold off all the assets."

"Which is how Adam's company ended up with this building," Sunny explained. "From what Adam says, they hadn't planned on making big changes, but what they didn't realize is that the income from the rent isn't enough to cover the expenses and pay the investors a rate of return."

Alice frowned. "It should be. Before we moved in, Ralph and I compared the rent to other places we'd viewed. It's just a little bit higher than what we'd pay for a comparable apartment, but it has more amenities, what with the extra room in the facilities and the gardens and all the activities Sunny puts together. If other properties can make a go of it, I don't see why this one can't. We're all living independently, so it's not like we're paying for assisted living services."

"My rent hasn't gone up since I moved in two years ago," Bonnie said. "Maybe when the leases come up, they just need to raise the rent by the rate of inflation."

Linda had stopped sorting books to fully listen to the conversation. "If you don't mind my asking, what are you paying in rent?" she asked Alice.

Alice quoted a figure, and Bonnie nodded

in agreement. Linda shook her head. "I'm paying half that."

"Me, too," Rosemary volunteered. "I wondered how they were able to keep the rent so low. I didn't realize we weren't all paying the same."

"My rent is seventy percent of Bonnie's and Alice's," Bea admitted.

"Mine is about that, as well," Molly said. "It must be based on income."

"So all these years," Linda mused, "Oscar Ravenwood was subsidizing us, without us knowing. What a kind man."

"Unfortunately, he didn't make arrangements for it to continue after his death," Sunny told them. "And that's why Adam is trying to calculate a way to make it work."

"What if he can't?" Rosemary asked.

Sunny frowned. "Then they'll either sell the building or they'll raise the rents."

Rosemary sighed. "With my income from the Saturday market in the summer, I could probably cover what Alice and Bonnie are paying, but I'm not sure how I'd manage the rest of the year."

Sunny knew Rosemary's organic honey and crystal jewelry were popular sellers at the Saturday markets in Anchorage, but when the tourists left, so did her income stream.

Linda pushed her glasses up her nose. "Maybe I could find a part-time job. I think I remember seeing a 'now hiring' sign at the bookstore."

"It's for the evening shift," Alice told her. "And even in Palmer, no one wants to be closing up a store and driving home alone late at night."

Bonnie squeezed Linda's arm. "Besides, you've earned your retirement. We all have. At our age, we should be working on what we want to work on, not what someone is paying us to do."

"What about your job?" Molly asked Sunny. "Would they keep you on if they raise the rents?"

"I don't know. Adam asked me to stay, at least for now."

Bea rested her hands on her round hips. "Well, I'm still disappointed about the oils class, but it doesn't sound like making a scene will help. Do we trust Adam to figure out a way to keep the Easy Living Apartments going?"

"It seems to me," Alice said slowly, "that Adam can probably use all the help he can get. I'll make tea and coffee."

"And I'll get plates for the scones." Bonnie set the bakery box on the table. "Sounds like we need to do some brainstorming."

CHAPTER SEVEN

ADAM CLOSED THE spreadsheet he'd been reviewing and rubbed his temples. After going over yet another set of expenses item by item, he'd found very little he could cut from the budget. He had to give Lou credit for running a tight ship.

Every expense was carefully documented, down to the nineteen dollars and eighty-two cents Tilly had spent on flowers for the front desk and coffee and sodas for the office staff the week before they left. Adam had at least eliminated that expense—no one had questioned the lack of fresh flowers, and he could buy his own coffee—but twenty dollars a week wasn't going to make a dent in the overall financial picture.

His phone rang, and his father's name popped up. He'd been hoping to put off this conversation a little longer, but he was going to have to fill him in on the situation at some point. He crossed the room to close the office door as he answered. "Hi, Dad. Aren't you supposed to be on a cruise?"

"We are, and it's been fun. But after a day of sightseeing, your mother headed for the spa, and I decided to get a little work done while we're in port. How's it going in Alaska? Must be pretty up there. Your mom said you asked her to send your camera."

"Yes." Adam looked out his window across the grounds to a mountain peak shining in the sun. "It's beautiful. The camera came in today, so tell Mom thanks."

"Will do. So where are we on this building?"

"Well, first of all, suing the Ravenwood estate for misrepresenting the facts is completely off the table. I found the information they submitted, and the situation was all spelled out, if Chad had bothered to read it."

"I figured as much. We should probably list it sooner rather than later."

"We already got an unsolicited offer," Adam admitted.

"That's good. See if you can shine the place up and cut the fat from the outflows before we talk to any interested purchasers."

"So far, I haven't found much to cut in the way of expenses."

"What about staff?"

"Cleaning is contracted, the administrative

assistant left with the old manager and I haven't replaced her. That means it's just me and the activities director."

"Activities director? That sounds like a frill."

"Maybe, but she's very popular with the residents."

"That's nice, but if the numbers don't add up—"

"I'm not going to cut any positions until I've done a full analysis." Adam's voice was sharper than he'd intended.

"O-kay." Dad sounded puzzled, as he well might.

Adam never snapped. And he'd never hesitated to make necessary staffing cuts, which always came with a generous severance package and job counseling. "What's so special about this activities director?"

"She's— It's—" Sunny's smiling face set the tone for the whole building. She was the very essence of this place. But how could he explain that to his father? "This isn't your average apartment complex. The people here aren't just neighbors, they're like family. And Sunny is the glue that holds it all together."

"Sunny?"

"Sunny Galloway. The activities director."

"All right. I'll leave that decision up to you,

then. How long do you think it will take to make this full analysis?"

"A while. The books are a bit of a mess." They weren't, but it was a common enough situation that Dad would buy it, and it would give Adam a little more time to come up with a solution. Yikes, now he was lying to his dad—who was also his boss.

"It sounds like we should just sell. Even if we have to take a small loss on the deal, it gets us out from under it and frees up capital for other projects."

"Not yet. Give me a little time."

"How much time?"

"Hmm." How much time could he reasonably ask for? "Two months?"

"Two more months? You've already been there almost three weeks. I don't know that I can spare you for that long." There was a pause, no doubt while Dad checked his calendar. "You'll be coming here for Thanksgiving in six weeks. Can you finish by then?"

"I think so." He would have to.

"All right, then. By Thanksgiving, I either want the building on the market or well on its way to earning a reasonable payout. Agreed?"

"Yes. Thank you."

"Quicker would be better. We've got a new prospect that could use your touch. A medical complex in Casper, Wyoming. I could put Fallon on it, but—"

A knock sounded, but before Adam could answer, the door opened a crack and one-half of Piper's eager face appeared. He smiled and beckoned her into the room. "Excuse me, Dad, my three-thirty appointment is here. May I call you back?"

"That's all right. We'll be sailing soon. But wrap up this project as quickly as you can and come home. We need you."

"Okay. Talk with you soon." He ended the call and turned to Piper, who carried a padded computer bag. Her camera dangled from a strap around her neck. "Hi there."

"Hi. I brought you something." She reached into the bag and pulled out a slightly crooked ceramic cylinder. It had an imprint of a duck on the side, pressed into the clay with a stamp. "It's a pencil holder. We made them at school. It's to say thank you for helping me with the camera."

"That's very sweet of you." Adam set it on his desk and pulled a few pens and pencils from the drawer to fill it. "It works great. Thank you." He smiled at Piper. "I see you brought your camera. Are you ready to learn how to download your photos?"

"Yes." She spoke decisively. "Mommy says I can use her laptop if I'm very careful."

"We'll take good care of it, then. Why don't you sit here?" He indicated his desk chair and moved his own laptop out of the way. "And we'll set up your mom's computer on my desk." While Piper climbed into his chair and removed a slightly battered laptop from the tote bag, he carried a guest chair around so that he could sit beside her.

"May I see the pictures you've been taking?" he asked.

"Okay." Piper pulled the camera from around her neck and handed it to him, watching his face in anticipation. He turned on the screen and paged through the snapshots. Most were of the residents here, going about their activities. Linda shelving books. Ralph and one of the other men playing checkers in the lobby. Francine holding up two of the new kittens, followed by a whole string of kitten photos, some just catching the tip of a tail or a blurry shape, but one or two really cute ones. The angles and framing weren't perfect, but for a first attempt, especially by a nine-year-old, these were pretty darn good.

"You've got some nice shots here," he told her, earning him a smile. "Let's get them on the computer, where we can see them full-screen."

She opened the laptop, clicked on the penguin icon and signed in. Adam couldn't help noticing that the other user icon, presumably Sunny's, was a yellow daisy with a smiley-faced center. Because of course Sunny would choose the most cheerful icon she could find.

Once Piper was in, Adam showed her how to create a folder for her photos and then how to plug in a USB between the camera and computer and transfer all the pictures. "Once they're all there, we'll tell it to remove them from the camera so that you'll have room to take more."

She caught on quickly, obviously no stranger to her mother's laptop. Once the pictures were downloaded, he showed her how to look at them, one by one. "I really like this shot of the striped kitten pouncing on the gray one," he told her. "Do you want me to show you how to crop it so that the kittens are in the middle?"

"You can do that?"

"Sure. Your computer has some built-in photo-editing software." It wasn't nearly as sophisticated as the software he'd installed on his own machine, but it could do basic edit functions. He only had to show Piper once how to crop and adjust the brightness before she jumped in and did it herself.

She pulled up another shot of a kitten chasing a laser dot across the floor. She pulled the cropping lines, so the kitten was in the exact center of the picture, but he stopped her. "Can you see how, when you center the picture on the kitten's body, he's sort of running out of the picture?"

"Uh-huh."

"Now watch." Adam redrew the crop so that the kitten's face was in the center. "Now he's running into the photo. It's more dynamic that way."

Piper looked up at him in puzzlement. "What does that mean?"

"Dynamic? It means moving, changing, energetic. Even though the camera has frozen the action, you still get the sense that the kitten is moving. See?"

"I see. Let's look at the one where Bea was showing Mommy how to twirl a baton. I bet that one's dyna-manic."

"Dynamic," he corrected her. "And I'll bet you're right." He had no trouble believing that the brash woman with a penchant for temporary hair dye had been a majorette at some point in her life.

They located the shot. Bea, dressed in bright pink and orange, was indeed twirling a baton, while Sunny stood and watched. Piper had caught her in the moment when the baton was flipping over Bea's hand, the slight blurring of the baton indicative of the speed it was spinning. Piper had cut off the tops of their heads, but she'd captured Bea's expression of intense concentration. Adam was more interested in the expression on Sunny's face, her smile open and generous, her eyes wide with delight at Bea's antics. This wasn't just a job for her—these people were her friends. Family, really, with Bea playing the role of eccentric great-aunt.

"Super photo."

"I'm going to take a lot of pictures on Saturday. Mommy's taking me to goat yoga."

"That should be fun. You've inspired me. I got my camera in today, so I think I'll plan an outing to take photos this weekend, too."

"You should come to the farm!" Piper exclaimed. "It's so cool. There's goats, and cheese, and pretty flowers in the summer. And the people are really nice."

"I don't know." He was still trying to wrap his mind around the concept of yoga with goats. But he had to admit, it sounded like a gold mine for photo opportunities. "Maybe."

"It's fun. You should totally come."

"You should." Sunny was standing in the open doorway. "If you're not busy Saturday afternoon, that is."

"I've never done yoga."

"Don't worry about it. It's more of an excuse to play with the goats than a workout. Many of the people there will be beginners. Crystal, the instructor, keeps it simple. Do you like cheese?"

"Sure. All kinds."

"Now and Forever Farms has won awards for their cheeses. They have a tasting room on the premises, and they sell gift packs and cheese by the pound."

Hmm, gourmet cheese from an Alaskan goat farm. That would take care of a big chunk of his Christmas shopping and earn him points for originality. "Maybe. I'll see if I can make it."

"Great. It starts at two. I'll email you the details. Piper, you've probably taken up enough of Adam's time today."

"But we were gonna crop more pictures."

"She's not bothering me," he assured Sunny. "We're having fun." And they were, he realized. It had been a while since he'd taken time for fun.

"I'm glad, but we're about to make autumn leaf wreaths. Do you want to help?"

"Yes!" Piper jumped up, but then she turned to Adam. "Sorry, I have to go. My mom needs my help with the class. Thank you for teaching me how to put the pictures on the computer."

"Thank you for reminding me how much I like photography."

"You're welcome." Piper packed her mom's computer carefully in the bag and returned the camera to her neck. As she left the room, she called, "See you Saturday!"

ADAM SPOTTED THE herd of goats in the field just off the road a minute before he saw the Now and Forever Farm sign with a picture of a goat at a split-rail fence in front of a mountain. The two cars in front of him turned in. He still wasn't entirely sure whether goat yoga was a real thing or an elaborate ruse of some sort, but if it was a joke, a lot of people seemed to have fallen for it.

The farm itself was worth the trip, with a large red barn and two other buildings painted the same color set against the background of rugged peaks. The trees at the base of the mountain sported shades of gold and russet. Not the brilliant autumn foliage of an eastern hardwood forest, but the warm colors glowed in the sunlight.

He followed the cars to another pasture and parked his rental there, grabbed his camera and followed the crowd. All ages seemed to be represented, from an infant in a baby carrier to a pair of gray-haired women crossing the path in front of him. When he got closer, one of them turned to say something to the other, and he recognized Alice and Rosemary. That's right, Sunny had told him the six ladies were in a yoga club. What was it called?

Mat Mates. That was it.

When he got closer to a pavilion where everyone seemed to be heading, he saw that the other four members of the club were already there. They were checking people in, directing them to step inside the fencing, select a mat and find a place to spread it out. A definite chill was in the air, but the sun was shining, and the yoga participants seemed comfortable in sweatshirts or long-sleeved tees and fleece vests.

Among the buzz of conversation, a familiar laugh rang out. He spotted Sunny and Piper next to a smaller adjoining pen, which held a dozen or so little goats, most of whom wore bright ribbons around their necks. Two of the goats had put their front feet on the railing and thrust their faces toward Piper. Sunny reached out to scratch one under the chin.

Piper picked up her camera and snapped pictures of the goats. She was too close, and Adam knew the goats' faces would look out of proportion from the rest of their bodies, but he would explain that to her later, once she saw the photos. It was the sort of thing a photographer learned from experience. In the meantime, he slipped around to the other side of the pen and changed to his longer telephoto lens to get some close-up candids of Sunny and her daughter laughing and interacting with the goats.

Another woman about Sunny's age wearing a green polo with the farm's logo embroidered on the left side came over and said something to Piper. She opened the gate to the goats' pen, let herself and the girl inside, and retrieved a purple ribbon from the ground. The woman handed the ribbon to Piper before catching one of the unadorned goats and holding him still while Piper tied the ribbon around his neck. The bow came out a little lopsided, which just made the whole thing cuter.

And Adam caught it all on his camera.

A minute later, Piper spotted him and waved. Sunny turned and flashed that amazing smile. "Adam! You made it."

"I did," he called back, and moved a little closer. "Beautiful day."

"I know. We're so lucky. We don't get many of these cloudless days this time of year. That's why Lauren decided to do one bonus yoga session. Come meet her." She gestured toward the woman with the goats.

When he stepped up to the pen, Sunny announced, "Adam Lloyd, this is Lauren O'Shea. Lauren is Bonnie's granddaughter-in-law. She runs the farm and is a master cheesemaker, as well as all-round goat expert. Wait until you taste her white cheddar."

"I'll look forward to that. Hello, Lauren. You have a beautiful place here." He offered a hand. Lauren took it willingly. That probably meant either she didn't realize he was managing the apartments where her husband's grandmother lived, or that Sunny hadn't shared his company's dilemma about the fate of the Easy Living Apartments. Either way, he was grateful. It was too nice of a day to mar with arguments. "I'm glad to meet you."

"You, too. Are you doing yoga today?"

"You know, if it's okay with you, I'd just as soon take pictures, instead."

"Sure. As long as you don't plan to post them publicly without permission from the subjects, I don't mind. In fact—" Lauren's already smiling face brightened even more "—I've been considering hiring a professional to get publicity shots of the farm and the different activities. Up until now, I've been posting photos I took from my phone on the website, but I think we're ready to step it up. Are you interested?"

"I'm not a professional photographer. It's just a hobby."

"Oh. I saw the fancy camera and I thought—"

"Adam is the temporary manager for the Easy Living Apartments. He's working for the new owners," Sunny explained. "But he's good enough to be a professional photographer. I've seen his work. Maybe he could let you see what he comes up with today, and if you like the images, you could buy some?"

"That sounds good," Lauren agreed.

Adam shook his head. "That's not necessary. I'd be happy to let you use any images you want for free."

"No, if we use the photos, we'll pay," Lauren insisted. "I believe it's important to pay people for their work, especially artists. Oh, excuse me. Looks like they have a question for me." She let herself out of the goat pen and crossed to Linda and Bonnie, who were waving her over to the folding table where they were checking people in.

"Why did you tell her you'd seen my photography?" Adam asked Sunny.

"Because I have. Those two pictures on your desk are your work, aren't they?"

"Why would you think that?"

"I just assumed. I know you're passionate about photography, and it's obvious the photos were taken by someone who cares about the people in the pictures. They seemed like your style. Was I wrong?"

"No, I took them." Adam was touched. Those two photos were favorites of his, but he'd never thought of them as having a certain style.

"Oh." Sunny looked at him uncertainly. "If you don't want to share your photos with Lauren, I can explain—"

"No, it's fine. I don't mind. In fact, it might be fun. And it gives me an excuse to watch instead of attempting yoga."

"Okay, then." Sunny grinned. "But I warn you, once you see how much fun everyone else is having with the goats, you might change your mind."

He looked at the people spreading their mats, mostly women with some kids and several husbands or boyfriends or friends, some of whom looked as though they'd been dragged along under protest. "I doubt it."

"You'll see. Come on, Piper, it's almost time to start. You'd better put your camera away and grab a spot." Their two matching ponytails swayed as they bounced over to select mats and spread them on the ground. It was hard to decide which of them was more excited.

At first, Adam couldn't see too much to get excited about. The leader gave some sort of instruction, and everyone sat cross-legged on their mats. But then, after they'd moved to their hands and knees, Lauren opened the gate and the goats gamboled into the pavilion. The goats, recognizing it was playtime, wasted no time jumping onto the backs of various people. Two of them chased each other across the pen, jumping from one back to the next. Adam would have thought those sharp little hooves might hurt, but no one seemed to mind. In fact, they seemed delighted, even the few guys who'd looked disgruntled before.

The little goats were seasoned performers, moving from person to person, nuzzling hands like dogs hoping for petting, and then unexpectedly jumping onto someone's back. As the instructor gave a different instruction and the participants stretched forward, two of the goats raced up Sunny's back and then one jumped on top of the other. Adam managed to snap two shots before Sunny, shaking with laughter, sent both goats tumbling down, only to land on their feet. Piper, on the mat next to hers, had given up following the instructor and was literally rolling on the ground, laughing.

On Piper's other side, Bea continued to follow the instructor and moved to her hands and feet, thrusting her bottom into the air. She wore clover-green yoga pants and had streaked her hair to match. It proved to be an unfortunate choice when a black-and-white goat with a red bow leaped onto her bottom and then marched down her back and began chewing on her hair, probably wondering why it didn't taste like clover.

Lauren rushed over, snatched up the offending goat, and after a quick apology, moved it to the other side of the pavilion. The goat, not so easily dissuaded, immediately ran back, weaving between participants and jumping over others, to return to that tempting green hair. After two more tries at distraction, Lauren gave up and returned him to the goat pen, where he stood and bleated his frustration.

The rest of the session went relatively smoothly, with as much laughter as yoga. Everyone there seemed to be having a great time. Adam got a variety of shots, some taking in the whole crowd with the trees and mountains in the background, and others close-up. He could hardly wait to go through them all later, to see what expressions he might have captured.

At the end of the class, Lauren, Bonnie and Alice circulated among the participants, offering to take pictures with their cell phones of them posing with the goats. Adam thought about offering to email photos he'd taken to the subjects but decided it would be too complicated to collect all the email addresses and sort out the names. But judging by the group's enthusiasm, if Lauren were to set up some sort of souvenir photo opportunity like the ones offered at theme park rides and cruises, she would get plenty of takers.

Once the photos were done and Lauren had rounded up the goats, most of the crowd gravitated toward the nearby tasting room. Picnic tables were scattered around the sunny area outside, surrounded by the flower beds. Adam didn't know much about flowers, but he recognized a few shrubby bushes with bright orange rose hips. The beds probably boasted quite a floral show in the peak of summer. In the wilder area in front of birch trees, with a few golden leaves still clinging to the branches, cottony seeds were the only remainder from the tall wildflowers that had been blooming already. Even without the flowers, the green valley backed by rugged mountains was a spectacular setting for the red barns and the white farmhouse with its wide front porch.

Lauren and a couple of others dressed in matching polo shirts moved several of the picnic tables into the pavilion. Meanwhile, people were coming out of the tasting room carrying plates with various combinations of cheese, fruits and crackers. Several also carried shopping bags printed with the farm's logo that matched the sign at the road.

Adam snapped a few photos of them gathering at the picnic tables. He noticed Bonnie, Linda and Bea—her hair looking a bit ruffled from her goat encounter—had claimed a table with ten chairs set a bit apart from the others.

Lauren came to stand beside Adam. "Have you, by chance, ever done any food photography?"

He let his camera dangle from its strap and turned to her. "Not a lot, but I took a workshop several years ago." It had been a fluke. He'd signed up for a weekend workshop on portrait photography, but through some mix-up, he had somehow been assigned to the wrong class, which he hadn't discovered until he'd shown up that morning. The sponsor had been apologetic and allowed him to attend a future session of the portrait class as well, but Adam had enjoyed discovering some of the techniques involved in creating mouthwatering photos of food. "Why do you ask?"

"I was talking with my sister-in-law, Rowan, who runs the Now and Forever Farm food truck. She wants to post photos of the menu items on the side of her truck, to help people understand what she's offering. I think we should do the same in the tasting room. Not only would pictures help entice people to try something new, but it should also speed up the ordering process. Is that something you might be interested in doing? I know you have a day job, but there's no huge rush for the photos. We would just want them in place before next summer."

"You haven't seen my work yet. How do you know I'm even any good?"

"Sunny vouched for you. She said you've already taught Piper a lot about photography. I figure if you know it well enough to teach it to a nine-year-old, you're probably pretty good."

"So, you don't subscribe to the 'those who can't, teach' theory?"

Lauren laughed. "It's not what I've found. The people who taught me to make cheese did it because they were very good at what they did and wanted to spread the craft."

"How about you? Sunny says you're a master cheesemaker. Are you teaching?"

"Up to now, I've been swamped getting the farm set up for my business, but I am toying with the idea of offering a few classes this winter through the community schools program. But we were talking about you. Could we hire you to do our food photography?"

It would be fun to try his hand at something new. "I'll tell you what. Once I've had a chance to look over today's photos and work on them a bit, I'll send them to you. If you like what you see, I'll take a stab at your food photos, and you can decide if they're worth paying for. If not, just say so. No hard feelings."

"Sounds like a deal. Rowan will be thrilled."

"We'll see." Adam didn't want to overpromise. He'd never really considered charging for his photography before. Well, that wasn't entirely true—there was a brief period in high school when he'd thought he wanted to be a professional wildlife photographer, but Dad had pointed out that Adam's talents in math and logic would make for a successful career in business, a much more secure profession. Once he had graduated, summa cum laude, with his degree in business analysis, Dad had hired him at Western Real Estate Investments, and he had never looked back.

"Adam, over here!" Bea called, as if he could possibly miss her with that green hair. She was waving a bright pink towel. "Come join us!"

Lauren grinned. "Looks like you're being summoned. Give me a call later and we can schedule something for those food photos."

"All right. Thanks." Adam made his way to the table, where all six of the Mat Mates were gathered around several cheese platters, leaving four empty chairs.

"Sit down here." Molly patted the chair next to her. "So, what did you think about goat yoga?"

"After watching the fun everyone was having, I can't imagine why anyone does any other kind of yoga," he replied as he settled into the chair.

"Don't let Crystal, the instructor, hear you say that," Alice warned. "She keeps it easy for the goat sessions, but she's a bear in regular classes. In our session last Tuesday, I swear she had us holding tree pose for fifteen minutes."

"It was two minutes," Rosemary corrected her. "It just felt like fifteen."

Adam wasn't sure what tree pose was, but if it kept a bunch of eighty-something-year-olds looking and acting as young as these ladies did, it must be magic.

"Here, Adam, try some of Lauren's incredible cheese." Bonnie set a small plate in front of him and pushed a platter closer. He put some grapes, slices of cheese and whole-grain crackers on his dish. Bonnie was watching him expectantly, so he set a slice of cheese on a cracker and bit into it. Wow, they weren't kidding. This cheddar was amazing—tangy, but incredibly smooth.

"That is great," he commented, and shoved the rest of the cheese and cracker into his mouth.

"So." Alice pulled a folder from the tote by

her side and slapped it on the table. Everyone immediately set up straighter, as though she'd banged a gavel. "We understand the Easy Living Apartments are in trouble."

Adam almost choked on his cheese. From Bea's smirk, he got the idea they'd purposely waited until his mouth was full to spring this on him.

"Don't worry," Molly said, patting his arm and handing him a glass of water. "We're here to help."

Rosemary pushed her braid behind her shoulder and smiled at him. "Sunny assures us that you're trying your best to keep the place going, and we want you to succeed. Take this." She handed him a black oval stone, polished until it was perfectly smooth.

"What is it?"

"Hematite, for grounding. It helps reduce mental clutter and provide clarity."

"I see. Well, thank you." Adam slipped the stone into his pocket rather than insult her by refusing it. He supposed he could use all the clarity he could get.

"Anyway, to start with, we've made a list of possible places to trim expenses." Alice passed a stack of papers to Linda, who distributed them to everyone at the table, including Adam. "But before we get into that, we want to make ourselves clear. No matter what else you have to cut, you can't eliminate Sunny's position. She's not just the activities director at Easy Living, she's the heart of the place. Without her drawing everyone together, we'd just be a bunch of old people who happen to live in the same building."

"If Sunny goes, I go," Bea declared. "And so would most of the others."

The other women all nodded in solidarity.

"I have no intention of cutting Sunny's position," Adam assured them. "But I'll be frank. If I can't figure out how to get the numbers to add up by Thanksgiving, the building is going on the market, and I already know of one firm that is interested in buying it and turning it into an office complex."

Alice didn't look surprised. "Well then, we'd better get busy. Item one, you can cut the floral budget completely. We'll organize a sign-up sheet for volunteers to decorate the entryway table weekly."

"Since it's almost time for the first freeze, item two won't affect the budget much until next summer, but you can cut back on the landscaping as well," Rosemary explained. "I'll lead a group who can prune shrubs and keep the garden beds planted, mulched and weeded.

You'll just need someone to mow regularly. I'll take care of the indoor plants, as well."

"I have a lead on snowplowing," Bonnie volunteered. "You know Chris and Marissa Allen, from the reindeer farm? They took part in Rowan's fundraiser for the wild animal rehab last summer, remember?" At the others' nods, she continued. "Well, Chris owns a commercial snowplow business in Anchorage and they're planning to open a branch in Wasilla this winter. He said they would plow our parking lots for free if we put up a sign advertising them."

"We could also set up a volunteer rotation to sweep the lobby and public rooms and take out the trash every day," Bea suggested. "So you could have the cleaning service come in a little less often."

Linda, the former librarian, cleared her throat. "I know Francine has already been helping out at the office. Alice and I both have administrative experience, as well, so we would be willing to donate our time so that you don't need to fill that position. We can work out a schedule with you."

Adam was impressed. If their organization at rounding up volunteers was anywhere as good as it was at brainstorming solutions, it would make a good dent in the deficit. Still, it wouldn't close the gap. "Thank you. I really appreciate this. I'll look at the numbers when I get back, but—"

"We know it's not enough," Linda interrupted. "We didn't realize until recently that we're not all paying the same rent. I don't know how many of us are paying less…" She paused to let him fill in the blank, but that was confidential information. When Adam didn't say anything, she continued. "But we hope that by reducing expenses that can buy us some time to come up with a more permanent solution."

"Linda and I have been researching grants," Alice said. "So far, we haven't found any specifically targeted for this situation, but—"

"What about that one you mentioned to encourage more housing for seniors?" Bonnie asked her.

"It turns out that one is about encouraging more assisted living facilities," Alice replied. "It doesn't apply to independent units."

Bonnie scoffed. "That's about as helpful as hip pockets on a hog. The whole point of the Easy Living Apartments is that we can live independently while joining together for group activities."

"I know. We're still researching. There are lots of opportunities out there—we just need to find them." Alice turned to Adam. "Once we have zeroed in on grant possibilities, we'll either need access to the financial information for the building, or else you'll need to apply for the grant. I feel it would make for better optics, though, if this were a collaboration between the owner and the residents."

Despite his misgivings, he was beginning to feel a surge of optimism. "I think something could be arranged."

Piper and Sunny approached the table, laughing together. Both wore crowns made from twigs with golden birch leaves attached. They took the two vacant chairs at the end of the table. "Sorry we were so long," Sunny told the ladies, "but Piper insisted I had to pose in front of the autumn trees and then she wanted to make crowns…" Sunny frowned as she noticed the papers in front of everyone. "Am I interrupting— Uh-oh. I'm sorry, Adam. When I was talking to Molly about the class budget, I let it slip—"

"Don't you feel bad." Bonnie patted Sunny's hand. "You spilled the beans—so what? It was bound to come out sooner or later. This way, we can hang our troubles out there where we can all take a swing at them."

The other women nodded in agreement. Piper looked wide-eyed around the table, her gaze coming to rest on Adam. "Is my mommy in trouble?"

"No," Adam assured her. It wasn't as though Sunny had promised to keep the information to herself, and besides, he had a feeling that once the Mat Mates got a whiff of trouble, she hadn't stood a chance at keeping the secret. "Your mommy's not in any trouble at all. In fact, Sunny, I should be thanking you. This has been a very productive meeting." He nodded to Alice. "We can certainly implement most if not all of these suggestions, and we'll move forward from there."

"Linda and I will keep you abreast of our research on grants," Alice said.

"Excellent."

"In that case," Bea put in, "would somebody please pass that fruit and Brie plate over to me? I'm starved."

As everyone put away their papers and began to fill their plates, Lauren strolled over, carrying a platter of what looked like tiny cheesecakes and set it in the center of the table. "The last yoga session of the season was a great success, thanks to all of you." She sat in the last remaining chair. "So, what did I miss?"

"Oh, nothing much," Bonnie told her. "Just solving all the problems of the world."

Lauren laughed. "I don't doubt that for a second."

CHAPTER EIGHT

AND HERE HE was again. After spending all day Monday working up another projection, including the budget cuts the Mat Mates had suggested and cutting the expected rate of return to the bone, Adam found the building was still in the red. Not hemorrhaging money like it was before, but still bleeding. And Dad had only given him until Thanksgiving to turn it around. Was there anything else he could cut?

He'd already removed the administrative assistant's salary and his own. One thing about the hours he'd been working the past few years—it didn't leave a lot of time for spending money. As a result, he'd saved up a nice chunk. He could get by on his savings for three months. That left Sunny as the only paid staff member. But Alice had put it well: Sunny was the heart of the Easy Living Apartments. Without her, what would be the point of saving them?

He absently reached for his coffee mug, only to find the remaining inch at the bottom had gone cold. Maybe a fresh hit of caffeine would help him think. He walked to the outer office and crouched down to reach for the bag of French roast he'd picked up on the way to work that morning. Footsteps tip-tapped into the office from the hallway, too quick to be Francine's. Besides, it was after five o'clock. She would be home in her apartment preparing her dinner and playing with her foster kittens. The steps went around the assistant's desk and into his office. When he stood up, he saw Sunny standing behind his desk, frowning at the screen.

"Were you looking for me?"

She jumped at his voice and pressed her hand to her chest. "Oh, Adam, I didn't see you there. I, uh…" She gave a guilty grin. "I'm afraid this is exactly what it looks like. I saw the computer open, and I was curious."

"That's okay. I was going to share it with you anyway. Go ahead and look it over." He spooned grounds into the filter. "Want some coffee?"

"No, thanks. If I drink coffee in the afternoon, I have a hard time winding down at night."

Adam had never seen her wind down at all. She was like a hummingbird, darting from flower to flower. Except, instead of extracting sweetness, Sunny spread it, making life better for everyone around her. If they didn't work together, he would be tempted to ask her out, but he had a strict no-dating policy when it came to coworkers. Even more so when they reported directly to him. Still, the thought of spending some alone time with Sunny, of kissing that lovely mouth—it was hard to resist.

She paged down to the bottom of the spreadsheet and for once that incredible smile faded. "It's not enough, is it?"

"No. It's not."

She took a fortifying breath. "Then, I come bearing what I hope is good news. Linda has zeroed in on two possible grants we may be eligible for. However, the deadline for the first one is next Friday, so they wanted me to ask if Alice and Linda could have immediate access to all the figures. I know it's sensitive information, including the residents' income and the rent they're paying, but they'd be very discreet." She grinned. "Unlike me, they can keep a secret."

"We could arrange something, maybe gather permission from all the residents, but the fastest and easiest thing would probably be for me to gather the statistical data they need without linking the information to the individual. I'll talk with Alice about it. But can they really write up a grant proposal in four days? I understand the process can take weeks."

"They say they can, and I've never known Alice not to deliver what she promises. But there's a hitch. Molly says you told them you have to have the apartments profitable before Thanksgiving or they'll be sold."

"That's correct." And his dad had a policy. Once he set a deadline, it never moved. If someone had an emergency, he might shift the responsibility to someone else, but deadlines were sacred.

"Trouble is, we might not get a decision for those grants before the end of the year. So," she added, before he could explain that the deadline was nonnegotiable, "the Mat Mates have come up with a stopgap. The residents are going to organize a craft fair. The money will go into a fund to subsidize the rent for the people who can't afford the market price until the grant kicks in."

Sunny smiled as though she and the Mat Mates had solved that pesky little problem and were ready to move on to world peace.

"Hmm." Adam was no authority on craft fairs, but he had a hard time imagining they could raise more than a few hundred dollars. Hardly enough to subsidize one person's rent for a month, much less half the residents. Still, they were trying. "That's great, but it sounds like a lot of work. Are they sure it's worth—"

"They're sure." She laughed. "I know what you're thinking. You're picturing a card table in the lobby with a few crocheted doilies and some painted vases. Don't underestimate the residents here. They think big."

"Okay. I'll look forward to this."

"Good. I'll tell them it's all on. Alice and her crew will check in with you first thing in the morning to get started."

"I'll be here."

"Oh, and I have one more favor to ask."

"More kittens?"

Sunny laughed. "No, Francine's got her hands full with those five."

"Okay then, what's the favor?"

"Piper was showing me a couple of the pictures you'd taken of the residents with her camera while you were teaching her. They're so good. Anyway, then we got to talking about Thanksgiving. Since most of the residents visit their families on Thanksgiving Day, we always have a group celebration for the whole building the Tuesday before, and I've always done a slideshow highlighting some of the projects and activities we've done through the year. But Piper had this idea that instead of just using group pictures, you could take a picture of each resident doing something they're particularly good at. Then I'd put them all together for the show."

"How many would that be?" It sounded like fun, but he'd already made an appointment with Lauren for a food photography session next Saturday. He didn't want to overpromise. "Let's see, we have forty-two apartments."

"Yes, sixty residents. Eighteen couples and twenty-four singles. I know it's a huge undertaking and you already have plenty on your plate, but Piper and I thought—"

"Mommy!" Piper walked into the outer office, gingerly carrying a large food container. "Ms. Rowan was here, and she gave us soup for supper!"

"Mmm, is that her cheese and broccoli?" Sunny took the container and set it on the desk. "It is! Adam, Rowan is Bonnie's granddaughter, who operates the Now and Forever Farms food truck. She takes Lauren's cheeses and makes them into the most incredible foods."

"Sounds delicious." He was supposed to meet Rowan this coming Saturday. "That cheese we had at the farm was some of the best I've ever tried."

"You've got to taste this soup." She looked around the office as though a soup bowl would suddenly materialize.

"Mr. Adam should come eat supper with us," Piper declared.

"That's a great idea." Sunny shot him that amazing smile. "This is a lot more soup than Piper and I can eat, and Francine gave me a loaf of her famous sourdough bread today. You and Piper can talk about 'f-stops' and 'depth of focus' and all those other photography words Piper has been telling me about that I don't understand."

"In that case, thank you. I'll be doing a little photographic work for them next weekend, so I'd love to try this soup with you before I do that."

"Oh, good. Lauren told me she was going to ask you. Are you ready to leave now?"

"I am."

"All right, then. Let's go!"

SUNNY GLANCED IN the rearview mirror to make sure Adam was close enough behind them to see her put on her blinker before turning into her driveway. Had she crossed a line, inviting him to her home? Technically, Piper had invited him, but she'd endorsed the invitation. She pulled into the single-car garage on her side of the duplex and checked the mirror again, taking a moment to smooth a few strands of hair that had come loose from her ponytail. She wished she'd taken thirty seconds to apply mascara that morning. Well, too late for that. Adam was here.

And that was fine, she decided. After all, she'd had Lou and Tilly over several times, because they were friends as well as coworkers. No reason she and Adam couldn't be friends as well. A voice inside her pointed out that Lou and Tilly's visits had never induced hair smoothing or made her heart beat faster in anticipation, but she ignored it and looked back at Adam.

Piper slipped from the car and ran back to take his hand. "This way, Mr. Adam. It's my job to set the table." She led him straight through the laundry room into the kitchen, and all Sunny could do was grab the soup and follow. He glanced around the kitchen. "This is exactly how I would have expected your kitchen to look."

Sunny set the soup on the counter and noted the open shelves stacked with mismatched colorful pottery she'd picked up here and there, the sunflower-print café curtains at the window, the markers Piper had left scattered on the island and the cluster of Piper's drawings that Sunny had framed and hung on the wall. "Is that a good thing?"

"A very good thing," he assured her. "It's a happy place."

"What a nice thing to say." She moved a bouquet of paper sunflowers—samples for a class she'd led—out of the way so that Piper could set the table. Meanwhile, Sunny preheated the oven to warm the bread and transferred the soup to a pot. "It will take about ten minutes to heat everything up."

"Come on, Mr. Adam," Piper said after she'd set the last spoon in place. "I'll show you my room and where I keep my camera."

"All right." He exchanged an amused glance with Sunny over Piper's head as he allowed her to tug him toward the end of the hall. Sunny used the few minutes alone to gather up a few stray toys, books and other clutter in the adjoining living room.

She could hear her daughter introducing Adam to each of her stuffed animals. "This is Humphrey. He's a tiger."

"I see that. Why is he named Humphrey?"

"He just is. And this is my favorite, Gladys. See, she's a loon, and she's very, very soft. You can pet her if you want."

"She is soft."

"I take her to bed with me every night."

Sunny returned to the kitchen and stirred the soup. "Dinner's ready," she called, ladling it into three bowls. Piper and Adam returned immediately. Sunny took the warm bread from the oven, set it on a wooden cutting board in the center of the table and poured a glass of milk for Piper.

"Adam, what would you like to drink?" He was probably used to nice dinners with wine, or at least a craft beer, but she had nothing like that in her refrigerator. "I have, um, orange juice or I could make coffee—"

"Milk's great if you have enough."

"Sure." She wasn't sure if he really preferred milk or was just being an agreeable guest, but she wouldn't argue. She poured two more glasses of milk and set them on the table. "Help yourself to some bread. Francine is really a wonderful baker."

"I know. She brought me some pumpkin muffins the other day." Adam cut a slice of bread and spread it with the butter Piper handed him.

Sunny cut another slice for Piper and one for herself. "I heard you shared your muffin stash with Phil after he came in to complain."

He laughed. "You are plugged in."

"Francine told me." She'd also described how Adam had offered Phil a cup of coffee and a muffin while he patiently listened to Phil's long list of grievances, most of which were imaginary. "Phil can be a challenge. Lou and Tilly had a system. When he'd barge into Lou's office, Tilly would wait three minutes and then text him with some emergency repair request, so he'd have an excuse to cut it short."

"I figured Phil mostly needed someone to listen. Seemed like he was in a better mood when he left, but I credit that mostly to Francine's muffins." He lifted a spoonful of soup, blew on it and tasted it. His face lit up in that expression Sunny had seen so many times when people first tried Rowan's food. "This is fantastic."

"I know." Sunny laughed. "I can't figure out how Rowan turns broccoli and cheese into something this good. And it's not just the soup. Everything she makes is wonderful. We're so lucky to have her here in Palmer."

"Where can I find this food truck?"

"They're in Wasilla several days a week, but they're always in the parking lot next to the Palmer library on Mondays for lunch."

"I'll put that on my calendar." Adam pulled out his phone and did just that. "And speaking of scheduling, I was thinking maybe Miss Piper and I could schedule a few photography sessions." At Piper's look of delight, he smiled. "Your mom told me about the Thanksgiving

project, and I think it's a great idea if you partic-
ipated too, a couple of afternoons should do it."

"Yes!" Piper held out a hand, Adam slapped
her a high five and just like that, Sunny's heart
melted. She could resist Adam's good looks,
his kindness toward people like Phil, and even
his efforts to save the apartments, but if he
was going to go around making her daughter's dreams come true, who could possibly
resist that?

"Tomorrow?" he suggested.

"Oh! I can't tomorrow. I'm going with Ms.
Francine and Thor to 'visit the elderly.'" Piper
quoted Francine without a hint of irony, not
realizing that most people would use that particular word to describe Francine and the other
residents.

"A nursing home in Wasilla," Sunny said,
clarifying. "Francine usually visits every week."

Adam's eyes crinkled at the corners, but he
didn't laugh. "I see. I don't believe I've met
Thor. Is he a resident?"

Piper laughed. "He's a dog! He's too big to
stay in Ms. Francine's apartment, so he moved
to a farm. Ms. Francine brings him to visit
people."

"I see. We'll just have to schedule those
photography sessions for a different day. Any
chance I might get seconds on that soup?"

"You bet," Sunny answered.

Once they'd finished eating, Sunny began clearing the table. "It's almost your bedtime," she told Piper. "You'd better go finish your math worksheet."

"But I—" At Sunny's look, Piper's protest died away. "Will you check it for me when I'm done?"

"Of course." Sunny set the dishes next to the sink. Adam brought his bowl and spoon over.

Piper went to her room, but almost immediately called, "Mommy, I broke my pencil and I can't find the sharpener."

"Excuse me," Sunny told Adam. It took a few minutes to locate the missing sharpener in the very back corner of Piper's desk drawer. When she returned to the kitchen, Adam had loaded the dishes into the dishwasher and was scrubbing the pot she'd used to heat the soup.

"You didn't need to do that," she protested.

"I don't mind." He rinsed the pot and reached for the dishtowel hanging on the oven door. "Do you always check Piper's homework?"

"I try to. She likes to get it right."

"After my mother remarried, my stepdad used to do the same thing for me. It made all the difference. When I knew he was going to be looking at it, I was motivated to do my best work. My grades went from C's to A's."

"He sounds like a great dad."

"Yes. He's a great boss, too, CEO of Western Real Estate Investment. There's hardly an employee in the company who wouldn't jump through fire for him." He looked thoughtfully out the kitchen window while he finished drying the pot. "He's been hinting that he's thinking of retirement."

"If he's as popular as you say, the employees must be nervous about getting a new boss."

"They don't know yet." Adam handed her the pot. "I'm hopeful that when the time comes, the board will offer me the position."

"Wow, head of the company at your age? That's impressive."

"I've been with them for almost fourteen years now, so I've had plenty of time to learn the business. But there's no certainty I'll get the job. There's at least one other obvious candidate in the company, or they could bring in someone from outside. But it would mean a lot to my dad if I could follow in his footsteps."

"Obviously, it would mean a lot to you, too."

He nodded. "It's been my goal since college. I've given up a lot to advance in this company. I don't want to let him down."

"What have you given up?"

"Leisure time. Hobbies. Relationships. Working sixty-hour weeks and traveling constantly doesn't leave a lot of time for a social life. Usually, I don't regret it, but sometimes…" He looked at her and their eyes locked.

For an instant, she was tempted to take a step closer. To put her arms around him and tilt her face up to his and—whoa. Where was this coming from? He was her boss, and she shouldn't forget it.

She turned away to set the pot in the cabinet. When she turned back, she said, "I don't think you need to worry about letting him down. If your stepfather is the kind of man you've described, I know he's proud of you and all you've accomplished. And whether you end up as the CEO or not, he'll still be proud of you."

"You're right. But that just makes me want it more. You know?"

"I do." She smiled. "And for what it's worth, I think you'd make an excellent CEO."

"Oh? Based on what?"

"On your people skills. You've got the folks at Easy Living feeding you, kidnapping you for tours, and dreaming up ways to help you balance the budget. Even Phil told Ralph you weren't a bad sort, and that's high praise coming from him. After this, running a company should be a breeze."

He laughed. "Maybe I should get you to talk to the board."

"Maybe."

"I suppose I should be going. Thank you for dinner. And for the talk."

"Anytime."

He handed her the dishtowel, and their fingers touched. "Goodnight, Sunny." He said the words, but his eyes never left hers, and he still held the towel.

"Goodnight, Adam." She felt herself swaying slightly in his direction.

"All finished!" Piper came out of her bedroom, sending Sunny and Adam jumping apart as though they'd been burned.

Sunny moved to the front door. "Adam has to go now, so come say goodbye."

"Bye, Mr. Adam," Piper chimed. "I'll see you tomorrow."

"Goodbye."

Sunny locked the door behind him. But instead of immediately starting to check Piper's math, she went to the window and watched until his taillights disappeared.

THOR TURNED OUT to be the tallest poodle Adam had ever seen. He happened to be outside when Piper emerged from the building. The second the dog spotted the girl, he jumped up from where he was sitting beside Francine on the lawn in front of the apartment building and dashed toward her skidding neatly to a stop in front of her. She threw her arms around the dog's neck. Obviously, they were old friends.

Francine followed at a more judicious pace. "I'm so pleased you could come today. The residents will be thrilled."

Adam walked over to greet them and ran his hand over the dog's head. "So this is Thor. May I take a few pictures of him?"

"Sure." Francine and Piper played with the dog for a few minutes while Adam snapped away.

"Okay, I think I've got enough. If there are any really good ones, I'll send them to you."

"Thanks. Piper, are you ready to go?"

"I'm ready." She followed Francine across the parking lot to her car.

On the way, they waved to Sunny, who was loading something into her hatchback. Apparently, she still hadn't fixed the lifts since the broken ski pole was holding up the door. "Have fun!" she called.

"We will." Piper's response left no room for doubt.

CHAPTER NINE

ADAM LOOKED UP to see Bea wrestling a large box through the office door. "Something just got delivered for you." Bea had volunteered to take a turn as office assistant today since Linda and Alice were neck-deep in writing grant proposals and Francine was taking Thor to an elementary school to teach the children about therapy dogs.

Adam jumped up to take the box from her. "Thanks." He set it on the visitor chair in front of his desk and reached for scissors to cut the tape.

Without any pretense of minding her own business, Bea read the return address. "Car parts? I thought you were driving a rental."

"I am." The parts were new lifts for the hatchback of Sunny's car. Every time he saw her using that ski pole to prop it open, he gave a mental shudder. What if the pole were to break and it closed unexpectedly and caught Sunny's hand? Or Piper's?

Adam didn't know if Sunny received child

support from Piper's father, but he knew her salary and he understood that nonurgent car repairs wouldn't be particularly high on her list of priorities, so he'd decided to take matters into his own hands. But Bea didn't need to know any of this.

"Did Francine place that order for paper towel refills for the public bathrooms?"

She had, and he knew it, but checking might keep Bea busy for a few minutes.

Bea gave a little snort. "Fine, if you don't want to tell me, you don't have to." She stepped from his office to the outer office. "If Francine said she was going to place an order, I'm sure she did, but I'll double-check."

"Thank you." Adam shut the door behind her. He rarely did that, but if Bea saw the parts he'd ordered, it would take her about two seconds to figure out who they were for. And he didn't want the residents here gossiping about how he was giving an employee inappropriate gifts. He chuckled to himself. If he were trying to woo a woman, he suspected jewelry might be a better bet than car parts.

Not that he was trying to woo Sunny, even though she was gorgeous and funny and a terrific mom and by far the most positive person he'd ever met—whoa. He reined in his galloping thoughts. Yes, if Sunny was someone he'd just met randomly, he would ask her out in a minute. But he didn't date coworkers. And even if he and Sunny weren't working together, he would only be here in Alaska until Thanksgiving at the latest, and he had a hard time imagining her anywhere else, so it's not as though they would have any kind of future together.

No, this purchase was just a matter of employee safety. If Sunny or Piper were to be injured in the parking lot here, the company might be held liable. And even if they weren't liable, it would be a lost time accident. So really, he was just doing what any good manager would do. The fact that he'd used his own credit card rather than charge it to the company was irrelevant. And fortunately, there was no one else there to point out that he'd never been concerned about the repair status of any other coworker's car before.

He opened the box and pulled out the packing slip and the two long boxes containing the new lift struts. The parts number looked correct. Now the trick was going to be how to get Sunny to let him fix her car without making her feel as though she owed him something. She might be one of the most generous people he'd ever met, but generous people were often the most reluctant to accept others' generosity.

Maybe he could sell it as a thank-you for inviting him to dinner the other night. He'd enjoyed the delicious soup, but even more he'd enjoyed spending the time with Piper and Sunny. Eating alone didn't bother him, but a real family dinner was a nice break.

Or maybe he could just sneak out and fix the car while Sunny was otherwise occupied. He wasn't much of a mechanic, but according to the video he'd watched on the website where he'd ordered the parts, it was a five-minute installation, or at least it would be once he'd collected the tools he needed. But only if Sunny left her doors unlocked, and surely nobody did that anymore.

A gentle knock sounded at his door, and a moment later, Molly's face appeared around the edge. "Excuse me. Am I interrupting?"

"No, it's okay." Adam stuffed the parts back into the box quickly, closed the lid and stepped in front of it so she couldn't see the label. "What can I help you with today?"

"We thought you might need these." Molly held out her hand, a set of keys on a yellow daisy key chain dangling from her fingers.

"Are those—"

"Sunny's car keys."

"Where did you get Sunny's keys?" Lots of people came and went here, not only residents. If Sunny was leaving her purse laying around where just anyone could get it, she might want to rethink that.

"Sunny is dropping off some art supplies for me at my friend's house later. I said I'd load them into her car while she was at oldies' karaoke, so she gave me the keys."

"Oldies' karaoke?" Adam was having trouble following Molly's train of thought.

"Yes. Everything from big band to the Beatles. Very popular. Anyway, Bea said you'd gotten in car parts. We figured they must be for Sunny's car, and you'd want to surprise her." Molly checked her watch. "She will be tied up for another twenty minutes before she'll expect her keys back. Ralph is fetching his toolbox. He'll meet you in the parking lot."

"But how did—" At Molly's knowing smile, he just shook his head. "Never mind. I'm just going to have to get used to the idea that you and your friends know everything."

Molly laughed. "That's the image we like to project. This is a very nice thing you're doing for Sunny, and we like to encourage that. Now, if you're going to do this, you'd better get started. You can bring the keys to my apartment when you're done."

"Yes, ma'am." He tucked the carton under one arm and accepted the keys. "Thank you."

"You're welcome. Move along now. Karaoke won't last forever."

THE REPAIR WASN'T quite as quick or easy as the video had led Adam to believe, but with Ralph's help, along with his tools, he managed to get the new lift struts installed. "Okay, that's it. Shall we give it a try?"

"Go for it," Ralph ordered.

Adam pushed the latch and watched with great satisfaction as the hatchback lifted itself gently into the air and remained open. "It works!"

"I never doubted you." Ralph returned his flathead screwdriver to his toolbox and closed the lid.

"I appreciate all your help." Holding the door up while wrestling the new parts in place by himself would have been impossible.

"No problem," Ralph assured him. "We all love Sunny. Now, if this is supposed to be a surprise, we should get out of here."

"You're right." Adam closed the hatchback and hit the button on the key fob to lock the doors. "We'd better get these keys to Molly."

They started across the parking lot, but before they reached the entryway, Sunny came dashing outside, digging through her purse.

"Where did I put those keys?" She looked up and saw Adam and Ralph, still carrying the toolbox. "Hi. What are you two up to?"

"Adam was just helping me replace a fuse in

my car," Ralph answered smoothly. "All done now."

"Oh, good. I have to pick up Piper from school, and I can't find my keys." She snapped her fingers. "That's right. I gave them to Molly so she could put something in my car." She started to turn back.

"Wait." Adam reached into his pocket and took out the daisy key ring. "Molly mentioned something about having to run out, but she gave me the keys to return to you."

"She went out? I thought her car was in the shop."

"Was it?" Adam hadn't gotten that part of the cover story. "Well, maybe someone was taking her to pick it up. I don't know. She just gave me the keys."

"Oh, okay. See you in a few." Sunny took them, bestowed her ever-present smile on the two of them and hurried across the parking lot.

"Fast thinking, son," Ralph remarked once she was gone. "Wonder how long it will take her to notice?"

"Not too long." Adam held the door. "Molly's art supplies were back there, so whenever Sunny drops them off, she'll need to open the hatch-back."

He and Ralph parted ways in the lobby. When Adam returned to his office, Bea was holding court at the front desk, talking to two other residents who had settled into the visitor chairs. Both of them were knitting away.

"Oh, Adam. You're back. We were just talking about the craft fair. We're thinking November 7, getting close to the holiday season but not so close to Thanksgiving that we run into conflicts. Are you free that day?"

"Should be." Adam checked his calendar to be sure, but as he expected, that Saturday was blank. "Where are you having it, in the multipurpose room or the lobby?"

"Oh, we don't have room here. We're having it in the barn at my son's farm. It's heated and everything. He just finished building it, and I convinced him to delay moving everything in until after the craft fair."

"A whole barn? How big is this craft fair?"

"Big. And growing. We have twenty people from here alone, plus we're renting out tables to outside crafters for a fee. Rowan, Bonnie's granddaughter, is organizing that. She says she's already got twenty-seven commitments, and getting more every day. My son says I can use his Clydesdales, so if there's enough snow, I'll be giving sleigh rides. If not, we'll do a hayride instead."

"Your son keeps Clydesdales? Here in Alaska?"

"That's right. Mostly for parades and such,

but he recently started a side business pulling a carriage in downtown Anchorage in the summer. The horses will be moving into the new barn once the craft show is over."

"I'm doing hats," one of the women explained, holding up her knitting made with a heavy wool in shades of rust and brown.

"I do scarves," the other one said. Her creation was light and lacy, in soft grays and blues.

Adam took a minute to admire them both. "Very nice. I'm sure they'll be popular at the sale."

Alice came in from the hallway, carrying a folder. "Hi, ladies. Adam, may I have a minute?"

"Sure." He ushered her into his office and closed the door. "Did you get those figures I sent?" He'd stayed until almost midnight last night putting together all the information Alice and Linda had asked for.

"We did, and it was invaluable. My eyes are starting to blur from all the numbers, but we have both grant proposals ready to go." She opened the folder and handed him a stack of papers. "I'll email you copies as well, but I always find it easier to work off a hard copy. As owner's representative, we'll need your signature, of course. Please read over these, and if you have any concerns, let us know."

"Of course. Thank you for putting in all this work."

"It's well worth it if it means we can stay together. The first grant is a long shot. We're not their target audience, but they might come through. The second, though, could have been custom-made for us, and I happen to know one of the insiders there. I gave her a general outline of our situation, and she's almost sure the committee will approve the grant by the end of the year."

"That's excellent news." Adam glanced at the papers in his hand. "I'll look forward to digging into these. I know time is of the essence, so I'll take them home tonight and if I have questions, we can meet up tomorrow."

"Sounds good."

"And thank you for loaning me your husband."

Alice chuckled. "Yes, he's handy to have around sometimes." She bestowed a proud smile onto Adam. "You did a good thing, there." She straightened the remaining papers in her folder and stood up. "I'll leave it to you, then, until tomorrow."

"Mr. Adam!" Piper called as she threw the door open and came in, Sunny's laptop bag over her shoulder. "Oh, hi, Ms. Alice. Sorry.

I'm supposed to knock when the door's closed. I forgot."

"It's all right," Adam told her. "We were done, anyway. So, what are you so excited about?"

"Mommy's car fixed itself!"

"Really?" He tried to look amazed.

"Yeah. The back door's been falling down for a long time, but all of a sudden it works. She says maybe it's because the weather's colder or something, but I think it's a miracle."

"A miracle, huh?"

"Yeah, like when something good happens, even though it's not supposed to," she explained. "Kinda like magic."

"Oh, wow."

"I think it's a birthday miracle."

"Is today your birthday?"

"No, but Mommy's birthday is next week, on Halloween. So maybe it's like an early birthday present miracle."

"That makes sense to me," Alice said. "I've already bought the candy for trick-or-treaters that day. Francine is making your mom's favorite chocolate cake, as usual."

"Yay! Mr. Adam, I want to give Mommy a picture I took for her birthday. Can you show me how to make it come out of the computer on paper and everything?"

"Of course."

"Well, I'll leave you two to your photography." Alice ran a fond hand over Piper's head. "See you later, kiddo."

"Okay. Bye, Ms. Alice."

"Do you have a picture picked out?" Adam asked once Alice had gone.

"I think so." Piper opened the computer and pointed out one of the photos she'd taken of Sunny leaning down to help someone with a craft project. Piper had chosen well. With a little cropping and editing, it would be amazing.

"Nice choice," Adam told her. "Let's get started."

SUNNY WAS AN ENCHANTRESS. At least that was the only explanation Adam could come up with as to how he found himself looking in the mirror, straightening the funnel he wore on his head that matched his silver face makeup and clothes. He didn't do costumes, at least not since he was about twelve and still young enough to trick-or-treat himself. And yet, here he was, getting ready to make a fool of himself in front of the entire population of Easy Living, plus all the children at the Halloween event and their parents, just because Sunny had asked.

He greeted Francine at the door of the multipurpose room, which had been transformed with cobwebs, hanging bats and orange-and-black crepe paper into party central. Beside her, a clear box with a slotted lid marked "donations" was more than half full. The room buzzed with conversation and laughter, young families mingling with the residents. It didn't seem to disturb Bob, though, who snored away under the table at Francine's feet.

As soon as Adam stepped into the room, a gingham-clad Piper ran to greet him. "Here you are! I was afraid you weren't coming!"

"Sorry I'm late," he told her, although according to the clock on the wall, it was four thirty now, the posted starting time for the party. "It took me a little longer to get into the costume than I thought it would."

"You look good," she assured him.

"So do you." In fact, she was adorable, with her hair in braids tied with blue ribbons and sparkling red slippers on her feet. She carried a basket on her arm, with a dog—a stuffed animal—peeking out from under a napkin. For once, she wasn't sporting the camera. Adam had his, underneath the barrel chest of his silver costume, but he decided that his primary job today was to be a sidekick for Piper, not an event photographer.

He'd been spending plenty of time on photography this week. Piper's photo project had mushroomed to a collection of several pictures for Sunny, and Adam was more than pleased with the result. They'd also done portrait sessions for a few of the residents last week. And he'd sent Lauren and Rowan several photos for their website and proofs from his first food photography gig. Their enthusiastic response was encouraging. Once they'd chosen their favorites, he would send the files to a professional printer to make the posters they wanted for the food truck.

Someone in a tawny jumpsuit with a lion's mane on the hood and shoulders popped up beside Piper. "You made it."

Adam recognized Ralph's voice before he could make out his face underneath the lion makeup. Apparently, Adam wasn't the only one Sunny had coerced into becoming part of Piper's entourage.

"I did. Where's the scarecrow?"

Ralph pointed across the room, where a floppy-hatted figure was setting out rows of pumpkins and paints along two newspaper-covered tables. Even with her back turned, Sunny's bouncy walk was unmistakable.

A moment later, Sunny climbed onto a step stool and waved her arms. Conversation stopped as everyone turned toward her. "Happy Halloween!" she called, and in almost one voice, the crowd returned her greeting.

"Thanks for coming to our trick-or-treat party, and thank you for your generous donations. The residents here are really excited to have you come to their doors." Sunny made a little shooing motion, and most of the residents began slipping out the back of the room, no doubt to return to their apartments and get their candy ready. "Remember, though, only knock on the doors that have a pumpkin like this." She held up a paper cutout of an orange jack-o'-lantern with a cartoon kitten peeking out the top.

"Why?" a child dressed as a ninja called out.

"Because they're the ones with the treats!" Sunny replied, smiling. "Linda is at the door with tote bags for everyone, so write your names on them. We'll meet back here in forty-five minutes for pumpkin painting, apple bobbing, games and scary stories. Then we'll have cake and punch. So, who's ready to trick-or-treat?"

"Me!"

"I am!"

The kids and families surged toward the doorway.

Adam moved closer and offered Sunny a hand while she climbed down from the stool. She gave him a once-over and nodded approvingly. "Wow, the costume fits you so well. Thanks for filling in. Our original tin man had to bow out."

"Cheap last-minute flight to Phoenix for a golf weekend," Ralph whispered to Adam.

"Glad to help. Happy birthday, by the way."

"Oh, thank you. Who told you?"

Not wanting to ruin Piper's surprise, he answered, "Not sure. Somebody mentioned it."

"Can we go now?" Piper urged.

"Sure. This way." Sunny and Piper linked arms and skipped across the floor. Ralph and Adam exchanged glances. Ralph shook his head. They followed, but without skipping. Sunny looked back and grinned. "Party poopers."

"Let's start downstairs and work back up," Piper said, skipping toward the stairs without waiting for agreement. At her mother's insistence, she slowed and walked down the stairs, but went back to skipping as soon as she reached the first floor. She passed several other groups already knocking and led her group to the far end of the hallway, to apartment 102.

"What about 101?" Adam asked Sunny, looking at the bare door across the hall.

"That's Phil's apartment," Sunny said, which was answer enough. Adam was sure Phil bahhumbugged every holiday and special occasion, just out of principle.

The door to 102 opened and Rosemary, dressed as a fortune-teller, peeked out. "Oh, my. You look like you're on the yellow brick road."

"Trick or treat," Piper chanted, unnecessarily, since Rosemary was already dropping some sort of organic fruit snack into Piper's basket. "Thank you!"

"You're welcome. Good to see you joining in on the fun, Adam. Happy Halloween!"

As they moved on to the next apartment, a movement caught his eye. The door to Phil's apartment was open a crack, and the old man was peering out for a glimpse of the children. If Adam wasn't mistaken, he even had a slight smile on his face before he shut the door again. It was as if the man wanted to be part of the group, but had been contrary for so long, he didn't know how to join in.

Adam, Ralph and Sunny followed Piper from door to door like a costumed Secret Service detail. Unlike Rosemary, the other residents handed out high-sugar treats with a free hand. Adam only saw three other apartments that didn't sport the pumpkin cutouts inviting trick-or-treaters. Ralph happened to mention that one belonged to the man who had originally been drafted to wear Adam's costume and the other two were at another function.

Which left Phil as the only resident who had deliberately chosen not to participate.

Once all the children had made the rounds and collected enough candy to keep a dentist in business for years, they all gathered back in the multipurpose room. Sunny divided them into two groups, so that some could paint pumpkins or participate in other activities, while others listened to Linda, dressed as a sorceress, reading a selection of not-too-scary stories. Then they switched activities.

Since Piper was occupied, Adam pulled out his camera and slipped around the room, snapping a picture of a little girl in a brown dog costume happily painting sharp teeth on the scary monster pumpkin she was creating. Of a wide-eyed unicorn waiting in suspense while Linda turned the page. Of the residents, who seemed just as enraptured with the story as the children were.

Meanwhile, Francine set a beautifully decorated sheet cake on a buffet table, which already boasted a platter of colorful veggies arranged in the shape of a jack-o'-lantern, and an assortment of mini pizzas. The chocolate icing on the cake had been decorated with orange rosettes and happy-looking ghosts and wished everyone a "Happy Halloween!"

After all the pumpkins were painted, other crafts and activities finished, and stories read, Sunny called the children over for refreshments.

Adam snapped a few more pictures. His own grandparents lived across the country from where he and his mom had settled in Idaho. The handful of times he'd visited as a child, most of their conversation consisted of warnings not to make noise, track in dirt, or threaten any of the fragile glass collectibles that covered every flat surface in their house. In his young mind, old people were as fragile as those figurines, and he'd avoided both as much as possible until he was an adult himself.

But the experience here was completely different. These seniors seemed comfortable with squirmy, noisy, messy kids. They didn't hesitate to correct the children when their behavior got out of line, but it was done as a friendly reminder, not a reprimand. The children soaked up the extra attention like happy little sponges. He noticed that most of the seniors were sticking to vegetables and pizzas, leaving the cake for the kids and parents.

Once the kids finished their goodies, their parents rounded them up, collected their bags of loot and herded them toward the door, where Linda was handing out scrolls with Edgar Allan Poe's *The Raven* printed inside. Once they were gone, Linda shut the doors to the room.

"Time for the after-party!" Bea shouted. "Happy birthday, Sunny!"

"Happy birthday!" the others repeated as Francine emerged from the kitchen carrying a new chocolate cake topped with raspberries and lit candles. Everyone joined in, most with more enthusiasm than skill, to sing the birthday song to Sunny.

With all the scarecrow makeup, Adam couldn't tell for sure, but he had a feeling Sunny was blushing as she listened to them all sing for her. She looked his way, and their eyes locked for a moment as Adam sang along. Sunny gave a little smile, and somehow he felt it was meant just for him. At the end of the song, among more shouts of "Happy birthday!", Sunny blew out the candles. Thirty-four, if Adam's quick count was correct.

"Thank you all so much!"

"Did you make a wish?" Piper asked.

"I did."

"Don't tell anyone, or it won't come true," she warned.

"I won't," Sunny promised.

"Now it's time for gifts," Alice announced. "Sunny, you come sit here." She indicated a chair at the head of the table.

"You shouldn't have done all this," Sunny protested, even while she allowed herself to be led to the place of honor. "You've already put in so much work on the Halloween party."

"Nonsense," Bonnie told her. "At our age, we know to celebrate every chance we get. Throwing a party for you makes us as happy as a dog with two tails."

"That's right." Molly set a basket of wrapped gifts in front of Sunny. "There's a lot here, so you'd better get started if you want any of Francine's raspberry dark chocolate cake."

"Yes, ma'am." The gifts ranged from a trio of hand-crocheted dishcloths to a gift certificate for a deluxe treatment at the local beauty spa–hair salon. Sunny greeted each gift with delight. She kept popping up to run around the table to hug each giver. Finally, Piper emerged from the kitchen carrying the package Adam had helped her wrap earlier in the day.

At the local arts-and-crafts cooperative, he had found a collage frame made of polished birch with room for seven photos. The largest, center photo was a candid one he'd snapped of Piper and Sunny together in an animated conversation. He was proud of that one. The expressions he'd caught on their faces illustrated the sparkling energy and love between the two of them. The rest of the photos were Piper's, of Sunny leading classes, decorating doors, playing with Francine's kittens and interacting with the residents. Piper had an intuitive grasp of what would make a good picture, and with a little judicious cropping and editing, the photos had turned out quite well. He was eager to see Sunny's reaction.

"What's this?" Sunny asked.

"Your birthday present from me." Piper thrust the package into Sunny's lap. "Mr. Adam helped."

"Oh, he did, did he?" Sunny flashed a smile at Adam before ripping into the package. "Let's see what we have here." When the last shred was torn away, Sunny gasped. "Oh…" She blinked, but a tear escaped and ran down her cheek.

Adam might be dressed as a tin man with no heart, but he felt his own heart swell at the emotion on Sunny's face.

Piper looked alarmed. "Mommy? Are you crying?"

"No." Sunny wiped away the tear. "I mean, yes, but only because I'm so happy." She pulled her daughter into her arms for a hug. "Oh, sweetie, it's beautiful!"

"I thought you'd like it."

"I love it! Thank you!" Over Piper's shoulder, Sunny's gaze met Adam's. "Thank you," she repeated.

"Wow, look at that!" Bea exclaimed. "Oh, there's me. Almost everybody's here. You even caught Phil in the background of one of the pictures, and he's not even frowning."

"Let's see," Alice said, standing to examine the photos. "Amazing! Piper, when did you take this one in front of the building?"

As the rest of the group huddled around and Piper explained the backstory of each photo, Sunny slipped away and came over to Adam. "Thank you so much for helping Piper put this together. You have no idea how much it means to me."

He wiped another stray tear from her cheek, her skin soft under his touch. "I have some idea."

She looked up at him, her eyes still glittering with unshed happy tears, and suddenly the noises around them receded to the background. Adam was hit with the overwhelming urge to kiss the cheek he'd just touched and then that delectable mouth to see if Sunny's kisses were as sweet as her smile.

She blinked and sucked in a tiny gasp of air, as though she could read his mind. But before he could act on his impulse, she put her arms around him and pulled him in for a hug. "Thank you," she whispered.

He hugged her back, noticing how well she fit in his arms. "You're more than welcome," he whispered back. Neither of them made any move to end the embrace until Piper's voice cut through the fog.

"It's time for cake!"

Reluctantly, Adam released Sunny and she turned to Piper with a smile. "I thought you already ate a piece of cake."

"That was Halloween cake, and this is birthday cake. Besides, I just had an itty-bitty piece."

Sunny chuckled. "All right. I'm glad I didn't eat any because I'm going to have a big piece of Francine's cake. It's my favorite." She returned to the table, but as she slipped away from Adam, she let her hand trail down his arm and gave his fingers a squeeze.

He stood there for a moment, realizing that if Sunny hadn't initiated the hug when she did, he would have kissed her. In the middle of a party. In front of her daughter. And the worst part was that he wasn't entirely sure he was glad her hug had stopped him, because holding her in his arms only intensified his desire to kiss her.

Adam just might be in deeper than he'd realized.

CHAPTER TEN

SUNNY PAUSED IN the hallway outside Adam's office, feeling every bit as awkward as that first day when she'd discovered the man she'd thought was Linda's grandnephew was really her boss. They'd gotten past that and developed an easy working relationship, but somehow, after her birthday yesterday, everything was different. It all came down to that hug.

Sunny was a hugger. She hugged her daughter at every opportunity, hugged the residents at Easy Living and had even been known to hug the mail carrier when he delivered a long-anticipated package. But yesterday, when she'd hugged Adam, it was different. When his arms came around her and she'd breathed in the woodsy scent of his aftershave, it all felt so warm and inviting and…right.

It had been all she could do to pull away instead of snuggling closer. Did he feel the same? For a second or two before the hug, she'd almost gotten the feeling that he'd wanted to kiss her, but maybe she was wrong. It wasn't as though she was tuned in to that sort of thing anymore. Ever since the fiasco with Piper's father, when she'd come to realize just how little she really mattered to him, she'd deliberately avoided anything close to romance. She'd probably just imagined that nonkiss because of her own attraction to Adam.

And yes, she was attracted. No use lying to herself. But obviously there was no future in a relationship with her boss—who was only in town temporarily. Just because he looked good and smelled good and gave nice hugs was no reason to lose her common sense.

"Sunny?" Linda came to the door. "You've been standing there for five minutes. Are you okay?"

"Sure, just remembering something I need to take care of later." Sunny walked into the outer office. "I just need to talk to Adam for a second."

"Okay." Linda seemed perplexed, as well she might since Adam's door was standing open behind her and Adam had long established that when the door was open, everyone was welcome.

"Hi, Sunny," Adam called through the doorway. "Come on in."

"Thanks." Sunny stepped into his office, but hovered at the door.

"Do you want to sit down?" He motioned toward the visitors' chairs in front of his desk.

"No, I just, um…" Sunny closed the office door behind her. "I just want to thank you again for the wonderful birthday gift. And for all the time you've been spending with Piper lately, teaching her photography."

"It's been a pleasure. And I mean that. I'd forgotten how much enjoyment I get out of taking pictures. And Piper's an excellent student."

"She's really into it. She's been doing portrait sessions with her stuffed animals and explaining the difference between key lights and fill lights to me."

Adam grinned. "That's great."

"Yeah. Anyway, that one picture you took of Piper and me? Would you mind sending me the digital version of that?"

"Sure. Although if you just want to print more copies, I'd be happy to do that for you."

"No, I just want a backup, in case something happens to the original." Her glance fell to the two framed photos on his desk. "You see, I lost almost all my childhood pictures of me and my family, and I want to make sure there's a digital backup so that Piper never loses hers."

"What happened to your pictures?"

"When I was younger our house burned down and they were destroyed."

"Oh no. I hope everyone made it out okay."

"Um…" Sunny felt a lump forming in her throat, which was silly. It was all so long ago. She'd moved on, made a good life. She went to the window and looked out to give herself a moment to steady her voice. "No. My bedroom was on the first floor and the firefighters were able to get me out, but my mom didn't make it. It was just me and her."

"Oh, Sunny." He came around the desk, and she turned toward him. "That's devastating. I'm so sorry."

He reached out to hug her, but she put a hand on his chest to stop him. If she let him take her into his arms, she would dissolve in a puddle of tears.

"I'm okay but thank you. It was…hard."

He dropped his arms, but he didn't back away. "I can't even imagine. How old were you?"

"Fourteen."

"Did you move in with a relative, or—"

Sunny shook her head. "No, there was no other family. I went into foster care."

He looked shocked. "After all that, how do you keep such a positive outlook?"

Sunny took a long, fortifying breath. "I was lucky. After the fire, I landed with a wonderful foster mother. She'd lost her husband not long before that, so she understood what I was going through. She told me that losing our loved ones was completely unfair, but we couldn't change the past. We could sit around and rail against fate, or we could be grateful to have had those people in our lives for as long as we did and move forward. And so, that's what we did. Eventually."

"Just like that?"

"Oh, we had setbacks. Lots of tears. But she showed me that the world was still good. She said life can be short, so we should live every day of it."

"She sounds amazing. Are you still in touch?"

"No. She passed away twelve years ago." Sunny sniffed and managed a smile. "So, anyhow, that's why I want a copy of the photograph. I didn't mean to get into all that other stuff."

"I'm glad you did. And of course, I'll send you the file." He reached for her hand. "Sunny, if you ever—" A knock sounded at the door.

Adam dropped her hand and stepped back. "Come in."

Alice stepped inside, her face uncharacteristically flustered. "Adam, I—oh, Sunny. I didn't mean to interrupt."

"It's fine. We're done," Sunny assured her as she started to move around Adam toward the door, but Alice continued talking.

"Adam, we have a huge favor to ask. Ralph's

granddaughter is getting married in Girdwood this Saturday, but the photographer she hired had an emergency appendectomy today, and apparently there's not another wedding photographer in the state who is free this weekend. Is there any chance you could fill in?"

"I've never done wedding photography. I wouldn't know what to shoot."

"From the weddings I've attended and wedding albums I've seen, I think it's mostly getting ready photos, shots of the ceremony, family groups afterward, and then candids at the reception," Sunny chimed in. "Right, Alice?"

"That sounds about right. They've already done a photo session at Exit Glacier, so this would just be the actual wedding pictures. Say, Sunny, if you're not busy Saturday, why don't you and Piper come to the wedding as well, as Adam's assistants? That is, if Adam is willing." She turned pleading eyes toward him.

"Okay, I'll give it a shot. I hate to risk messing up someone's wedding album, but if it's that or no photographer at all—"

"Thank you! And I know you'll do great. That picture of Piper and Sunny is wonderful, by the way." She reached into her pocket and pulled out a piece of paper. "Here's the address, timetable and contact information. Sunny, are you and Piper in?"

"Sure."

"Great! All right, then. I'll call the bride and let her know she can relax. Thank you both so much. You're lifesavers!" She hurried out of the office.

Sunny looked at Adam. "Well, looks like Saturday, we're going to a wedding."

A FEW RAINDROPS pattered on the roof of the wedding gazebo as Adam took a few prewedding close-ups of the bridesmaids wrapping deep red-and-gold flower garlands around the pillars, but the bride seemed surprisingly unconcerned. Not so the mother of the groom. "I told them an outdoor wedding was a risk, but they said if we got precipitation in November, it would be snow," she said to Adam. "And yet here it is, fifty degrees. Can you check your phone again and see if they've changed the forecast?"

Adam had already checked twice for her, but he did it again. "Still calling for the sun to come out an hour before the wedding. I think it will be fine," he assured her, but she didn't look convinced.

Sunny came over and touched the woman's elbow. "Christine, Chelsea was telling me that you sewed all the bridesmaid dresses. I'm so impressed. How long did it take you?"

She led her to the other side of the gazebo,

leaving Adam free to continue with the photography. He could see them chatting, and Adam suspected from the slight smile on the woman's face that Sunny was convincing her everything would be all right. Sunny tended to have that effect on people.

The wedding wasn't for another three hours, but according to Sunny, some of the most treasured photos would be the ones he took of the preparations leading up to it. Sunny had been a huge help, researching and putting together a list of "must-have" photos, as well as information about the site and scheduling. She'd already arranged a couple of informal group photos of the family members and was natural at making people laugh and putting them at ease.

This seemed to be something of a do-it-yourself wedding, with various family members and the wedding party unloading chairs, arranging flowers and testing the music on the sound system. Adam was having fun capturing all the activity and family dynamics as everyone laughed and talked while they worked.

Piper had already been absorbed into a group of kids playing a game of tag in the adjoining meadow who were ignoring the sprinkles. When Adam had picked them up that morning, he'd wondered why Sunny and Piper wore casual clothes and carried their wedding attire on hangers, but now he wished he'd done the same. He'd shed his suit jacket and replaced it with a fleece anorak, but he still felt over-dressed.

The bridesmaids, identified by matching peach-colored sweatshirts over their jeans, fluffed the bows they'd tied around the pillars. Meanwhile the bride, wearing a similar sweatshirt with *Bride* spelled out in rhinestones, consulted a clipboard and checked something off.

She looked up. "That's it then. Everything looks awesome!" Her groom, dressed in jeans, a flannel shirt and down vest, came to stand beside her, and she stood on tiptoe to give him a quick kiss, which Adam managed to catch on camera. "I'll look completely different next time I see you," she told the groom.

"Can't wait. But then, you always look beau-tiful to me." He smiled and kissed her again, and Adam mentally gave the guy bonus points. Judging by the beaming bride, so did she.

Once the bride and her entourage had disap-peared into the cabin next to the gazebo, the rest of the group began rounding up kids and loading into cars until Adam was left alone with Sunny and Piper. "Now what?" he asked Sunny.

"Now we have a little time to kill. You'll

need the obligatory photos of someone putting on the bride's veil and pinning the boutonniere to the groom's lapel, things like that, but we should give them time to shower and do their hair. Meanwhile, do you want to have some lunch? There's a great little sandwich shop here in Girdwood. And maybe you'd like to get a few general photos of the town."

"Sounds good."

At Sunny's direction, they drove uphill and parked in a lot close to the bottom of one of the ski lifts.

Piper jumped out of the car. "I'm going to get grilled cheese and clam chowder. Or maybe vegetable soup. Mr. Adam, what are you getting?"

"I don't know. I'll have to see the menu first."

"Oh, that's right. I forget you don't live in Alaska. It's like you've always been here." Piper skipped on ahead.

Adam chuckled. "That's one of the nicest things anyone has ever said to me."

"She's right, though," Sunny said. "You fit in here. All that traveling to different places must have made you adaptable."

"Maybe." But it was more than that. Adam usually slid into various positions with ease, but he'd always been aware that the positions were temporary. He'd never gotten to know the residents personally, the way he had at Easy Living. And he'd never felt the urge to reach for a coworker's hand, the way he was tempted to do right now. But he didn't. Instead, he took advantage of a brief sunny break in the clouds to take a picture of the snowcapped mountain rising up behind them. Variegated shades of gold, brown and red painted the lower mountain, and a few leaves from several mountain ash framed the edge of the vista.

"Whatcha doing?" Piper tapped on his elbow. "Isn't that tree in the way?"

"No, I like catching a little of the foreground to establish depth. Especially if I use a larger aperture so that the leaves in the foreground are a little blurred while the mountain is in focus. Let me show you." He knelt and passed the camera to her so that she could look through the viewfinder. "See, focus straight at the mountain. Now look at it with a few leaves from the tree around the edge."

"It looks bigger," Piper agreed, "and farther away. I like the colors."

"Me too." Sunny agreed. "Autumn is one of my favorite seasons."

Adam laughed. "One of? What are your other favorite seasons?"

"Summer, of course, because everything is

green and warm and blooming. And winter because the snow is so beautiful."

"So spring is the only season excluded from your favorites?"

Sunny wrinkled her nose. "Instead of spring, we have breakup, when the snow melts and everything is a soggy mess. But when the first rhubarb leaves start pushing through the ground and the birch leaves go from tiny yellow buds to full green leaves in just a couple of weeks, it's magical. So, maybe spring is a favorite, too." She grinned. "Can't I have multiple favorites?"

"Absolutely." Her favorite season was the one she was experiencing at the time, just like her favorite resident would be whichever one she was talking to in any given moment. He admired that trait in her. "You can have all the favorites you want."

"Good because I'd hate to have to choose between you and Piper as my favorite photographer. Come on, everyone. Let's get some lunch!"

A FEW DAYS LATER, Adam sat at his desk, making a final adjustment on the color balance of the bride and groom's first official photo as a married couple. The minister had just pronounced them husband and wife, and he'd managed to get an especially good shot of the groom's face, just before he kissed his bride. The guy looked as though he'd just won the lottery, and maybe he had. Adam had heard lots of out of control wedding stories, but this couple seemed relaxed and happy, more concerned about each other than about achieving a perfect event.

The next photo he pulled up to work on was one of Alice and Ralph dancing together. The look on Ralph's face wasn't too far from the one on the groom's. Maybe that was the young couple's secret—they had good role models. Alice had once confided in Adam about how, upsetting all her plans at the time, she'd somehow fallen in love with the rough-hewn bush pilot a few years after he lost his first wife. She and Ralph had celebrated their thirty-fifth wedding anniversary not too long ago, but they still held hands like teenagers.

Would Adam ever have that kind of love? He wanted a wife and family, in theory anyway, but with all the travel involved in his job, he barely found time for an occasional date, much less time to find a woman he'd want to spend his life with. If Dad was serious about retiring and Adam were to step into that job, he'd finally be in one place long enough to settle down and look for a wife. But the idea of a deliberate search for a wife, like a job candidate, didn't sit well with him. He was a practical man, but the hidden romantic in him hoped that someday he would meet his soul mate, and everything would fall into place.

Suddenly his eye was drawn to the background behind Alice and Ralph, where Sunny and Piper twirled in circles, sending the skirts of their dresses flaring out around them. He zoomed in, taking a moment to study Sunny's face. She was lovely, from the delicate curve of her cheek to her big brown eyes, to her ever-present smile.

At first, he'd assumed her relentless positivity was because she'd never experienced the dark side of life, but after their talk the other day, he realized it was just the opposite. Sunny had experienced the worst. She knew that everything could be taken away in an instant, and yet instead of letting a fear of loss shape her life, she had the courage to hope for the best. Always. He'd never known anyone like her, and he suspected he never would again.

Footsteps in the hallway alerted him to a possible visitor. Piper skipped into his office. Judging by her jacket and backpack, she was on her way out. "Hi, Mr. Adam."

Sunny was just behind her. "Hey. Working late?"

"Just doing some editing on those wedding photos. They're coming out great." He glanced at his phone. Already nearly seven. "What are you two still doing here?"

"I was working with the Mat Mates on final arrangements for the craft fair next Saturday. You're coming, right?"

"Sure. In fact, I've given Molly a few photo prints to sell. Maybe they'll bring in a couple bucks."

"Oh, good. Well, we saw the light and I thought I'd turn it off if you'd gone home, but obviously you're still here. We'll see you tomorrow." She turned to go, and Piper followed.

"Wait." When they looked back, Adam realized he didn't really have a follow-up except that for some reason, he didn't want them to leave. A sudden growl from his stomach gave him a handy excuse. "Do you have dinner plans?"

"Mommy said we could pick up pizza and take it home," Piper told him.

"Pizza sounds good. How about if we all go to that place across the street for dinner instead?"

"Ooh, yay!" Piper jumped up and down. "If we eat at Ptarmigan Pizza, they bring us coloring place mats."

"Pizza *and* coloring place mats. Even better." Adam turned to Sunny. "Unless you need to get home for another reason."

"No, Piper already finished her homework, and other than a date with an overflowing hamper, I'm free. And I suppose the laundry isn't going anywhere."

"Okay. Let me lock up and we can walk over." Adam grabbed his jacket and slid his laptop into his satchel, locked the office door and walked out with them. He felt the chill as soon as they stepped outside. The temperature had dropped considerably since yesterday. Overhead, no stars were visible in the sky. "Feels like winter's coming."

Sunny nodded. "Finally. We're supposed to get several inches of snow in the next couple of days. Hope you have your snow tires on."

"Yes, I traded in the rental car for an SUV last weekend, and it has winter tires. Are you all set?"

Sunny nodded. "I got new ones last week. By the way, did I tell you my lift gate fixed itself? It just suddenly started working."

"Yes, Piper mentioned that. Really odd." Adam tried to keep his voice casual.

"I know. I'm glad I didn't spend the money to have it repaired, because the snow tires weren't cheap. I'm kind of excited, though, to try them out on the snow this week. Too bad it didn't arrive in time for the wedding."

"Snow would have been pretty, but the groom's mom was just thrilled that it didn't rain during the ceremony."

"It was fun, wasn't it? I really like the family. Even though they're only related by marriage, Ralph's granddaughter is a lot like Alice, don't you think?"

"I do. It was fun." Adam chuckled as they followed Piper toward the restaurant. "I used to look at those wedding photographers and think it must be boring to do the same old shots over and over, but it wasn't like that. Sure, the family group shots were pretty standard, but the festivities gave me an opportunity to see into the relationships and try to capture it all."

Sunny glanced up at him. "You like that best, don't you? Photographing people, I mean. At least from what I've seen, you're great at landscapes and such, but you have a gift for being able to capture someone's personality in a single shot. Like the picture of your parents on your desk. You can tell your mom is full of fun, and that your dad adores her."

"You're right. That is my favorite." He gave a wry smile. "But it takes a lot more than a single shot. Thank goodness for digital photography because otherwise I'd go through film like—"

"Like a sharp-toothed beaver through a cottonwood tree?" Piper suggested as she skipped back to them. "That's what Ms. Bonnie always says."

"Exactly like that." Adam laughed as they reached the corner and paused, waiting for the light to change.

Adam looked up at the dark sky. "I hope the snow doesn't put a damper on the craft fair."

Sunny followed his gaze. "The clouds are supposed to clear by Friday. That should give the road crews plenty of time to plow. In fact, if we get enough snow for sleigh rides, it might even attract more people."

Adam laughed. "That's you. Always looking for the bright side."

"Why not? The bright side is the fun side. Right, Piper?"

"Right! Can we get pepperonis on our pizza?" she asked him.

"We can get anything you want." He glanced at Sunny. "Assuming your mother agrees."

Sunny chuckled. "Be careful what you promise. Last time I let Piper pick the toppings, we ended up with green peppers, pineapple and barbecued chicken."

"How was it?"

"Surprisingly delicious," Sunny admitted.

The light changed and they all crossed the

street. The aroma of cheese, tomatoes and garlic met them at the door. Piper led them to an unoccupied table near the window, and a waitress appeared almost immediately with glasses of water, a mug of crayons and paper place mats.

"Hi, Doralie," Sunny greeted her. "How's your mom?"

"Much better," the waitress answered, setting paper place mats in front of all three of them. "Surgery went well, and the doctor says without her gallbladder, she should be feeling herself in no time. Did I tell you we put her name on the waiting list for Easy Living?"

"No. Sharleen would be a terrific addition to the place. Doralie, this is Adam. He's managing the apartments right now."

"Oh, then I suppose I'd better take good care of you, and maybe you'll move Mom to the top of the list." She laughed to show she was joking and handed them menus. "Can I get your drinks while you decide?"

"Water's fine for Piper and me," Sunny said.

"I want milk, please," Piper interrupted.

They'd all had milk with the soup the other day at Sunny's house. Adam wondered if she'd just ordered water to save money, planning to give Piper her milk later at home. In fact, that's probably why she'd originally planned carryout instead of dine-in—to save the cost of drinks and tips. Adam's mother used to do that when times were lean.

"I'll have milk, too, please," he told Doralie.

At Sunny's nod, Doralie wrote down their selections. "Good choice. Good for your bones." She patted him on the shoulder, then headed off toward the kitchen.

Adam opened his menu. Choosing toppings took a long time and a lot of good-natured discussion, but they finally settled on pepperoni, mushrooms and olives, along with a side of salad. Once their order was in, Piper picked up a purple crayon, and Adam noticed for the first time that the three mats weren't identical. His featured a dog, Sunny's had turtles and Piper's had penguins. Sunny chose a crayon, too, a bright pink one, and handed the mug to him. He chose a green one and went to work solving the maze to lead the cartoon dog to the doghouse, which he then colored in with his crayon.

They all laughed as they read the silly riddles aloud to each other, and then, following Piper's suggestions for crayon choice, Adam colored in the rest of the pictures on the page, while Sunny and Piper did the same for theirs. Adam noticed when another family came in, only the children received activity place mats. Apparently, Sunny was special.

Of course, he already knew that.

Piper looked over her shoulder at the family who had just come in. "It's Livy!" She slid out of her chair. "Can I go say hi?"

"Sure." Sunny turned and waved at the family, who waved back. Piper skittered across the room to greet her friend.

Sunny turned back to Adam. "Livy is in Piper's class in school. I met her mom when I helped chaperone a field trip to the museum downtown."

Adam smiled at Piper's enthusiasm as she greeted her friend. "You've got a really great kid."

"I know. I'm very lucky."

"You're obviously doing a great job raising her."

"I can't take the credit. Piper's just awesome all by herself."

"Maybe, but it's because she feels secure and happy with you that she can be herself. I know it's not easy, raising a child alone. Does Piper's father help out at all financially?" As soon as he said it, Adam realized he'd crossed a line. "Never mind, that's none of my business. It's just that my mom raised me without any child support, and it wasn't until I was grown that I realized how tough she had it."

"Oh? How old were you when your mother married your stepfather?" He noticed she didn't address the question of child support, which probably meant she wasn't getting any. She was all about giving credit where credit was due. Still, as he'd said, it was none of his business.

"He came into our lives when I was thirteen, and it made all the difference. Don't get me wrong, my mom was, and is, a great parent, but I'd reached that age where I needed more direction. I'd gotten in the habit of just sliding by in school. Dad made me realize I could do better."

"By checking your homework."

"Yes, and by talking with me. He made me believe I had a bright future if I put in the work."

"Good on you that you were willing to listen. Not too many teenagers would."

He laughed. "Oh, there were tense times, believe me. I give him full credit that he hung in there no matter how obnoxious I became."

"I can't picture you ever being obnoxious."

"Then you know how much he's influenced my life, because there was a time when my sole focus was to drive him away. Thankfully, for my sake and my mom's, I wasn't successful. They've been happily married for longer than twenty years now."

"Any more word about when he plans to retire?"

"Not directly, but when he and my mom were telling me about the cruise they just took, it sounded like it might be sooner rather than later."

"So, if you're going to get that top job, you'll need to impress the board with your performance."

"Yes."

Sunny tilted her head. "If the Easy Living Apartments are losing money, that can't be good for your reputation."

"My reputation is built on turning around underperforming assets." And he'd been very good at it. Up until now.

"How do you do that?"

He shrugged. "Usually, it's a matter of sprucing up the place, attracting new tenants and getting an effective management team in place."

"And how long does that usually take you?"

"Oh, it often takes several months to implement, but I usually spend anywhere from a couple weeks to a month on-site, get the ball rolling and new management on board, and then oversee it from a distance while I move on to the next project."

"And yet you've already been here a month

and a half, and you said you'd stay until Thanksgiving."

"This a special case."

Sunny's brown eyes met his. "Why?"

Why, indeed? Because it was a senior living center, and it would be bad for the company's public image to shut it down? If it were only that, they could sell it to the interested company and wash their hands of it. No, it was because unlike other projects he'd worked, Adam had gotten to know the people who lived there. He cared about them. And he wanted to do right by them.

He wondered about some of those other projects he'd led. He'd always assumed that fixing up the units, increasing the occupancy and replacing poor building managers was to the benefit of the current tenants, but of course when the building was upgraded, rents went up as well. Had he displaced other seniors on fixed incomes and never known about it? Quite possibly.

It made him even more determined to help these residents stay where they were. But even though Alice had said the grant was on track to come through, it was far from a done deal. And Adam didn't have a plan B. Everything still might fall through. But how could he explain all that to Sunny? She had such high hopes.

Fortunately for him, before he had to answer, Doralie brought their pizza to the table and Piper came scurrying back, licking her lips. "Yummy."

"It does look good," Adam agreed.

Sunny's eyes crinkled a little at the corners, like she knew he was purposely changing the subject. He had a feeling the discussion wasn't over. For now, he just wanted to enjoy dinner and forget about work for a little while.

Once Sunny had distributed slices of pizza to each of their plates and they'd eaten a few bites, he turned to Piper. "Your mom was telling me you've been photographing your toys."

Piper nodded eagerly while she chewed the bite of pizza she'd just taken. "I made a triangle with the lights just like you said, with one twice as far as the other. I wish I'd brought my camera, but I left it at home. I can show you tomorrow."

"I'll look forward to that."

They chatted easily for the rest of the meal. When Doralie brought the check, Sunny reached for it, but Adam was faster. Sunny shook her head. "Let me pay. There are two of us and only one of you."

Adam refused. "I ate more pizza than the two of you put together, and you know it. Besides, it's my turn. You fed me soup and sour-dough bread, remember?"

"You mean Rowan's soup and Francine's bread?"

"Still my turn." Adam reached into his pocket for his wallet.

"Thank you."

"You're welcome." While he signed the charge slip, Sunny and Piper stopped by their friends' table to say goodbye, leaving Adam a minute to watch them. A typical small-town scene, running into a friend, stopping for a quick chat.

How long had it been since he'd stayed any-where long enough to make a friend, much less enough friends that he was likely to bump into one randomly? Come to think of it, when was the last time he'd made contact with one of his old friends? Work had crowded out his photography, his friends, any sort of dating life—was it worth it?

But things would change once he'd stepped into the CEO job. Dad worked long hours, but he always made a point to eat dinner with the family every evening. He'd always attended Mom's performances in community theater and Adam's baseball games, and for two summers, he'd even made time to coach. Dad was happy with his life.

Adam would be, too.

Piper and Sunny returned to the table and shrugged on their coats. They all crossed the street to walk to the apartment parking lot, but just as they reached the street corner, the first few snowflakes drifted down, swirling under the streetlight like a snow globe.

"The first snow of the year!" Piper exclaimed.

She and Sunny looked at each other conspiratorially. "Come on." Sunny grabbed Adam's hand and tugged him onto the brown grass.

"What are we doing?" he asked as he allowed Sunny to pull him to the edge of the pool of light.

"If you can catch a snowflake on your tongue from the first snow of the season, you get a wish," Piper explained.

"Is that so? I've never heard that before."

"It's a very old tradition," Sunny said, but by the twinkle in her eye, he got the impression the tradition didn't predate Piper.

"Well, we can't go against tradition, can we?" Adam glanced up. A wet flake landed on his forehead, nowhere near his mouth. He looked over to see Piper turning slowly in a circle, leaning left and right, following the path of a single snowflake as it drifted from the sky. The way the streetlight fell on her face… His hand went to his chest, instinctively reaching for his camera, but he'd left it in his office.

Sunny bumped his shoulder with her own. "I know," she whispered. "You want to freeze this moment in time, hold on to it forever. But sometimes, if you try too hard to capture the magic, it slips away. Just go with the moment. You'll remember."

"I missed that one." Piper frowned. "It hit my nose."

"You'll get the next one," Sunny replied. "Oh, there's a good one!" She moved under a large flake still a few feet above her head and worked to position herself in its ever-changing path.

Adam laughed and joined in, tilting back his head and sticking out his tongue as far as he could while trying to zero in on a particular snowflake. They were coming faster now, big fluffy bits of snow.

Sunny and Piper bumped into each other, and in the ensuing fit of giggles, both missed their targets. The three of them must be quite a sight, turning in slow circles with their tongues sticking out, laughing. If anyone at the home office could see Adam at that moment, they'd never believe it.

And then it happened. A fluffy snowflake landed right on the tip of Adam's tongue, instantly dissolving into a fleeting caress of cold. "I got one!"

"Yay! Make a wish!" Piper instructed him.

Standing here on the grass, laughing with Piper and Sunny, Adam couldn't think of anything else he wanted than to have more moments just like this.

Piper squealed. "I got mine!"

"Me, too!" Sunny called, her smile radiant as snowflakes drifted down harder and began to collect on her hair and shoulders. And Adam knew Sunny was right. He didn't need a picture. This scene, with the three of them happily making fools of themselves in the snow under the streetlight, was one he'd never forget.

CHAPTER ELEVEN

THE RISING SUN washed over a field beside the country road Adam was driving on. It was Saturday morning, and he was on his way to the craft fair. Only a single line of animal tracks and the long shadows from bare trees at the end of the field marred a blanket of pink-tinted snow.

Unable to resist, he pulled over on the next wide spot on the road, took out his camera and walked back to the field. As he snapped a photo, the maker of the tracks, a white fox, emerged from the woods and regarded Adam, his head tilted to one side. Adam quickly zoomed in and snapped three more photos before the fox turned and disappeared.

Meanwhile, several cars had passed, more traffic than he would have expected on a rural road at eight forty-five on a weekend. As he went back to the road, a blue truck slowed, and the window lowered. "Everything all right?" a male voice called out. Adam could see a woman beside the man driving, leaning forward to get a good look at Adam and what he was doing.

"I'm fine, thanks. Just stopped for a picture."

"It's pretty, all right. On your way to the craft fair?" the woman asked.

"I am."

"Well, you'd better get a move on," she told him. "They open at nine and the best stuff goes fast. I hear Francine Lopez only made four chocolate cakes, and we aim to get one of them."

Another car was approaching from behind, so with a wave, the couple moved on. After waiting for three more cars to pass, Adam returned to his rented SUV and followed Sunny's directions.

At the farm, he recognized Margaret, all bundled up in a knit hat, down coat and orange safety vest, waving traffic into a nearby field where a man around Adam's age was directing them into neat rows. Adam parked and got out. The man, after gesturing the next car into place, walked over to Adam.

"You're the new director at Easy Living, right? Gran mentioned you'd be bringing your camera."

"Yes, Adam Lloyd."

"Patrick O'Shea. Bonnie's grandson, Lauren's husband, and Rowan's brother. Lauren loves the food photos you did for her and Rowan."

"I'm glad. Your wife makes incredible cheese."

"Yes, she does." Patrick grinned. "She's got a booth inside. Oh, and the food truck will be here from eleven to two."

"Do you suppose they'll be selling any of that broccoli cheese soup?"

"I'm sure they will. It's one of Rowan's best-sellers. Here." He handed over a lanyard with a red striped card attached.

"What's this?"

"Your pass. Residents and staff of Easy Living get in free. Head over there—" he pointed to a sign on a tall pole labeled Wagon Stop "—and Bea will take you to the barn. Or you can walk if you'd rather. Just follow the path through the snow."

Before Adam could answer either way, another car turned in and Patrick left to direct it.

When the Mat Mates had mentioned a craft fair, Adam had never imagined anything like this. He crossed the field, snow crunching under his boots. Near the sign, someone had built a set of steps. Soon a family joined him there, a young couple with a preschooler, and a baby in a carrier who gurgled happily as they waited. A minute later, the sound of jingling bells rang out, and a pair of enormous horses came into view, the white "feathers" around their hoofs bouncing with each step. The little boy's eyes went wide in wonderment. Two middle-aged ladies hurried from the parking lot.

Adam lifted his camera and began snapping photos. As the horses drew closer, he could see Bea driving the wagon. He couldn't tell what color her hair was today, since she wore a long stocking cap, red with white snowflakes. She pulled up to the sign and expertly brought the Clydesdales to a stop so that the wagon was lined up in front of the steps. "All aboard for the craft fair!" she called, and favored Adam with a grin.

The couple and their preschooler climbed on and selected a hay bale. Adam ushered the two ladies up the stairs and then followed them, finding a handy hay bale just behind Bea. She shook the reins, and the horses moved forward. From the grin on the boy's face, simply getting to ride behind the horses was enough to declare his day a success.

"Looks like a good turnout," Adam commented.

"You bet! I've already taken fifty or sixty people, and the door only opened ten minutes ago." Bea guided the horses around a spruce grove, and he spotted the barn. It was made of metal instead of the traditional, red-painted wood. Farther back, a brown wooden barn looked like it might have been standing for decades. Both stood in clear relief against the snow-covered mountains behind them. People had lined up outside the new barn, waiting for their turn to get in. Adam also spotted Bonnie, leading a goat who wore a bow around her neck and a banner reading Check Out My Cheese in Booth 3B.

They passed maybe a dozen or so people who had chosen to skip the hayride and walk. Bea pulled up to another set of stairs a short distance from the barn and allowed the group to disembark. The preschooler dashed off toward the goat, with his mom in hot pursuit while the dad with the baby followed. The two ladies made their way to the back of the line.

Adam snapped a photo of Bonnie and the goat. A discreet but still convenient distance from the barn, a row of porta potties waited, and if the heavy cable running along the snow toward the barn was any indication, they were heated.

The organizers had thought of everything.

"Mr. Adam!" Piper was running straight for him, with Sunny not far behind.

"Hi there."

"You made it. I was afraid I'd given you bad directions," Sunny told him.

"No, the directions were good. I just got way-laid by a pretty sunrise," he confessed. "So, how can I help?"

"Take lots of pictures, please, because Piper forgot her camera today."

"I forgot to put it in my backpack last night," Piper explained. "But Mommy says it's just as well because I'll be busy all day anyway."

"Too bad, but you can edit some of the ones I take if you like. What else do you need from me?" he asked Sunny.

"I don't have any specific instructions, but I'm sure if you make yourself available, the Mat Mates will be tapping you in from time to time."

"Sounds good."

"And have fun. It's a party in there." Sunny looked up as a large red truck pulled past the barn. "Oh good. The reindeer are here. Rowan asked me to show them where to set up."

The three of them moved past the corner of the barn so they could see the red truck pull up and stop. The passenger door of the truck opened and Santa Claus himself climbed out. He went around to fold down the rear door of the panel truck, forming a ramp. Several other people dressed as elves spilled out of the truck after him. One by one they went into the back of the truck and came out leading live reindeer.

Adam blinked. "Wow." He lifted his camera and zoomed in for some close-ups of the majestic animals with their huge antlers.

"There wasn't enough snow for Bea to pull a horse-drawn sleigh," Sunny explained, "but Marissa, from the reindeer farm, said there was enough to do sled rides with reindeer for the kids. She and her uncle Oliver had already agreed to do family photos with Santa and the reindeer, so she just recruited the rest of the family to do the sled rides."

Piper jumped up and down. "I can't wait to go on a reindeer ride!"

"It's been especially helpful to have the reindeer farm involved because they've been cross-promoting this event on social media, and they have a huge following," Sunny explained. "I'll bet a lot of the people who show up today are as interested in the reindeer as they are in crafts."

Adam looked back toward the doorway. Bea was dropping off another load of potential customers. The line at the door seemed to be moving quickly, although some of the people waiting were so enthralled with Bonnie and her goat, they had to be nudged to move forward, and they hadn't even spotted Santa and the reindeer yet. "They've really organized this well."

"I know," Sunny agreed. "The Mat Mates did a lot of the work, but Rowan, Bonnie's granddaughter, is directing the whole thing. She used to be in international marketing before she became a chef, but she still organizes an annual auction fundraiser for her husband's wildlife rehabilitation charity every July. It's too bad you weren't here then. It was amazing."

"Looking at everything going on here, I can believe it. And I haven't even been inside."

"You have to see." Piper took his hand and tugged. "Francine is doing a dance-off and Molly is giving classes and there's a lady who's doing face painting, too. Come on."

"You two go on ahead," Sunny said. "I'll be along in a few minutes."

Adam didn't recognize the two youngish women collecting entry fees at the door—probably friends or relatives of some of the residents—but after seeing the badge Patrick had given Adam, they waved him and Piper on through.

Inside was a buzz of activity that would put Rosemary's bees to shame. Table after table of baked goods, homemade candy, and even jerky lined one of the walls. Then came the crafts, everything from hand-knitted scarves

and hats to scented soaps, polished wood bowls
to exquisite quilts, and jewelry. Lots of jewelry, ranging from miniature turkeys dangling
from earrings to some beautifully done mar-
quetry bracelets, inlaid with jade, turquoise and
coral. He snapped several photos of the colorful
items. When he could, he also got some snapshots of the crafters, with their approval, their
faces as varied and interesting as their wares.

"There's Rosemary." Piper pointed her out.
Rosemary's table straddled the food and craft
categories, with pots of honey and jams, and
different kinds of crystals and crystal jewelry
for sale. He reached into his pocket and rubbed
the smooth hematite stone she'd given him. For
clarity, she'd said. He'd taken to carrying it
around with him, not wanting to disappoint
her if she asked about it. A pair of teenagers
stopped at her booth, and she smiled a welcome.

More people poured through the door, and
despite the enormous space, it began to get
crowded around some of the tables. "Good
morning, everyone."

Alice's voice came over a loudspeaker. Adam
looked around until he'd spotted her standing in
the far corner of the barn, near tables and chairs
set up in a U-shape. "Welcome to the Easy Living craft fair. You should have received a flyer

with today's schedule when you arrived," she said, holding up a long, narrow slip of purple paper, "but if you've misplaced yours, the schedule is posted up here. In thirty minutes, artist extraordinaire Molly Handleson will be offering a class in calligraphy." She gestured toward Molly, who was seated at one of the tables. Molly waved.

"Spots are limited," Alice continued, "so if you're interested in participating in any of the classes, better sign up now. The dance-off will be starting up soon, and photos with Santa are scheduled to begin at ten. If you have any questions, look for someone with a badge like this." She held up a badge identical to the one Adam was wearing. He hoped no one would ask him for information, but if they did, he'd just have to find someone who had the answer.

Alice waved. "Enjoy! Have fun!"

The people responded with a short round of applause, but they were too intent on shopping or hurrying to get in line for activity sign-ups to stand still for long. Adam made his way to the sign Alice had indicated. It looked like Molly would be teaching a drawing class that afternoon, as well as a class for children on making a Thanksgiving centerpiece. Others offered various classes and demonstrations.

"There's Mommy and the reindeer!" Piper

pointed toward a rear door Sunny was holding open while Santa and two of his elves, along with three reindeer, came inside. "I'm gonna go see her." Piper sprinted off before Adam could stop her. Fortunately, the reindeer seemed to take crowds and excited children in stride, calmly walking beside their handlers. Sunny led them to one of a few enclosures in the back of the barn, probably the future stalls for the Clydesdales.

Adam wandered around, snapping photos. Near the classes, a couple of volunteers were staffing an art booth. On the easel out front, an excellent still life of a basket of fresh herbs beside a potted red geranium bore Molly's signature. More paintings and a few hanging textile art pieces were displayed on temporary walls.

Someone had set up a rack featuring Adam's contribution, a dozen or so photos he'd mounted with mats ready to slip into standard eleven-by-fourteen-inch frames. He'd mostly chosen local landmarks he thought people might appreciate, like the rail station, the mountains and several from his trip to the farm, but he'd mixed in a few of his own favorite shots.

According to the sign, his photos were priced at thirty dollars each. Would anyone pay that? He considered asking them to lower the price, but before he could get closer, two women stepped up and began flipping through the photos.

"Oh, look at the goats!" the older of the two women exclaimed. She pulled out a close-up of one of the young goats with a red bow around its neck. "So cute."

"I like this one," said the younger woman who had to be the daughter, judging by their similar features. She'd selected a photo of a goat peering around a corner. "You think Aunt Judy would like it for her collection?"

"She'd love it. You know how much she likes goats."

"Well, she is still married to Uncle Billy," the daughter quipped, and they laughed together while the daughter paid for the photo. Meanwhile, more people had gathered and watched while another woman flipped through the remaining photos. When she reached Adam's personal favorite, one he'd taken just before Piper had gone out visiting with Francine with Thor, she paused. The photo was a close-up of Francine's hand, marked and wrinkled with age, resting on Thor's head, with Piper's hand, pudgy and smooth, on top of hers. Adam had printed it out and mounted it for himself, but decided to throw it in with the others at the last minute, figuring he could always make another print if this one happened to sell.

The woman flipping through started to move on to the next picture, but a man reached for the photo of the hands. At the same time, a blond woman in a gold puffy coat on the other side of her reached for it, too.

"I want this one," the blond woman declared.

"I reached for it first," the man on the other side claimed.

"Is there a problem here?" One of the volunteers who'd been writing a receipt for the woman buying the goat photo stepped up to the table.

"I'd like to buy this picture, please." The blond woman tugged it out from under the man's hand.

"I touched it first," the man insisted. "And then she grabbed it."

"What's the price, thirty? I'll pay forty," the woman in the puffy jacket insisted.

"Fifty," the man countered.

"Fifty-five."

"Sixty."

"Seventy-five."

"One hundred," he proclaimed, with an air of finality.

The woman glared at him. "One twenty."

"Now hold on." The volunteer held up her hands. "I just sell the art. I'm not authorized to auction it off."

"Ha. Then, you'd better get somebody over here who is," the woman huffed.

"Excuse me," Adam said, stepping forward. "Maybe I can help."

"Are you in charge?" the woman demanded. "Because I want this photo."

"I'm not, but I took the picture. If you like, I could print another one."

"You're the photographer?" The man looked him up and down with interest. "Could you make me a larger print? Say an image size of sixteen by twenty-four?"

"Sure." Adam had shot at a high resolution and done minimal cropping.

The man turned his palm up in a gesture of surrender toward the blond woman. "It's all yours. One hundred and twenty, I believe you said?"

She opened her mouth to protest but seemed to think better of it. "All right. One hundred and twenty it is." She opened her wallet, counted out six twenty-dollar bills and handed them over to the volunteer, who wrapped the photo for her.

Meanwhile, the man gestured to Adam that they should step a little farther from the table. "I'm Mason Jasper. Call me Mason."

"Adam Lloyd."

"Good to meet you, Adam. How soon can you get me that print?"

"I could print it tonight. Oh, I take that back. I don't have the capacity to do a print that big, so I'll need to have it professionally printed. It might take a day or two."

"All right." Mason looked surprised, but he reached in his pocket and pulled out a card case. "Do you have a website with links to your portfolio?"

"Uh, no. I don't have a portfolio. Or a website."

"You're not a professional photographer?"

Adam shook his head.

Mason paused for a moment. "You're very talented."

"Thank you."

"With your permission, I want to offer this print for sale in my gallery in Anchorage." He handed over a business card.

"Oh?" Adam had just assumed the man was buying it to display in his own home. He looked down at the tasteful card with the name of the gallery. "You think it will sell?"

"Absolutely. The juxtaposition of the child's hand over the old woman's—it touches the heart. People will pay for something that really speaks to them. Well, you saw." He nodded toward the blond woman, who was now walking away carrying the wrapped package, a smug smile on her face. "If you decide you have more to sell, I'd like to look at them."

"Thanks. I'll keep that in mind." Not that Adam had any plans in that direction, but it was flattering to know a professional gallery owner considered his photography good enough to sell. "I'll call once the print is ready, and we can make arrangements to get it to you."

Mason chuckled. "We haven't settled on a price."

"Oh, you're right."

"So, let's see. If you will agree to a five-edition limit—"

"Five edition?"

Mason smiled and shook his head. "You really are an amateur. That means you agree to never sell more than five of that particular print at that size."

"Okay." As far as Adam was concerned, he would probably never sell another print, period.

"All right, with a five-edition limit, you print and mount, but I pay for the framing…" He paused for a moment, as he made a mental calculation. "I can offer three hundred."

"Three hundred dollars?"

Mason laughed. "I usually deal in dollars, but if you'd rather take it in camera store credits or something—"

"No, dollars would be fine." The three hundred could certainly go toward someone's rent subsidy while they waited for the grant to be approved. He'd just never considered himself that caliber of photographer.

"Good. Call me when it's ready."

"Will do."

"All right, then. It was nice meeting you, Adam. Have a good rest of the day." Mason moved on and Adam glanced back at the table. Only two of the prints he'd donated were still in the rack.

"Looks like your photos are selling fast." Sunny had slipped up beside him.

"Yes. In fact, someone just requested a bigger print of one of them." He looked down at the card in his hand.

"I'm not surprised. Your photos are great. I was looking through them when we were setting up yesterday." Sunny got a look at the logo on the card. "Jasper Gallery? In Anchorage? Wow!"

"Wow, good or wow, bad?"

"Good! They've got wonderful stuff. Not that I can afford anything there, but I've been in a few times on First Friday art walks. Are you going to do it?"

"I said I would."

"That's great! Which one did he want?"

"The one of Francine's and Piper's hands."

"Oh, I love that one. In fact, I was hoping to buy it. Is it still there?"

"Sorry, you're too late, but I will print another one for you." Just not at the size he'd promised the gallery.

"Would you? That would be nice." She looked past him at the class area. "Seems like the lines are backing up with people trying to register for classes. I'd better go help. I'll see you around." She turned and jogged toward the table where Alice and Molly were busy signing people up.

Adam lifted his camera and snapped a couple of shots of Sunny, her warm personality overflowing as she took a clipboard and greeted people in line. He moved on to other booths and activities, taking photos and eavesdropping on conversations. Most of the people there seemed thrilled with the variety and quality of the offerings. The upcoming holidays appeared to be a major motivator, with people either getting a jump start on their Christmas gift shopping or stocking up on autumn-colored table linens, quilts and kitchen items.

One of the most popular draws was a photo with Santa. The reindeer farm people had posted a take-a-number dispenser out front, and by the time they opened at ten and called number one, the next available number was twenty-six. They had a nice arrangement, a set with Santa front and center on a throne holding on to a lead rope of a reindeer beside him. A camera perched on a tripod was focused and ready to go.

"Mrs. Santa" would help arrange the family around Santa in the space and then take the photo with a remote. The camera sent the photos to a laptop, where an "elf" would do a quick check for closed eyes or other problems. If all seemed well, the family would move on to the second elf, who would collect their money, print out their photo and slide it into a red-and-green folder for them to take home.

Adam was looking over the printing equipment when a sudden wave of laughter drew his attention back to Santa. One of the people looked at the badge he wore and tapped his arm. "Excuse me, sir. It appears that reindeer isn't completely housebroken."

"Oh." Adam didn't have much experience with livestock, but it was pretty clear what needed to be done. "I'll take care of it." Fortunately, he'd noticed a flat-bottomed shovel leaning against a wall in one corner of the barn earlier. He fetched it and returned to the booth. Mrs. Santa, who looked to be around the same age as the residents of Easy Living, smiled at him. "Oh, thank you. I was about to run out to the truck." She reached for the shovel.

Adam wasn't about to turn over manual labor to someone old enough to be his grandmother. "That's okay. I'll do it." Once Santa had led the reindeer out of the way, Adam used the shovel to scoop up the pile of dark nuggets.

"Ho ho ho! Thank you, young man." Santa spoke in a warm, booming voice, and everyone cheered. Adam grinned and made his way outdoors, still carrying the shovel. Bea, who had just dropped off a load of new customers, spotted him and directed him on where to deposit his collection.

When he returned to the barn carrying the empty shovel, Sunny met him at the door. "Hey there. I just heard you saved the day over at the Santa booth."

He laughed. "I'm not sure shoveling fertilizer is particularly valiant, but it needed to be done."

"That's what makes it valiant." She stepped closer and went up on her tiptoes to kiss his cheek. "My hero."

Piper came running up. "Mommy, the make-an-ornament class is about to start. Hurry!"

"Oops, got to go," she told Adam. "And thanks."

He stood for a moment, looking after the two of them. He liked this hero business, the kiss on the cheek. Wondered what it would be like to experience a real kiss from Sunny.

"You want me to take that?" Ralph had popped up from somewhere while Adam wasn't paying attention.

"What?"

"The shovel. I'll put it back where it belongs."

"Oh. No, I can return it."

"She's a sweetheart, that one," Ralph commented.

"Who?"

"Sunny, of course. Isn't she the reason you're standing there with a goofy grin on your face?"

"I'm not—" Adam started to say before he realized that's exactly what he was doing.

"Yeah, I thought so. You'd be hard-pressed to find someone with a bigger heart than our Sunny." Ralph pressed his lips together and nodded. "Just make sure you handle it with care."

Adam shook his head. "Sunny and I aren't—"

"You're not? Well, I'd get going if I were you." Ralph chuckled as he walked toward the food booths, leaving Adam to wonder if the entire building was speculating on him and Sunny. This was why he didn't date coworkers. And yet...

"Adam!" Alice came striding over. "We need

three more tables for the next craft session. They're in the red van out back behind the barn. Would you mind carrying them inside?"

"No problem." He accepted the key ring she handed him.

Between taking photos, running errands and generally making himself available, Adam was busy for the rest of the day. He got some great shots of the reindeer rides. Elves would load the children onto plastic sleds and then pull them behind the reindeer. Even though they led the reindeer at a gentle walking pace, the children seemed to find the rides quite exciting. Especially Piper, but then Piper, like her mother, seemed to extract maximum joy from every experience. Adam did find time to grab lunch from the food truck, more of his favorite broccoli soup and homemade cheddar rolls, and to buy a beautiful handmade scarf for his mom and a wooden bowl for his dad.

The building closed at three, and by then the volunteers were beginning to look a little weary, but they also seemed jubilant at the success of the fair. In all the busyness, Adam almost forgot why they were doing this—to subsidize the rents for those folks who couldn't afford them until the grant money arrived. He had just carried a few heavy boxes to someone's car when he saw Bea returning from her last trip dropping off customers in the parking lot.

Adam went out to greet her. "You've put in a full day."

"Oh, I managed to get a few breaks while my son took over." She climbed down from the wagon and pushed her fists into her lower back in a long stretch. "But I have to say, I'm glad to be done. My husband and I used to drive horses on Mackinac Island every summer, but it's been a few years."

A man wearing heavy overalls came out from the barn. "All done, Mom?"

"Yes, I am, and thank you for the use of your barn and these beauties today." She stepped up to pat the two horses. "They have really earned their oats tonight."

"So have you." He rubbed her shoulder fondly. "I'll take care of the horses. You go get some rest." He led the horses and wagon off toward the older barn.

But apparently Bea had better things to do than rest. She immediately jumped into helping the others break down booths and fold up tables. If Adam hadn't grabbed the tables to carry them outside, she probably would have done that, too. The rest of the volunteers from Easy Living were equally busy turning the craft fair back into a barn, all except Alice and Linda, who were huddled together at one of the tables with calculators at the ready, counting money and charge slips.

Sunny and Piper were helping several of the residents pack up their leftover items and carry them out. There weren't a lot of leftovers, which was nice to see. By any measure, the event had been a success. Slowly, the volunteers and vendors trickled away. Adam lent Molly a hand to pack up her easels and the equipment she'd brought for classes. She'd sold all her art, including his photos. She drove away, leaving only a few cars parked behind the barn, one of which was Sunny's.

Sunny had been a whirlwind today, dashing from person to person, handling emergencies, filling in here and there so that others could leave their booths to shop or take classes, her smile never faltering.

The sun had slipped behind the horizon while he was packing Molly's car, but traces of magenta and pink still clung to the clouds in the darkening sky. Sunny slipped out the back door of the barn, activating the automatic light over it. She had several tote bags draped over her arms and was carrying a box. Adam hurried to take the box from her.

"Thanks!" She opened the hatchback of her

car and set down her load. "And thank you for fixing the lifts on my hatchback. You shouldn't have, but I'm glad you did, especially on days like today." She shifted the tote bags to make more room.

"How did you find out?" he asked.

She took the box from him and set it in the car. "The daughter of one of the residents mentioned it today. She saw you working from her dad's window when she was visiting, and she didn't know it was supposed to be a secret. Anyway, thank you. That was incredibly kind."

"Thank Ralph. He really did most of the work." Not quite true, but Adam couldn't have done it without him.

"I already have." Sunny closed the hatchback and turned to him, her eyes dancing in mischief. "And now, I'm thanking you." She reached out for a hug. He only hesitated for a split second before wrapping his arms around her, pulling her close.

What had started out as a friendly hug grew into something more. He swore he could feel her body heat, even through the heavy coats they both wore. She seemed to feel it, too. Her head tilted back, and she looked up at him, her eyes soft. And suddenly, all he wanted in the world was to kiss this incredible woman.

He lowered his head, and her arms tightened around his neck, pulling him to her. When their lips touched, happiness zinged through him, as though the joy Sunny always carried around with her was overflowing and spilling into him. He tilted his head just a bit, and the kiss deepened, their lips fitting together as though they'd been made to kiss each other.

He finally broke the kiss, lifting his head just enough so that he could look into her beautiful face and see the sparkle in her eyes. Did anyone else on earth have eyes in such a warm shade of golden brown, with little flecks of amber that made them look as though they were lit from within?

Or was it only Sunny?

The motion-sensor light flicked off, leaving them in the dark, but Adam still didn't let her go. When he held her, he felt impervious to the cold, to the rules, to anything except the rightness of being together. He kissed her again, easily finding her lips in the dark.

The back door opened. "Mommy?" The light flicked on as Piper stepped outside, looking down at something in her hands.

Sunny dropped her arms from his neck, and Adam reluctantly let her go. "I'm here," Sunny called.

"Ms. Linda gave me—oh, hi, Mr. Adam. I didn't know you were still here."

"I was helping your mom with a few things." He sneaked a glance at Sunny, who was hiding a smile. Fortunately, Piper didn't seem to notice.

"Look. Ms. Linda gave me a game she got today." She held up a classic ball and cup game, this one made of wood turned on a lathe and polished, with a wooden ball on a leather string. "You want to try it?"

"Very nice." Adam admired the polished wood and attempted to toss the ball into the cup. He missed, tried again and missed. Sunny chuckled as he missed the third time, and Adam grinned. "It's harder than it looks. Here, you try."

Sunny took the toy, and with a quick jerk of the wrist easily tossed the ball into the cup.

Adam bowed his head. "I yield to the master."

Sunny laughed. "As well you should. Come on, Piper. It's time to head home."

"Okay. Bye, Mr. Adam."

Once Piper was in the car, Sunny turned toward Adam, and once again, their eyes caught and held. Was there something different about her smile, something softer and more intimate, or was that just his imagination?

"Good night, Adam. I'll see you Monday."

"Good night." He watched her get into the car. Piper waved as they drove away, and he waved back.

Monday couldn't come soon enough.

CHAPTER TWELVE

"AND NOW RELAX your arms, shake out your hands and have a wonderful day." Sunny smiled and waved goodbye to the members of her morning stretch group, a little fewer in number than usual. All the Mat Mates were huddled in Alice's apartment with Bonnie's granddaughter, Rowan, adding up all the figures from the craft fair.

Sunny couldn't imagine how the event could have gone any better. Sure, there were the usual minor mishaps and a bit of grumbling when one vendor didn't like her table's location, but the team had sorted everything out. The vendors Sunny had talked to were thrilled with the number of customers and felt the fee they'd been charged to participate more than paid for itself. The crafts and foods the Easy Living residents had donated to raise money had almost completely sold out, and most of the classes had been filled to capacity. Marissa and the rest of the family from the reindeer farm had also donated all their net profits from the reindeer rides and Santa photos.

And then, out of nowhere, came that kiss. Just thinking about it sent a pleasant little shiver down Sunny's back. She hadn't intended for it to happen. Sure, she was attracted to Adam, but when she'd hugged him, it was simply a thank-you, just like the hug she'd given Ralph as soon as she'd found out he and Adam were responsible for fixing her car. But when Adam had put his arms around her, something had changed. And when he'd looked at her like that...

"Sunny."

She jumped and turned. "Oh, hi, Phil."

"I called your name twice." He scowled. "You can't claim you're hard of hearing like half the people around here do when they don't want to listen."

"Sorry, I was just thinking of something else." She smiled at him, ignoring the dig. "What can I do for you?"

"Can I have one of those?" He nodded to the stack of the activity schedules on the table, which Sunny had been about to distribute to everyone's apartment.

"Sure." As far as she could remember, Phil had never attended any activity except occasionally when there was food involved, so she wasn't sure why he would want an advance copy, but she handed over the top sheet, anyway.

Without glancing at the paper, he folded it and stuffed it in his pocket. "I hear that new manager has been taking pictures of everybody."

"Yes, but it's strictly voluntary. You don't have to have your picture taken if you don't want to," she reassured him.

He grunted. "Nobody asked me."

"Oh." So, Phil was feeling left out. Sunny was ninety percent sure that if Adam had contacted Phil and requested a photo shoot, he would have refused. "I don't know where Adam is on that project, but I'll be sure and let him know you're interested."

"I don't know if I'd say interested, but if everyone else is doing it…"

"I'll tell him to contact you."

"Say I'll be at home tomorrow at three."

"I'll relay the time. If he can't make it then, I'll have him call to set something else up."

"You do that." With a curt nod, Phil turned and left.

Sunny glanced at the clock. The turkey-stencil napkin-painting class she was leading didn't start for another hour. If she got these flyers delivered, she would have time to stop by Adam's office for a few minutes. To pass on Phil's request, of course. Not to kiss Adam, or anything. Because kissing at work would be inappropriate.

But fun.

Grinning to herself, she grabbed the stack of printed schedules and began walking down the hallway, sliding one under each door. A few of the residents, seeing the flyers, came to chat for a few minutes, but she was still able to finish with fifteen minutes to spare.

For once, nobody was at the desk in the outer office, so Sunny went on through and stopped in Adam's open doorway. He sat at the desk, his focus on something on his screen. "Knock, knock."

He looked up, and a slow smile bloomed on his face. "Sunny."

"Hi." She smiled back at him. He looked good today, in a navy crewneck sweater over a lighter blue shirt that brought out the blue of his eyes. Oh, who was she kidding? He looked good every day. For a long beat, she held his gaze before remembering she was supposed to be delivering a message. "Um, Phil happened to mention that you hadn't made any arrangements to photograph him yet."

"Oh, I assumed he wouldn't—"

"Me, too, but apparently he's feeling left out."

"Well, we don't want that. I'll get in touch with him."

"Actually, he wants you at his apartment tomorrow at three. I said if you couldn't make it, you'd call and reschedule."

Adam laughed. "Royal summons, huh?" He checked his calendar. "Three works."

"Good." Having delivered the message, Sunny could have gone on to prepare for her class, but she couldn't seem to turn away. Was Adam going to mention that kiss? Should she? But they were at work. She should probably play it cool. "How is the rest of the photo project going?"

"It's going well," he told her with enthusiasm. "This afternoon, I'm supposed to get together with the last two residents—well, besides Phil, I guess. In fact, I was just sorting through the photos, trying to pick out the best ones. Want to take a look?"

"Sure." She came around to his side of the desk and stood next to his chair, catching a whiff of his piney aftershave. He reached over to click his mouse and his sleeve brushed against her, sending a tingle running up her arm. She focused on the screen. Adam had hooked up his laptop to the larger monitor that Lou had always used. Three portraits showed on the screen. Wonderful portraits.

"Wow." The first was of Bonnie, leaning over a fence to give one of the goats a pat with her dachshund in her arms, reaching up to lick her chin. Francine was next, pulling a cake from the oven. Thor stood nearby with his nose raised, taking in the delicious aroma. The third photo was of Linda, dressed in her sorceress costume, reading to the kids. Arrows on the edges indicated there were more pictures. "May I?" Sunny asked, gesturing toward the mouse.

"Of course."

She bent down over the desk and clicked through, loving the expressions he'd caught on faces so dear to her. In most of the photos, the subjects were actively involved doing something they were passionate about. Even in the few where the residents were simply sitting in a chair or standing, their expressions seemed animated, as though they were in the process of telling Adam a story. "Oh, there's Rosemary and her bees. I didn't know you'd gone bee-keeping with her."

"Yes, early in October, she invited me to go along while she collected the final batch of honey for the year. It was fascinating, watching the process. The only problem is that you can't really see her face clearly behind the veil. So, I thought when you make the slideshow, you might want to pair it with this one I took of her at the craft fair this weekend—" he clicked to the next page "—selling her jars of honey."

"Perfect! And here's Rosemary pruning the rosebushes. Where did these aerial photos come from?"

"Ralph called me yesterday afternoon and asked if I wanted to go up with him. I didn't realize he was a bush pilot for so many years."

"Yes, he and his first wife were both pilots. They ran an air taxi service together. After she died, he sold that business and moved to Juneau, where he did flight-seeing tours. That's where he met Alice." With alarm, she noticed a photo of Ralph in the front looking out the windshield. "Ralph didn't fly the plane, did he? He's scheduled for cataract surgery next month. He's not supposed to be driving, much less flying."

Adam laughed. "No, it was Ralph's daughter's plane, and she flew us. She's a chemistry professor at the college, but also an accomplished pilot."

"I guess she takes after her parents. Did you enjoy the flight?"

"Very much. I didn't realize just how big the Matanuska Glacier was until I saw it from the air. From above, you can really see the river of ice."

"Did Alice go with you?"

"No, she dropped Ralph off but said she didn't like small planes. Something about them being incompatible with her stomach. Funny she would be married to a pilot."

"Well, there's no accounting for love." Sunny spoke before she thought, and then stole a glance at Adam. She'd not been hinting at anything, but now that she'd said it…

The corners of his mouth quirked up, and he leaned a little closer. Their lips were just inches apart when the sound of footsteps in the hallway alerted them.

Sunny straightened quickly. "Great photos!" she said, loudly enough to carry to the hallway. "But I'd better get moving. I have a class in…" She glanced at the clock. "Five minutes."

Alice came into the room, with the other five Mat Mates right behind her. "We have the final numbers. I think you'll be pleased." She handed a piece of paper to Adam. Sunny stayed, looking over his shoulder.

He looked at the paper and his eyes widened. "Wow! Yes, this should cover the subsidized rents for six months, easily, and according to the guidelines on that main grant, if it comes though, they should start funding in five. You've done it! Congratulations!" He stood up and gave Alice a hug, and then proceeded to hug each of the women.

Sunny hugged them, too. "You are amazing! I've got to go, but I want to hear all about it later." She slipped out of the room, leaving them to give Adam the details. They'd really done it! They'd saved the Easy Living family. That was marvelous news. Even if it did interrupt a kiss.

AFTER A LAST check to make sure he had the right lens and equipment, Adam knocked on the door of apartment 101. Unlike most of the other doors in the complex, this door displayed no autumn wreath, welcome sign, or even a paper turkey. After a moment, the door opened a crack and Phil's face peered out. "Oh, it's you."

"Yes. We had a three o'clock appointment, right?"

"It's two minutes after. I thought you weren't coming." Phil stepped back and opened the door.

Adam's phone said two fifty-nine, but he didn't argue the point. He followed Phil inside and, noticing a pile of shoes near the door, kicked off his own. They walked past the coat closet and around a corner into the main living room. The room itself was identical to all the other apartments in the building, a large room with space for a table at one end next to the kitchen and big windows looking out over the grounds on the living room end.

They all had hardwood floors, but in Phil's case, the living room floor was covered with an antique Persian rug that had faded into beautifully muted shades of red, gold and orange. On it sat a tufted and curving couch covered with coral-colored velvet, the nap worn smooth in places. Two buttery leather chairs perched on the other side of a brass coffee table. An upright piano was pushed against the wall, and a low glass-and-chrome bookcase supported a couple of green plants below the window. It all looked like the set of a glamorous movie from the 1930s, and was about the furthest thing possible from what Adam would have imagined he would find in Phil's place.

"This rug is incredible," Adam said, taking in the abstract floral pattern. No wonder Phil only wore socks inside.

"It was my mother's," Phil told him. "All of this." His gesture took in the living room furniture and the round dining table, which was made of white marble on a pale wood pedestal.

"It's beautiful." And quite high quality. Other than the wear on the upholstery, the furniture was in excellent shape despite presumably being almost a century old. Adam knew from his records that Phil was one of the residents receiving a deep discount based on his income, but it looked as though there had been money in the family at some point.

"I gather Sunny gave you my message. Hard worker, that one. Doesn't deserve the treatment she got."

"What treatment is that?" Was someone here harassing her? Adam would put a stop to that immediately.

"I mean with her old boyfriend before she came here. I don't usually listen to rumors…"

Adam suppressed a sigh. How often were those words followed by the most outlandish tales?

"But word is, when she came up pregnant, he took off. Never gave her a nickel of support for the baby."

"Hmm." Adam said nothing more, not wanting to encourage more gossip.

Eventually Phil cleared his throat. "Okay. Well, I don't have all day. Where do you want me?"

Adam noticed for the first time that Phil had dressed up for the occasion, adding a tweed blazer over his usual gray pants and plaid shirt.

"That chair would be good." Adam nodded toward the one angled slightly toward the window. Judging from the wear pattern on the leather, he'd guess it was Phil's usual seat of choice. "Or would you rather be at the piano? Do you play?"

Phil, on his way to the chair, stopped and frowned. "Of course, I play. Why else would I have a piano in my apartment?"

"I thought it might be a family heirloom. Do you play any other instruments?"

"Several. You?"

"Me? No. Other than a recorder in elementary school, I've never attempted to learn an instrument."

Phil shook his head. "That's a shame. Although a few of my students probably would have been better off if they'd stuck with a recorder."

"Students?"

"Yes, I gave private lessons in piano and woodwinds to pay the bills. Jazz musicians don't earn a lot." On the piano, Adam noticed two signed photos, one musician at a piano and the other holding a clarinet. Both gave Phil profuse thanks for teaching them to play. Maybe he had taught from necessity rather than choice, but apparently, he'd been good at it.

"I like jazz. Will you play for me?" Adam asked.

Phil shook his head. "Don't feel like playing today. Haven't in a long time." He gave the piano stool a spin, raising it about an inch.

"This stool belonged to my maternal grand-mother's mother. It's over a hundred years old."

"What a treasure." Family history must mean a lot to Phil. "Let's pose you sitting on it, with the piano behind you. I'll set up the lighting."

Phil ran the stool back to its previous height and sat. Adam flicked off the overhead light, which was creating a distracting glare. The low winter sun streaming through the window would be the main light source for his photo. Phil's lean face was full of sharp angles and deep lines, a thinker's face. Adam set up one of his lights as a fill to soften the shadows, but then realized the harsh shadows created a more interesting, if not flattering, portrait. He moved the fill light farther away and set up a tripod for his camera.

"You mentioned that this furniture belonged to your mother," Adam commented as he arranged everything. "Are you the oldest?"

"Yes."

Adam moved behind the camera. "All right if I take pictures while we talk?"

"That's what you're here for, isn't it?"

"Yes. How many brothers and sisters do you have?" Adam asked conversationally as he looked through the viewfinder, focusing on Phil's face, and snapped the first picture.

Phil's jaw tightened. "None now. My half brother died recently."

"Oh. I'm sorry for your loss."

Phil frowned. "Don't be. We hadn't spoken in almost sixty years."

"I'm sorry," Adam repeated. To him, that was an even greater loss. Growing up as an only child, he'd always wished for a brother. He couldn't imagine the grudge that would separate him from a brother for a lifetime. If this was Phil's younger brother, he couldn't have been very old sixty years ago. "What did he do to bring about this separation?"

"He did nothing."

"Nothing?"

Phil pressed his thin lips together. "I worked for my father one summer between semesters at college. Hated it. At the end of the summer, during a family dinner, my father laid down an ultimatum—said if I didn't want to join him in the family business once I graduated, I was no longer a part of the family. Oscar said nothing. Neither did his mother." Phil sat up straighter. "Of course, she was probably the one who put my father up to it in the first place. She'd been trying to push me out since the minute she married my father."

"What happened to your own mother?"

"She died when I was eight. My father didn't

even wait a year before he married again. Their son was born within a year. I suppose when I told my father I'd rather pursue music than go to work for him, I played right into my stepmother's hands, but I just couldn't do it. Real estate is a soulless business." He suddenly seemed to remember who he was talking to and had the grace to look embarrassed. "No offense."

Adam smiled to himself. Hard not to take offense when someone had just labeled the profession he had dedicated his life to as "soulless," but he was more interested in hearing the rest of Phil's story than arguing. "None taken. So, you refused, and he kicked you out of the family?"

"That's right."

"And you never spoke again?"

"Oh, my father contacted me a few times. Apologized, said he'd overreacted. But the damage was done. I wasn't going back. I even changed my name—took my mother's maiden name. And my father got what he wanted. His 'good' son had a knack for real estate and grew the company into one of the most successful in the state."

"How old was your brother when all this happened? This confrontation between you and your father, I mean."

"Let's see, I was twenty-one, so he would have been twelve."

"Just twelve?" It seemed to Adam that expecting a twelve-year-old to argue Phil's case with their father was unrealistic. "Did you ever try to contact him after he was grown?"

"I didn't. After our father's death, Oscar came looking for me. He'd inherited the whole company, but he said that wasn't fair, offered me half if I was interested, but I wanted no part of it. Decent of him to offer, though. When he was settling the estate, he found all this furniture in storage and realized it had been my mother's, so he made sure I got it. His wife used to send me an invitation to Thanksgiving dinner every year, but I never took them up on it. Got an annual Christmas letter with pictures of their two boys up until they were grown and gone."

"Is your brother's wife still living?"

"No, she died in the accident with my brother."

A real estate developer who had recently died in an accident along with his wife? "Wait, are you talking about Oscar Ravenwood, who owned this building? He's your brother?"

"That's right." Phil gave a sly smile. "After my band broke up and I retired, I heard about these affordable senior apartments in Palmer. When I found out Oscar was the owner, I decided to take a look, see what it was all about. I figured he'd cobbled together dinky little apartments so he could make money off old people on fixed incomes. That's what our father would have done. But I was wrong.

"The apartment they showed me was a good size, and the building was well-maintained. I didn't stay in the real estate business, but I learned enough that one summer to know he had to be losing money on them. So I decided to move in, try to figure out his angle. I kept waiting for the shoe to drop, to get a notice they were raising the rents, or selling the building, or something, but I finally decided he really was just doing it out of the goodness of his heart." Phil scoffed. "Don't know where he learned that generosity—not from our father or his mother. Maybe it was his wife."

Phil shrugged, a look of regret crossing his face. "Kind of wish, now, that I'd taken them up on their offer of dinner a time or two, gotten to know them a little bit. Always thought I might, someday. Guess I never thought about Oscar dying before me."

"Have you ever met your nephews?" Adam asked, as he snapped another photo.

Phil shook his head. "Not even sure if they know about me."

"I'll bet they do. Maybe you should approach them."

"They'd probably want nothing to do with me, especially after all these years."

"You might be right." Adam snapped another shot. "Or they might welcome a new family member, given they've lost their parents so suddenly. You never know."

"I suppose." Phil nodded slowly. "It might not hurt to say hello."

"What have you got to lose?" Adam asked him.

"Not a lot." Phil gave a mirthless laugh. "They can't very well kick me out of my apartment since they sold it to your company."

"That's true."

Phil looked toward Adam. "You really think I should contact them?"

Adam shrugged. "My opinion doesn't count. You never let other people dictate your decisions."

"You're right, there." Phil gave a curt nod. "All right, then. Get that picture you want and quit wasting my time. I've got things to do."

"Got it." Adam snapped one last shot, capturing an expression he'd never thought he would see on Phil's face—hope.

CHAPTER THIRTEEN

THE NEXT DAY, Adam sat in front of his computer, putting the finishing touches on the photos he'd taken of Phil. Funny how, starting from their first contact, he'd seen Phil as a nuisance, a troublemaker whose only purpose in life was to make things harder for everyone else. But apparently, he'd been a good teacher, good enough that a couple of his former students, who looked to be professionals now, sent him thank-yous. It sounded like it was his relationship with his father that had soured him, made him push people away before they could get close enough to hurt him.

It was a shame, though, that he'd allowed the resentment he'd felt for his father keep him from his brother, even after the father was gone. It was clear he regretted that decision.

Regrets. Was it possible to live a life without them? Adam and Phil had both been in the position of choosing whether to go into business with their respective fathers. However, while Adam's stepfather had made it plain he would welcome Adam into the business, he would have supported any career choice Adam made. Adam had been only too happy to go to work with the man who had made such a difference in his life and brought his mother so much happiness. But he did regret that he'd allowed the work to take over his life to the point where there was no room for anything else. Not hobbies, like photography. Not relationships. Just properties to be managed.

Until now, anyway.

He clicked through the pictures he'd taken since arriving in Alaska. The landscapes, the wedding photos, the food photos, and best of all, the portraits. He'd really enjoyed delving into photography, remembering the passion it had once held for him. It was as though his visit here in Alaska was a time-out, a chance to live a balanced life, to enjoy people and hobbies outside work. Once he moved on to his next assignment, he'd probably fall into his old patterns of working evenings and weekends, and it might be years before he picked up his camera again.

He clicked on to the next page, of pictures taken at the craft fair. The residents had done an amazing job putting it on, and they'd raised plenty of money to subsidize the below-market rents until that grant came through. The Easy

Living Apartments were on their way to a solid footing. If this were any other of the various properties Adam had evaluated and set on a new path, that would mean it was time to move on. There were certainly other properties that needed his attention.

But Adam dragged his feet, arguing to himself that until they got final approval from the grant, his job here wasn't done. Dad had given him until Thanksgiving to turn the property around, after all.

He glanced over the photos he'd taken at the fair, of arts and crafts, children on reindeer rides, the enormous horses pulling the hay wagon, and interesting faces of all ages, from a laughing baby to a grandmother in a wheelchair beaming when she received the cake she'd won in a raffle.

One photo caught his eye, and he clicked to enlarge it. In this one, he'd caught Piper's squeal of joy as she rode in the sled behind a reindeer. In the background, Sunny looked on, delighted to watch her daughter having so much fun.

He zoomed in to study Sunny's face. Her smile, so much a part of her. The sparkle in her eyes. Everyone around her was smiling, too. It was as though she created a little bubble of joy wherever she went, spreading happiness to everyone who met her. He felt it whenever she was close, and he missed it when she was gone.

Was Sunny the real reason he didn't want to leave?

He'd come to Alaska thinking it was just another assignment, one more problem property to get straightened out as quickly as possible before he moved on to the next. He'd never thought he'd find himself making friends with the residents, learning about their lives and talents as he photographed them. Or that he'd be sharing his love of photography with a precocious and talented nine-year-old. And he'd certainly never thought he would meet someone as warm and caring and extraordinary as Sunny. She was one of a kind.

"The mail's early today." Bea cruised into the outer office, pushing a folding dolly with a box and a bundle of mail on top. She set the mail on the desk and looked at the label on the box. "For Rosemary." Bea shook her head. "Rosemary's niece's daughter in Arkansas always looks for children's books at garage sales for the reading program, but half the time she forgets to include the apartment number so her box ends up coming to the office. I'll run upstairs to the activity room in a minute. You know, oddest thing. Yesterday, Rosemary heard this beautiful piano music coming from

Phil's apartment. We never even knew he had a piano in there."

Interesting. Yesterday, Phil told Adam he hadn't felt like playing in a long time. What could have changed?

Bea picked up the mail and walked into Adam's office, sifting through the envelopes without any pretense of privacy. "Water bill. Coupon ads. Oh, here's one to you from Boise. Looks like a card. Beverly Lloyd. Your mother, I'd guess? Isn't that nice. Oh, here's something that might be about one of the grants." She frowned. "Hmm, looks like a thin envelope, which probably means it's a no."

She arrived at the desk and Adam reached for the stack. "Thanks, Bea." He waited for her to leave, but it soon became clear she wasn't going to budge until he'd opened the letter about the grant. It was from the foundation that Alice had deemed a long shot, so Bea was probably right about it being a rejection. He reached for the Iditarod letter opener. Inside the envelope was a one-page letter with the grant's logo across the top. He skimmed it. "You're right. It thanks us for applying, but we don't meet the current criteria, blah, blah, blah, wishing us luck in finding other funding."

Bea shrugged. "Too bad, but we pretty much

knew it was coming. It's the other grant we're counting on."

"Yes. Hopefully, we should hear something from them soon."

Bea nodded. "I'll let Alice and the others know about this one while I take Linda her books for the kids. Don't forget to open the card from your mom." She grabbed the grant rejection and bustled out. Presumably Bea would bring it back to file once she'd reported to the Mat Mates and the other residents. He'd noticed that the prevailing attitude among his various volunteer "assistants" was that they knew better than he did how things should be run. Admittedly, they were usually right.

He slit open the envelope from his mom, which contained a card with a vintage photo of two children playing "telephone" with cans and string. Inside was a clipping announcing her role in an upcoming Christmas play. He smiled. She'd be great as the wisecracking grandmother in a house full of children. She loved working with kids, and often mentioned ever so casually that she would be a terrific babysitter should he ever find himself in need of one. *Can't wait to see you at Thanksgiving. Love, Mom.*

Thanksgiving. He looked at his calendar. Just under a week until the Easy Living early

Thanksgiving meal on Tuesday, when Sunny would be unveiling the portraits he'd taken. They had managed to keep them under wraps, despite various residents trying to cajole and bribe them into letting them take "just a peek." He couldn't miss that. Which meant he'd need to fly to Boise on Wednesday, if he planned to be there for his family's Thanksgiving dinner on Thursday. He should have booked a flight weeks ago. Oops.

He started to put aside the rest of the mail and open a travel app on his computer, but then noticed an envelope from Jasper Gallery. Inside was the promised check, which he set aside to give to Alice later. Mason had also enclosed a handwritten note, mentioning that they'd sold the print almost immediately and reminding Adam that if he wanted to sell more photographs, Mason was interested.

Adam picked up the check again. It was exciting, thinking of his photograph hanging on someone's wall somewhere, just because they loved the image he'd captured. It was a dream he'd had as a teenager when he first fell in love with photography, and even though he'd long ago chosen another route, it was still gratifying.

Below that one was another letter with a return address that was simply a post office box. Probably an invitation to a house-flipping seminar or something similar. But then he realized the PO Box was in Juneau, which was where the philanthropic organization they'd applied to for the second grant was located. He reached for his letter opener.

A light patter of footsteps sounded in the hallway, and instantly, he knew it was Sunny. No one else danced through the hallways like she did. Sure enough, her face appeared at the door to the outer office. "Hi. I was looking for Bea."

"She's taking a package to Linda. She should be back shortly."

"Oh. Okay." Sunny came through to his office. "Any word on the grants?"

"The one in Anchorage turned us down," he told her.

"Alice said they would."

"Yes. I was just about to open this other letter. I think it might be from the one in Juneau."

"And you were just going to open it?"

"Um. Yes?" What else was he supposed to do with a letter?

"After all the work everyone has put into this? Come on! This is worthy of an awards show–type announcement. The Mat Mates should be there when you open it. After all, they've put in more work than anyone on getting this done."

"You're right." Adam was so used to working alone he hadn't even considered that. "Are they here?"

"Yes, they're in the multipurpose room putting together Thanksgiving goody bags to send home with the reading club kids this week. I was coming to ask Bea about stickers she had for them. Come on!" She took his hand and tugged playfully.

"Okay." Her enthusiasm was catching. He picked up the envelope, which did seem to be a little thicker than the rejection letter from the other organization. "But what if it's bad news?" he asked as they hurried to the elevator.

"Then we'll all find out together. Good news or bad, it's better with people you care about. Besides, Alice said we meet all the criteria. I have a good feeling."

"Me, too." Although that good feeling might have as much to do with the fact that Sunny was still holding his hand as it did with the letter he carried.

"By the way," she said as they rode the elevator to the second floor. "I need to work on the slideshow for Thanksgiving this evening. Can you send me the pictures?"

"Sure. Or I can give you a hand choosing pictures if you like."

"I was hoping you'd say that. I started chili

in the slow cooker this morning. If you're free tonight, you could have dinner with us."

"I'd love that. Thanks," he said as the elevator door opened. Bea almost bowled into them with her now-empty dolly before realizing the elevator wasn't empty.

"Sorry."

"It's okay. Come with us to the multipurpose room," Sunny urged. "Adam is going to open the letter about the grant."

"He already opened it." Bea waved the letter she was carrying. "It was a no."

"No, this is from the other grant," Sunny explained.

"At least I think it is," Adam said.

"Let's find out." Bea spun the dolly around and wheeled it back down the hallway, leaving Adam and Sunny to follow in her wake. As soon as she burst through the doors of the multipurpose room, she let out a loud whistle. The rest of the Mat Mates, who were standing at tables sorting items into paper bags, turned toward her. "Adam has a letter about the big grant," she announced.

"Maybe," Adam said, clarifying. "Here, Alice, you wrote most of the application. Why don't you read it?" He handed off the envelope.

Alice pulled a pair of reading glasses from her bag and put them on. "This is the address, all right." She picked up a pair of scissors someone had been using to cut ribbon, slit the envelope and pulled out the letter. The room went perfectly quiet, while Alice read the letter. After a moment, she smiled. "We're in!"

"Yes!" Sunny threw her arms around Adam's neck. "Easy Living is saved."

"Thank goodness." Adam hugged her back, relief flooding his body. He hadn't realized how afraid he'd been that it wouldn't work out, that all the efforts the residents had put in had been wasted, and that he would end up being the bad guy who brought about the downfall of this community. It would still be hard to leave, but at least he could go knowing that the people he'd come to care about would be all right.

"It's not completely official yet," Alice warned. "This says the selection committee has approved us for the grant, but it's not final until the board signs off at their next meeting, which won't be until January. Looks like we won't be getting any funds until the end of March, so it's a good thing we raised all that money through the craft fair."

"Still, it's wonderful news!" Sunny released Adam and went to hug Alice and the other Mat Mates. "You did it!"

"With Adam's help," Linda pointed out. "He's the one who got all the figures together."

"I'm just so pleased it came through," he said.

"I'm as thankful as a squirrel in a walnut orchard," Bonnie declared. "We're all going to have a whole lot to celebrate this Thanksgiving."

THAT EVENING AFTER DINNER, Adam and Sunny sat side by side at her table going through the photos. "So, which two for Bonnie? This one, right?" Adam indicated a close-up of Bonnie with the mountains behind her and copied it to a folder he'd set up to share with Sunny.

"Yes, and this one where she's holding Wilson and he's licking her chin. Although—" Sunny leaned closer to the screen "—I love this one of her with the goat at the craft fair, with her kneeling down and talking to that little boy."

"You said you're limiting it to two photos per person."

"I know." Sunny sighed. "But it's so hard to choose. I love every single one of the photos you took of the residents. Are you sure we can't use them all in the Thanksgiving presentation?"

"Only if you want it to last until Christmas. People do have a limited attention span, especially after they've just eaten a big meal."

"I guess you're right. But put the one at the

craft fair in the folder, too. I might use it in sort of a collage about the craft fair in general."

Adam added the picture. "By the way, how do you handle the logistics of Thanksgiving dinner? That little kitchen in the multipurpose room isn't big enough to prepare dinner for the whole building."

"No, several people roast turkeys in their apartment ovens and everyone else brings something to share. Originally, it was a true potluck, but apparently one year they ended up with fourteen types of sweet potatoes and no stuffing, so after that Linda created a sign-up sheet with all the traditional Thanksgiving foods, plus a wild card category, which is lots of fun. Last year, someone brought crab-stuffed halibut rolls. They were incredible."

"I'll bet. Does Francine bring her famous chocolate cake?"

"No, she makes pies. Pumpkin, rhubarb, apple, pecan and usually a few more. But no matter how many she bakes, they're always all gone by the end of the day."

"Francine's apple pie is my favorite." Piper, who had been off brushing her teeth and changing into her pajamas, came bouncing back into the room. "Especially with ice cream."

"Apple pie is my favorite, too," Adam told her.

Piper came to sit on her mom's lap but rested

one hand on Adam's arm. "Did you choose the one with Rosemary and her funny bee hat?"

"Yes, we did," he assured her. "But maybe you can break a tie. For your mom's picture, she wants to use this one." He enlarged a shot of Sunny in the middle of a group of residents, leading a stretch. "But I think this one is better."

The next photo was a close-up of Sunny's face. He'd taken it with Piper's camera that first day when he was showing her how everything worked. Sunny had been outside with her dance class. The breeze had caught her hair, lifting it from her shoulders, and she'd tilted back her head as though to drink in the sunshine from above. It somehow captured the unique way Sunny managed to combine energy and peace into one amazing package.

"That one!" Piper agreed. "You're so pretty, Mommy. You look like one of those ladies in magazines!"

Adam didn't agree. Sunny was more than a model who knew how to arrange her face and body to present the image some advertiser wanted to convey. Her smile was genuine. Her ability to find the good in every situation, to open her heart to the moment, that's what was reflected on her face. All the residents at Easy Living, even Phil, knew that smile. That heart. And they knew what a treasure they had in Sunny.

"All right. I liked the other one because it has more people in it, but if you both want this one, we can go with it." Sunny got up from her chair and put a hand on Piper's shoulder. "Now, it's bedtime for you. Tomorrow is a school day."

"Can I read another chapter in my library book before I turn off the light?"

"Yes, but only one."

Piper turned to look up at Adam. "Can Mr. Adam help tuck me in?"

"Of course." Adam stood and swooped her into the air, making whooshing noises, which set off a fit of giggles. He gently set her on her feet, grinning.

Sunny laughed. "Come on, now. Don't get her all worked up before bedtime."

Together they tucked her in. Bob even came in to say good night, laying his head on Piper's bed for a head pat and giving a tail wag before padding back down the hall to his own bed. Sunny snapped on the bedside light, made sure Piper's library book was close at hand and leaned over to kiss her forehead. Adam, remembering when his own mother used to tuck him in, handed her the stuffed loon she'd introduced him to last time he was here. "Here's Gladys. Good night. Dream well."

"I will." Piper snuggled the loon closer. "Good night, Mr. Adam. I like your pictures."

"I like yours, too." He stepped into the hall. Sunny followed, snapping off the overhead light as she stepped out of Piper's room and closing the door behind her.

"Guess we'd better get those last few photos chosen so I can put this together before next Tuesday," Sunny said as they returned to the main room. She looked at him. "You'll be there, right?"

"Of course. I wouldn't miss it. The residents here have become very special to me."

"They are pretty great, aren't they? I love every one of them."

"They love you, too." Adam was sure of that. He noticed Sunny had hung Piper's collection of photos in a place of honor above the bookcase. Many more framed photos were scattered across the top of it, most predating Piper's interest in photography, so Sunny must have taken them. All seemed to be after Piper's birth, though, except for one formal portrait of a family with two adults and a little girl. Presumably, a dad and mom and daughter, who all looked a lot like Piper. He picked that one up. "Your family?"

"Yes, me with my parents."

Looking closer, he could recognize Sunny's smile.

"I was ten. My dad passed not long after that. Heart attack. Me and my mom, Rainey, grew even closer after that."

Adam raised his eyebrows. "Rainey and Sunny?"

Sunny chuckled. "I know. My father's idea. He loved corny jokes." Sunny touched the edge of the frame. "It's the only photo I have of them. In the book club once, we were reading about moms and daughters, and I mentioned my mother did a fancy braid for me once when we had a family portrait taken at a studio in Anchorage. Linda knew I'd lost all the family photos in the fire, so she contacted the studio, and they were able to find the negative and make a print for me. She gave it to me last Christmas."

"What a thoughtful gift."

"Yes. I was blown away."

"I can't help but notice…" He hesitated. Really, it was none of his business, but he was curious.

"Notice what?" she asked.

"I was thinking that there are no photos of Piper's father anywhere."

"No. He, um, opted out."

"What does that mean, *opted out*?" Like his father had, Adam supposed. Just disappeared and never looked back. Adam still didn't understand how a man could do that to his own child.

"He was a rock climber. Is a rock climber, I assume. He had a guide business, based in Anchorage, that took groups out and taught them to climb. I used to help sometimes."

"You were a rock climber?"

"Hardly." She laughed. "I get dizzy if I look out of a fourth-story window. But I helped manage the reservations and things, and I'd sometimes sort out the logistics, transport gear, things like that. He was really into it, though, ate, slept and breathed rock climbing and ice climbing. He was even a stunt double in a commercial they filmed up here. He did so well, the director offered him a job as consultant on a series he was filming of famous climbs around the world. It really was a dream come true for him."

"He left you behind?"

"Actually, he invited me along, but I'd just discovered I was pregnant, which was not part of the plan. To be fair, we'd talked about it. He'd been clear he didn't want kids and I thought I was okay with that. But once I became pregnant, I realized what I wanted more than anything in the world was a family of my own. So, he followed his dream, and I followed mine."

"I'm sorry. That must have been tough, going through the pregnancy and birth alone."

"It wasn't easy," Sunny admitted. "But once I held Piper in my arms, I knew I'd made the right decision. Every day, I'm reminded again of how terrific she is."

"She is terrific," Adam agreed. Her father was missing out on so much. "What happened with him once the filming finished?"

"I don't know. He left, and I never heard from him again. I think the series was released, but I haven't been curious enough to find out if he was in it. I've moved on."

She certainly had. And Adam knew, just from his own mother's experience, just how much strength and courage it took to do that. But before he could say so, Sunny sat down at the computer. "Let's get the rest of the photos chosen."

He would have liked to talk a little more about Sunny's history, but obviously she *was* ready to move on. Just like she'd moved on from her family's tragedy and from her boyfriend's abandonment. And she'd done it with a smile on her face and an optimistic attitude. With all she'd been through, she could have easily become a fearful and clingy mother, but instead she encouraged Piper to grab life, the same way she did.

Sunny pointed. "I love this one of the early-morning walkers with the sunrise behind them."

Adam added it to her folder. It didn't take too long to check the last few residents off Sunny's list, along with a sampling of the different events and activities. He would leave it up to her to caption the photos and arrange the order of the presentation.

"I think that about does it." Sunny stood and stretched. "The residents are going to love this. You've captured them all so well."

"Thank you. I've enjoyed it. It's been a long time since I got my camera out. I'd forgotten how much I love it."

"Alice says the wedding couple was absolutely thrilled with their photos. They've even had friends asking for your contact information to hire you for their weddings."

"She told me. It's gratifying to know people are enjoying my photography. I probably won't have much time for it once I leave here."

"Where will you go next?"

Sunny's smile seemed a little dimmer tonight. Could she be dreading their separation as much as he was?

"The company is about to close on a town-house development in Mountain Home that will need updating." It was a property Adam had found and recommended to the company. "It's only an hour from the main office, so I'll probably stay in my own condo in Boise, for a change."

"That's good. I imagine you're eager to get home."

Adam shrugged. His condo was remarkably similar to the hotel rooms where he spent most of his nights. It would be nice to be in the same town as his parents, to be invited to the occasional Sunday dinner. He should be eager for the next assignment, to demonstrate his ability to find good properties, update them and make them profitable. To impress the board with his abilities. But for the first time in a long time, he wasn't looking forward. Instead, he'd been dragging his feet, finding things to keep him here. But now that the grant had been approved, his excuses had run out.

Sunny's smile faltered for a second. "When will you be leaving Easy Living?"

"My last day at work should be the Wednesday before Thanksgiving, although I still need to hire the new manager." He'd interviewed several and was down to two good candidates, both of whom were able to start immediately. "Are you sure you don't want to apply?"

She shook her head. "No way. I love the job I have."

"Okay, then. I plan to go with the candidate Bea recommended. I'll probably have her start on Monday. The Thanksgiving celebration on Tuesday would give her a chance to meet everyone."

Sunny laughed. "If she comes back on Wednesday, you'll know she can handle it." She picked up a stray pencil from under the dining table and added it to a cup on a bookshelf. "So, you fly out that Wednesday evening?"

"I meant to, but no," he admitted. "I waited too long, and the flights are all booked. My mom was not happy with me, but I have a reservation the next Saturday, and we'll celebrate together a few days late."

"Then where do you plan to spend the actual holiday?"

"They're doing a turkey dinner at the restaurant at my hotel."

"You can't spend Thanksgiving in a hotel." She seemed appalled at the idea, but then her face brightened. "You should have Thanksgiving with Piper and me."

"I don't want to make a lot of extra work for you."

"It's no extra work. I always make the traditional turkey, but since we have the big celebration at Easy Living the Tuesday before, we don't get too carried away with the sides.

I get a paper tablecloth, and we draw pictures of things we're thankful for and then after the meal, we spend the afternoon playing board games. In the evening after turkey sandwiches, we put up Christmas lights on the porch and hang a wreath on the door."

"It sounds like fun." But then, everything did when Sunny and Piper were involved.

"It is fun. We usually have two or three residents with us—whoever has nowhere else to go. This year it's just Phil, Piper and me. We'd love to have you join us. And don't feel like you have to stay for the whole board game and Christmas light part of the day unless you want to. I'm sure Phil will head out right after dinner."

"I want to." Maybe it wasn't wise, but he wanted to spend as much time with Sunny and Piper as possible before he left for good. Maybe memories of a Thanksgiving celebration together would brighten future evenings when he was alone. "What can I bring?"

"Just yourself. You're all I need." Her eyes widened slightly, as though she hadn't intended to say the last part. Their eyes met and held.

"Sunny..." he whispered, and took a step closer.

"Adam?" She looked up at him, her lips parted just slightly.

"I'd like to kiss you now."

"What a wonderful idea." And then her arms were around his neck, and he was holding her close. Their lips touched, and then came together. It felt so good, so right. The way she fit in his arms. The taste of her lips. It was as though he'd been wanting this, needing this, for his whole life, and just never known it.

He wanted more. More time. More conversation. More kisses. But they both knew this couldn't last. He was leaving in just over a week. Soon, his time with Sunny and Piper would be nothing but a sweet memory. If he were smart, he would back off now, before either of them got in any deeper. Of course, if he were smart, he never would have allowed his feelings for Sunny to have crossed professional lines in the first place. Yet if he were smart, he would have missed out on all of this. So maybe this wasn't smart, but there were more important things in life than being smart. And a kiss from Sunny was one of them.

CHAPTER FOURTEEN

THE NEXT MORNING, Adam packed up his laptop and camera and did a visual sweep of his hotel room to make sure he hadn't forgotten anything before heading to work. It was a nice room, decorated in serene blues and grays, with plenty of space for a desk and a little kitchenette with a microwave and refrigerator. It also came with a few extra touches, like a selection of pillows and a basket of different flavors of coffee and tea pods. The housekeeper even left a fresh cookie every day. Little things to make his stay more comfortable. But it was still a hotel room. Not a home.

Not like Sunny's house, cluttered with dog bowls and books and Piper's half-finished art projects. Yesterday evening, Sunny and Piper had talked and laughed with him and with each other while eating a pot of chili. The conversation had continued in the kitchen, while Adam washed dishes, Sunny dried them and Piper wiped the table. It felt…real. Like a life being lived, not a temporary arrangement. Adam hadn't realized how much he'd been missing that feeling. Even his condo in Boise, neatly organized and conveniently located near his office, was just a place to sleep and maybe get in a few extra work hours.

What kind of life was that?

He needed more. Some reason to go home at the end of the day. Someone to talk to, and about more than just his job. Someone to listen to, to laugh with. He needed exactly what he'd found with Sunny and Piper yesterday evening. But they were here, in Alaska. And very soon, he would be somewhere else, working on his next project. And then the next. But eventually, if everything went the way he hoped, he would move into the job in Boise, and he'd finally be able to settle down, build a home, start a family. The timing was wrong to start any kind of a relationship right now.

He drove the familiar roads to Palmer, parked in his usual spot, and waved to the maintenance crew clearing and sanding the sidewalks before the early-morning walkers arrived. On the table in the lobby, Margaret was busy arranging several colorful squashes around a pot of purple chrysanthemums. "That looks festive," Adam commented.

"Thank you." Margaret moved the last squash and stood back to study the effect. "I figure they can work as decoration until I'm ready to make them into curried butternut soup."

"Sounds amazing."

"I'm making it for the Thanksgiving celebration next Tuesday. You'll still be here, won't you?"

"Yes. I'll be working here until Wednesday."

"And then what will you do?"

"I'll head back to Boise and move onto the next project."

Margaret shook her head. "No, not for work. I mean, what happens next with you?"

"I, uh, don't know what you mean. Work *is* what happens next."

"Oh." Margaret gave a little sigh and patted his shoulder. "Well, I hope you have a nice day." She turned and headed toward her apartment.

Adam wasn't quite sure what that was all about, but he hadn't yet had coffee this morning. Maybe once he was properly caffeinated, the world would make more sense.

After his first sip, he called the preferred candidate and offered her the manager's job, which she accepted immediately. She also agreed to start next Monday. Then he emailed the other candidates to let them know the job was filled. He hated sending out bad news, but it was better than leaving them wondering. Later today, he would put together the employment package for the new manager, with the forms to fill out and a detailed job description. His job here was almost done. Time to get a handle on what would come next.

He pulled up his notes for the town-house development in Mountain Home, but he couldn't seem to concentrate. With a history of mismanagement and neglect, this property was an excellent candidate for an upgrade, and when he'd recommended the purchase, he'd been excited about the possibilities. But now it was just one more assignment. One more thing pulling him from where he really wanted to be.

Adam blinked. Where had that thought come from? He would be able to handle this one from Boise, and Boise was where he wanted to be. Wasn't it? That had always been the plan. He would put in the hard work, the travel and the dedication so that eventually the board would see that he was the one they could trust to run the company after his dad retired. That's what he had been working toward all these years. Successfully handling this project in Alaska would bring him one step closer. The Mountain Home project was another step. So, what was his problem?

He pulled a pen from the holder on his desk, the one Piper had given him as a thank-you for teaching her to operate her camera. Maybe the problem wasn't so much where, as who. He clicked the pen's tip in and out. He could follow the plan—wait until he'd received the promotion to look for a lasting relationship in Boise. But whoever it was with wouldn't be Sunny. And she wouldn't have a daughter like Piper. The ones he loved.

Because yes, he realized, somewhere along the way, he'd fallen in love with Sunny. And he loved her daughter, too. Being with them made him happy.

Could he have it all? Sunny was an incredible activities director. There had to be places in Boise that needed someone like her on staff. Would she be willing to relocate? He could help her find a place in Boise, where she and Piper could settle in, get to know his parents. And then, when the time was right and he had the new position, he would ask her to marry him. He closed his laptop, picked up this week's activity schedule from his desk and checked the time. Looked like Sunny would have just finished a morning trivia challenge, and if he hurried, he could catch her before the book club meeting.

He headed down the hall and spotted her in the lobby, getting off the elevator. "Sunny, do you have a minute?" he called.

"Sure." She crossed the lobby to him. "I was just on my way to Francine's. She's hosting the book club this month." Sunny held up a thick volume and whispered, "Don't tell, but I had to skim the last four chapters to finish in time."

"Your secret is safe with me." Now that he'd found her, he wasn't sure exactly what it was he wanted to say. But whatever it was, it didn't need to be said standing in the lobby. "Can you come into my office for a minute?"

"Okay." She glanced at her watch as she walked with him. "But I need to be in Francine's in eighteen minutes. Alice is leading the discussion, and she waits for no one."

"Understood." They arrived at the office, and he touched her back to indicate she should go in first. Once he'd followed, he closed the door behind him.

Sunny raised her eyebrows. "Closed doors. Is something the matter?"

"No, I just wanted to talk to you about something. But first..." He stepped forward and touched her cheek, stroking her soft skin with his finger. "I wanted to do this." He leaned in, and she gave a little smile as she tilted her head to receive his kiss.

"Nice." Sunny laughed. "But it's been my experience that closing a door in this building sends out some sort of emergency beacon. I'd estimate we have less than five minutes before someone knocks. So if you need to talk about something, we'd better get started."

"You're probably right." He realized, belatedly, that this was the sort of subject he should be bringing up after a meal at a fine restaurant, not in an office sandwiched between appointments. Maybe this weekend. "I just wondered if you and Piper were free for dinner tonight. We could go to the pizza place she likes."

"Sure, we'd both love that." Sunny picked up the photo of his parents on his desk. "We might be a little late finishing up today, though. Piper plans to use some of the photos she's taken to make refrigerator magnets for all the volunteers in the reading program. She wants to complete them today so they can dry overnight, and she can deliver them at the program tomorrow."

She set the photo down and turned to him. "Adam, I don't know if I've ever thanked you properly for your part in getting that grant and saving Easy Living. This place is so special. The residents here are family to me and Piper. If it had closed or converted to some other type of residence and I lost my job, we would probably have had to move away from Palmer. And that would be like losing my family all over again. I'm so grateful to you."

She reached out for a hug, and he pulled her

close, glad she couldn't see his face. Because at that moment, he was feeling nothing but shame.

He'd only been thinking of himself. How could he have been so selfish that he'd been about to ask her to pull her daughter out of school and move away from all the people who loved her, just so he could see them occasionally? Because that's really all it would have been. Between the long hours he worked and the likelihood that most of his projects would be far enough from Boise to require living there, he would only have been able to see them on weekends, if that. That wasn't fair.

He wanted more than that for Sunny and Piper. They were happy in Alaska. And if that meant he couldn't be part of their lives, then so be it. Their happiness was more important than his. Because, really, that's what love was all about.

THE NEXT MORNING, Sunny sat in her office-supply room clicking through photos. After dropping Piper off for her Book Battles practice, she had decided to come in early to add the finishing touches to the Thanksgiving presentation. She couldn't get over Adam's portraits. It wasn't so much that they were high quality and flattering, although they were, but the wonder of them was the way they somehow captured the personality of every single resident. You could see the hint of mischief in Ralph's smile, the warmth in Linda's face as she read to the children, the love that Francine seemed to add to all her baked goods as she stirred something in a mixing bowl. Adam had even somehow caught a hint of vulnerability peeking out of Phil's crusty exterior. Each portrait was as unique as the subject.

And his talents didn't stop with photography. He was an excellent teacher. Piper had learned an amazing amount since he'd begun tutoring her. And according to Alice and Linda, the numbers he'd gathered and put together for them were probably the deciding factor that had cinched the grant deal. But most of all, he had a gift for kindness, for treating people with respect. That's what drew Sunny to him, that inner goodness. And on top of that, he was an incredible kisser.

It was going to be hard to let him go. She allowed herself one moment of despair before she pushed it away. She knew all about loss and pain. She'd experienced plenty of it. But she always came out the other side. Despairing of something that hadn't happened yet was as useless as wishing for a different past. The past was gone. The future was murky. But right now, she was here, in a job she loved, a job that

Adam and the residents had helped save. She had a lot to be thankful for.

Footsteps outside alerted her to a visitor. Bea popped her orange-and-yellow-streaked head inside the door, her face twisted in outrage. "Have you heard?"

"Heard what?" More footsteps sounded in the hallway. Since there was barely room for her desk, much less a crowd, inside Sunny's office, she closed her laptop and came out to the hallway. "What's wrong?"

"Did you tell her?" Bonnie asked, as she and the other Mat Mates congregated around her. Linda had a newspaper tucked under her arm.

"Not yet," Bea answered. The women all looked at each other, as though none of them wanted to be the one to break the news.

"What is it?" Sunny demanded.

Molly pointed to Linda's newspaper. "Show her."

Linda handed the newspaper to Sunny. The headline read "Embezzlement Temporarily Shuts Down Housing Assistance Foundation."

"Wait. Housing Assistance Foundation. Isn't that—"

"Where our grant is coming from," Bea interrupted. "Or rather, was coming from. Looks like they no longer have any money left to give out."

"But—"

"Apparently two of their top financial people have disappeared, along with all the money," Alice explained. "Police are investigating, but until they can recover the lost funds, assuming they ever do, the foundation is bankrupt."

"Bankrupt?" Sunny desperately tried to piece the fragments together in a way that meant Easy Living would still receive the grant. "But we got the approval. Could they have already set aside the grant money for us?"

Alice shook her head. "No, it was pending final approval by the board. Apparently, they had six grants on the agenda, and all of them are now canceled."

Was there any way to save this? "Does Adam know?" His organization had given him until Thanksgiving to come up with a solution, but surely in a situation like this, they would give them more time.

"I'm not sure if he's in yet," Alice said.

Sunny glanced at the time. Adam should be pulling into the parking lot about now, but sometimes he came in early. "Let's go find out."

The door to Adam's office was closed, but the coffee dripping into the pot in the outer office indicated he was somewhere close by. Before Sunny could suggest knocking, Bea threw open the door.

"—haven't had a chance to—" Adam looked up from his phone call. "Excuse me, Dad, I'll need to call you back. Some people are here to see me."

All the Mat Mates marched into Adam's office. Sunny followed. Adam caught her eye and gave her a weak smile. Poor man. It wasn't his fault someone had stolen the funds, but he was in charge and was going to have to deal with it.

"Have you heard—" Alice started to say, but Adam held up a newspaper identical to the one Sunny was still holding.

"I've been on the phone for the past hour, trying to get information," he told them, "but nobody at the foundation seems to know anything, and the police just say they're investigating. It's too early to know if there's much chance of recovering the funds or not. I think we're going to have to assume that the grant is a bust."

Molly sighed. "So, we're back to square one."

"What is wrong with people?" Bonnie burst out. "It's bad enough when someone steals from a business or a home, but to steal money donated to help others?" She huffed. "Why, I could chew up nails and spit out barbed wire!"

Rosemary patted her arm. "We all feel betrayed, but we can't let our anger get the best of us. This is a setback, but we've all faced setbacks before. We need to remain calm and make a plan. Where do we go from here?"

All eyes turned to Adam. An expression of frustration crossed his face. "I honestly don't know what to do right now. I don't know if Easy Living can survive this."

Sunny couldn't bear the disappointment she saw coming from her friends. "But you'll figure it out, right?" she asked Adam, trying not to let the panic she felt bleed through to her voice.

Adam nodded. "I'll try. That's all I can promise."

"And that's all we expect." Alice's voice was soothing. "We're not asking you to be a superhero, just to do your best. Come on, ladies. Let's get out of Adam's hair and let him work."

Bea frowned. "But what…?"

"Let's go." Alice gave Bea a little nudge toward the office door.

Sunny was the last one out. Before she left, she turned what she hoped was a reassuring smile toward Adam. "You'll think of something. This is too important. There must be a way."

"I appreciate your faith, Sunny." He smiled grimly. "But frankly, I'm all out of ideas."

ADAM CLOSED HIS office door, and for the first time since he'd arrived, locked it. The last thing he needed were more upset residents barging in and demanding answers he didn't have. The building was no doubt flooding with gossip, but there wasn't a lot he could do about that. He'd call a general meeting to answer all their questions as soon as he could, but first he needed some answers himself.

He crossed to the window and looked out onto the lawn, now covered with a blanket of snow. Across the street, the sign was dark at Piper's favorite pizza place, but as he watched, the light went on inside and through the window, Adam could see someone writing the special of the day on a chalkboard. Today was Tuesday, so the special would be Hawaiian pizza with ham, pineapple and green peppers. He'd never stayed on an assignment long enough to learn the local specials before.

What was he going to do? Ordinarily he would weigh his options, make an improvement plan, implement it and move on. While he always tried to consider residents and treat them fairly, he'd never gotten to know them how he had here. And then there was Sunny, with her faith that somehow he would save the day.

What did she expect from him? He'd already stayed far longer on this job than on any other he'd managed in the past. He'd dug into the books, finding the numbers they needed to qualify for the grant. He couldn't be responsible for the embezzlers at the foundation. And now the Thanksgiving deadline was looming, and he was back where he'd been on the first day, with not a single idea in sight.

He pulled out his phone and called the familiar number. "Hi, Dad. Sorry we were interrupted."

"That's all right. What did you tell them?"

"What could I tell them?" Adam shifted his phone to the other ear and paced across his office. "This is a disaster. The residents here have worked incredibly hard to save this place. They've volunteered their own hours so that we could cut expenses. They put together these grant proposals, which is a huge undertaking. And you should have seen this craft show they put on. They raised enough money to subsidize the below-market rents for a full six months while they waited for the grant. And now it's up to me to tell them it was all a waste of time."

"That's a shame. But this isn't your fault."

"Well, it isn't the residents' fault, either, but they're the ones who will pay the price."

"I know. From what you've told me, it sounds like this is a special place, but if the grant is gone, it's gone. We need to move forward. So, what's your recommendation? Should we investigate a private sale with the company that expressed interest or list the building?"

Adam tried to shift into his analytical mode, weighing which would be best for their investors, but his mind kept returning to the look on Sunny's face just before she left the room. "You gave me until Thanksgiving to come up with a transition plan."

"Yes, but that's barely more than a week away. What can you do in a week?"

"I don't know, but I want to try." He'd promised Sunny that much.

"Huh." Dad sounded confused, and why wouldn't he be? He had taught Adam to approach business logically, dispassionately, and that's how he'd always functioned in the past. "Wouldn't your time be better served lining up a real estate professional and getting a sales plan in place?"

"Probably," Adam answered honestly. "But I'm asking, anyway. Give me until Thanksgiving before you pull the plug."

Dad paused before answering. "All right. I'll

stick to the original agreement. Your mother said to tell you she has a big turkey in the freezer for our belated celebration."

"That's great, Dad." It would be good to see his parents, even if he did feel he was letting everyone down.

"She suggested a video call on Thanksgiving. She hates the thought of you being alone in a hotel."

"Tell her not to worry. A friend of mine has invited me for Thanksgiving dinner at her house."

"A friend, hmm? Your mother will be intrigued."

"Sunny is the activities director here." She was a lot more than that, but now was not the time to discuss it. His relationship with her was temporary. His life was in Boise, and hers was here. "It's not anything—"

"Don't say anymore." Dad laughed. "Let your mother enjoy the moment. We'll plan to pick you up from the airport a week from tomorrow. Until then, good luck on this project. I truly hope you can pull it out."

"Thanks, Dad." He was going to need every bit of luck he could get.

CHAPTER FIFTEEN

ALICE HAD GONE OFF, saying she needed to break the news to Ralph, but the rest of the Mat Mates and Sunny had retreated to the multipurpose room, where they were preparing Thanksgiving activities for the read-in tomorrow afternoon. For a long time, the group remained uncharacteristically quiet, each woman lost in her own thoughts.

Sunny picked through tubs of old crayons and sorted out those in shades of orange, gold and brown. Using a chef's knife and cutting board, she chopped the crayons into little pieces and added them to a plastic bin. Tomorrow, the kids would cut leaf shapes from paper, arrange these bits of crayon on top, and with an adult volunteer's help, iron them between pieces of waxed paper so that the crayons melted into the paper, forming translucent fall leaves they could use as suncatchers. But then she realized she'd mindlessly chopped up a blue crayon and added it to the mix. Now she would have to go through the whole pile to sort the blue pieces out. She pushed the bin away in disgust.

Bea broke the silence. "I can't believe Adam has given up on us. After all we've done."

Molly narrowed her eyes. "He said he'd try."

"Try is what you say when you know you're beaten." Bea paced across the room and back. "What kind of a company does he work for, anyway? Who kicks a bunch of old people to the curb? Especially after we worked our tails off raising six months of money so his company wouldn't be out a dime until the grant came in."

Sunny couldn't disagree. Intellectually, she understood Adam's explanation that his company had a duty to their investors to handle their money responsibly, but her heart just knew that people she cared about were in trouble.

Bonnie shook her head. "It's not fair to blame Adam or his company. It's those dirty embezzlers who are at fault."

"Assigning blame doesn't get us any nearer to a solution," Linda reminded them. "I believe Adam when he says he'll try, but what ideas is he going to come up with that we haven't already considered? I think those of us who have been paying less than market rent had better be looking into other alternatives."

"Let's not give up yet." Rosemary tossed her braid over her shoulder. "We need all the positive energy we can muster right now. We need to trust that there's an answer to this that we just haven't thought of yet."

"Trust." Bea snorted. "Maybe if the grant committee had been a little less about positivity and trust, and a little more about auditing their investment officers, we wouldn't be in this mess." At Molly's chiding look, Bea looked down. "Sorry, Rosemary. That was out of line."

"It's all right." Rosemary gave Bea a serene smile. "I understand. But it's almost Thanksgiving. The time of the year when we all come together in gratitude. Even if this does turn out to be our last Thanksgiving together, I'm thankful for my years here. With all of you."

Rosemary was right. If this turned out to be the end of Easy Living, well then Sunny should be grateful for the experience and move on. It's what she'd done over and over in her life. When she lost her parents. When Piper's father left her. But this time, it just seemed to be too much. She had already accepted that she was losing Adam. Why did she have to lose all the people she loved at Easy Living, too?

Sunny looked around the room. This was the family she'd been searching for ever since she'd lost her mom. Adam knew how important they were to her. Had he really given up?

She pushed the craft pieces aside and stood. "Excuse me. I'll be back to finish this in a little while. There's something I need to take care of."

ADAM POURED A fresh cup of coffee and returned to his desk. He'd been searching the web, looking for similar situations to see if the people involved had come up with any fresh solutions. So far, he'd found a couple of interesting ideas, but either they weren't applicable or would take too long to implement. But he'd just gotten started. He'd keep going until he hit pay dirt.

The next thing he knew, Alice had arrived at his office doorway, holding a folder. "I'm back."

"I see that." And he still didn't have answers for her, but he was trying. "Where are the rest of the Mat Mates?"

"Getting ready for the reading group tomorrow."

"Oh, of course." The children in the reading group: another gaggle of people who would be affected if he couldn't figure out a way to keep this community together.

"I just wanted to touch base, let you know

I've made some calls. I used to work in the governor's office, and I still have a few connections. Our local representative is quite concerned. Here's her contact information." She handed him a sheet of paper. "She wants to do something to help, but as you may know, the Alaska legislature meets in January for three months, so it would be at least February before she would be likely to bring something like this to the floor."

"I appreciate that, Alice, but I have to level with you. We don't have that kind of time."

"I thought the money we raised bought us time."

"Yes, in the sense that we could wait a few months for the grant to kick in, but I have a week to give the board a plan as to how Easy Living can carry on with at least a minimal return on investment after the money runs out. If I don't have a workable plan by Thanksgiving, I have instructions to begin the selling process."

A little squeak alerted them that Sunny had slipped in behind Alice. She stepped up beside the older woman. "Only until Thanksgiving?"

He nodded. "I'm afraid so."

"But nobody could have foreseen the foundation going bankrupt," Sunny said. "Can't you get an extension?"

Adam opened his mouth to say no. Dad never gave extensions. A deadline was a deadline. But he just couldn't look into those two faces and dash their hopes. "I'll ask. As you said, these are hardly ordinary circumstances. If I could just come up with something—some nugget of an idea—then maybe I could get the time to work on it. Alice has contacted your local representative. That's something."

He would follow up with the representative later, to get an idea whether this was really a possibility or if she was just placating a voter. Either way, it probably wasn't enough to convince Dad to abandon his long-held policy of no deadline extensions. "But I'm operating under the assumption of a hard deadline of Thanksgiving."

Sunny huffed, a sound Adam had never heard from her before. "But this isn't some board game with rules. These are real people, real lives. How can you work for a business who doesn't care about people?"

Adam shook his head. "That's just not true. Western Real Estate Investments has an excellent reputation for treating tenants well. They take good care of their properties and charge fair prices for rent, if only because treating people fairly is good business. But this is a different situation. We were blindsided. We had no idea, when we bought this building as part of a package, that Oscar Ravenwood had been running it with no return on his investment. He was a private investor, and he could do that. But Western doesn't have that option. They have a legal responsibility to their investors."

He stood up and met her gaze. "Sunny, if I truly thought Western treated people badly, I wouldn't work for them. In fact, if putting in my resignation would save Easy Living, I would do it. Gladly. But it wouldn't. Western would just send someone else." Probably Fallon, who, with her usual efficiency, would have the place sold within weeks, or maybe days. "So, my only option is to continue to look for some alternative form of funding and hope I can get it nailed down before Thanksgiving."

Before Sunny could respond, a grunt sounded behind her and Phil pushed his way between Sunny and Alice. "Let me through. I need to talk with Adam."

Sunny turned to the man and shot him a withering gaze, something Adam hadn't even know she was capable of. "Phil, Adam doesn't have time to listen to you grouse right now.

He's doing everything he can to keep Easy Living viable."

"I know," Phil shot back. "That's why I'm here. Now if you ladies would please excuse us—" Phil looked meaningfully at the door "—I think I might have the means to do just that."

SUNNY AND ALICE found themselves in the outer office, staring at Adam's closed door. Sunny turned to Alice. "Do you really think Phil has a plan to save Easy Living?"

"He seems to think so." Alice shrugged. "Phil isn't one to make rash promises."

Sunny snorted. "As far as I know, Phil doesn't make promises at all. He never interacts with other people."

"Still, Easy Living is important to him. Maybe he has come up with something. I hope so, because Adam didn't sound very confident about a deadline extension."

"No." Sunny blew out a breath. "Was Adam serious, do you think? I mean when he said he would resign if it meant Easy Living could go on?"

"I believe he was. Not that it matters. He's right. Resigning would just mean the company sends someone new to deal with us, and chances are they would be less patient than Adam has been. Adam is one of the good ones."

"He is. I just wish—" What did she wish? That Easy Living would be saved, of course. But even if it was, Adam would be leaving, heading back to Idaho to his next project. And she and Piper would go on just like before, as part of the Easy Living family. But it wouldn't be the same, not without Adam.

"I know." Alice patted her arm. "I know."

The door opened, and Phil marched out, a satisfied smirk on his face. Adam was right behind him, clutching his jacket with one hand and his computer bag with the other. "There's a plane leaving from Anchorage for Juneau in less than three hours, and Phil and I need to be on it."

"Juneau? What are you and Phil...?" Sunny started to ask, but before she could complete her question, Adam kissed her, a brief but deliberate kiss.

"I'm sorry. No time to explain. We'll be back as soon as we can. Wish us luck, and tell Piper goodbye for me."

And then he and Phil were out the door.

Sunny stared after them until they'd disappeared around the corner. She turned to Alice. "What was that all about?"

"I don't know." Alice's eyes crinkled in amusement. "But I'd like to know more about that kiss."

Sunny shifted her gaze away from Alice. "You heard him. It was for luck."

"Uh-huh." Alice smiled. "Well, we could all use some of that right about now."

CHAPTER SIXTEEN

ON THURSDAY AFTERNOON, Bob snoozed on his bed in Sunny's office while she went over her to-do list for the Thanksgiving celebration next Tuesday.

"Hi, Mommy." Piper came into the room and opened the bottom drawer of Sunny's desk. After the read-in, she'd gone off with Francine to help her "socialize" the kittens while Sunny went to her office to answer emails and get her paperwork done for the day. "I just came to get my camera. I helped Francine bake little, tiny pumpkin bread loaves, and they're so cute, I want to take some pictures."

Sunny laughed. "Just taking pictures? Not tasting?"

"Maybe," Piper admitted, as she draped the camera strap around her neck. "If she gives me one, I'll save you a bite."

"Thanks. I'll come get you when I'm done in about fifteen minutes or so." She watched her daughter skip away. Fortunately, Piper

didn't seem to have picked up on all the anxi-
ety Sunny was feeling.

Sunny had heard nothing from Adam since
yesterday, when he'd kissed her goodbye. Right
in front of Alice and Phil. Did that mean something? Or was it like she'd told Alice, just a kiss
for luck for whatever this mission was that he
and Phil were on.

The phone on her desk rang and a number
popped up. She didn't recognize the 208 area
code, but if her desk phone was ringing, whoever was calling must either know her extension or have gone through the phone tree from
the main number. "Easy Living Apartments.
How may I help you?"

"Hello. I'd like to speak to Sunny, please."

"This is Sunny."

"Oh, good. This is Adam's mom, Beverly. Adam
told Ken that you'd invited him for Thanksgiving
dinner."

"Oh. Yes, I did." In all the excitement about
losing the grant, Sunny had almost forgotten.

"That's very kind of you. I couldn't believe
he left it so late that he wasn't able to get a
flight home, and I hated the thought of him
having Thanksgiving dinner in the hotel restaurant."

"Well, Piper and I are glad to have him."

"Piper? Your husband?"

"No, my daughter. She's nine."

"A daughter. How delightful." And she really did sound delighted. "I was just calling to see if you'd like my recipe for cranberry relish. It's easy to make, just cranberries, oranges, and sugar, and one of Adam's favorites."

"Sure, I'd love that. Would you like to email it to me?" Sunny gave her the address and Beverly repeated it back.

"Wonderful. I'll send that right away. What kind of pie are you having?"

"I asked my friend, Francine, to save us an apple pie."

"That's Adam's favorite."

"He mentioned that. It's my daughter's favorite, too."

"Isn't that nice." Bob, who had been snoozing, suddenly let out a bark in his sleep. He woke up with a jerk and looked at Sunny sheepishly. She leaned down to give his ears a rub.

"Is that a dog I hear?" Beverly asked.

"Yes, that's Bob. He comes to work with me every day."

"Aw. I have a little Pomapoo, Trixie, who goes everywhere with me. Darling, we are going to get along just fine. I'll send you that recipe. Ta-ta."

"Thanks. Goodbye." Beverly sounded just

as cheerful and friendly as she looked in the pictures on Adam's desk.

Sunny couldn't blame Adam for wanting to please his parents by striving toward that future CEO job. He'd spent almost three months here in Palmer, far longer than his usual assignment, and now he had nothing to show for it. Would that count against him when it came time for the board to choose the new head of the company? Adam could have saved a lot of time and effort by selling the building right away, but he'd stayed on and worked hard to keep the place together for the residents here. For her. And now, if he and Phil weren't successful, it might end up costing him the job he wanted.

Sunny added oranges to her shopping list. She just hoped that he would be back in Palmer in time to eat Thanksgiving dinner, and that he and Phil would have good news to report.

TUESDAY MORNING, SUNNY and several volunteers set up chairs and tables for the upcoming Thanksgiving celebration. The smell of roasting turkey and sage wafted through the entire building from the various apartment ovens. People were already beginning to bring pies, cranberry sauce and breads to the long buffet tables near the windows. Soon those tables would be groaning under the load of platters and casserole dishes piled high with food. This was probably Sunny's favorite event of the year, when they all came together to acknowledge how grateful they were to be here. Would this be their last time?

She pushed that thought away. Whatever Phil's idea had been, Adam must have believed it had merit if he was willing to abandon his post and fly to Juneau on a minute's notice. All she and the others could do was to go on with their plans, assuming it would all come together.

She'd spent the weekend cleaning house, shopping for groceries and helping Piper with her crafts. Piper had decided the house needed more seasonal decoration since Adam was coming. All the front-facing windows were now embellished with crayon-infused paper leaves in autumn colors, and an elaborate papier-mâché turkey centerpiece was drying on top of the refrigerator. Sunny just hoped, after all her daughter's preparations, that Adam and Phil still planned to show up Thursday.

Monique Jackson, the new manager Adam had hired, was helping with the setup. She had come to work on Monday morning, as scheduled, and if she was put off that Adam wasn't there to greet her, she didn't let it show. A middle-aged woman with a kind face and unflappable attitude, she seemed like a good fit as office manager. Hopefully, if Western was forced to sell the building, Monique would be able to stay on with the new company.

Once the tables were in place, Sunny unrolled the first tablecloth from the big tube they used to store them. Molly stepped up to take the other end of the cloth and help Sunny spread it over a table.

"Still no word from Adam?" Molly asked.

Sunny shook her head. "Not a peep. I wish I knew what was going on." Adam had said he wouldn't miss the early Thanksgiving celebration today, but that was before he and Phil had taken off on their mysterious trip to Juneau.

"They haven't completely fallen off the face of the earth. Rosemary says Phil called her Saturday and asked her to let herself in with a key he'd hidden so she could water his plants."

"Really?" Phil asking for a neighborly favor? That was a first.

"He apparently was calling from the Juneau airport, about to catch a plane to Bethel."

"Bethel? Why in the world would Phil need to go to Bethel?" About four hundred miles from Anchorage on the Kuskokwim River, Bethel was a sort of hub city providing fuel, groceries and medical care for the surrounding villages. That was, if you could call a community of six thousand or so that wasn't connected to the road system a city. "Was Adam still with him?"

"Presumably."

"Did he give her any indication when they would be back?"

"No, but she got the impression he only wanted her to water them once, not on an on-going basis, so probably soon. Maybe they'll make it back in time for the dinner."

At a quarter till twelve, Sunny slipped off to take Piper out of school. The Easy Living Thanksgiving meal was one of very few activities she felt were more important than Piper's school attendance, and her teachers had always understood and agreed. When they returned to the Easy Living parking lot, Sunny checked Adam's usual slot, but it remained empty. It looked like he and Phil weren't going to make it, after all.

When she and Piper arrived upstairs, everyone had gathered. Sunny moved to the space in front of the big wall screen, where Linda had set up the portable microphone they liked to use when they had crowds. She tried to call for attention, but even using the microphone, her greetings were lost in the sea of voices. Bea put two fingers in her mouth and let out a piercing whistle.

Everyone turned. Bea gestured to Sunny. "All yours."

"Thank you, Bea." Sunny looked out at the group of people she loved so much. Other than Phil, every single resident of Easy Living was here today, in this room. If this was to be their last Thanksgiving together, they should make the most of it. "And thank you. All of you. On this day of Thanksgiving, I want you to know how glad I am to be here. You've all taken Piper and me in and made us part of your family, which is the greatest honor we could have asked for." She glanced toward the table. "That food smells wonderful, and I know you're eager to dig in, but first, let's all take just a moment to be grateful."

Sunny gave them a minute or so, and then, at her nod, Bonnie dimmed the lights and Linda started the projector. This, a teaser before the real show later, began with one of Adam's photos, a picture of the Easy Living apartment building with the sun rising behind it, the pinks and peach colors warming the snow around it.

Oohs and aahs sounded throughout the room. Instrumental music played in the background, while photos filled the screen showing the group activities and projects that had taken place since last Thanksgiving. Each photo sparked low murmurs and exclamations. Some pictures were snapshots Sunny or one of the residents had taken with their phones, but the more recent ones were mostly Adam's work. A few were even Piper's, which she gleefully pointed out to everyone.

Five minutes later, Linda cut the projector.

The moment Bonnie clicked on the lights and Sunny gave the word, a general stampede erupted. A good-natured stampede, though, as the residents laughed and joked while letting one another go ahead of them to the buffet line. "Hey, save some of those mashed potatoes for the rest of us!" someone in line called as one of the men helped himself to a large serving from the industrial-size casserole pan.

"Don't you worry," Ralph told them as he added a few serving spoons to the buffet table. "I've got a whole 'nother pan of them keeping warm in the oven. Nobody's missing out today."

"You're doing so well with your photography," Francine told Piper as they both waited in line. "My husband would be pleased that his camera is still making such nice pictures."

"Thank you!" Piper beamed. "Mr. Adam taught me how."

"He's a fine teacher, and a fine photographer himself." Francine looked over Piper's head to Sunny. "Still haven't heard anything from him?"

Sunny shook her head. "Not yet. Maybe that's good news. Maybe it means he and Phil are working so hard on whatever it is they're doing that they haven't had time to check in."

"Where is Mr. Adam?" Piper asked. "He said he was going to be here."

"He and Mr. Phil got tied up working on financial business out of town." Sunny had purposely not mentioned the possibility of losing Easy Living to Piper. If the worst happened, there would be plenty of time later to break the bad news.

"What does financial mean?" Piper asked.

"Money," Francine said, clarifying. "It takes a lot of money to run a large building like this. Good thing we have Mr. Adam to take care of it."

"Yes." Sunny looked around for something to distract Piper before she could ask more questions. "Oh, Ms. Jamie can't reach the sweet potatoes from her wheelchair. Piper, can you go move them closer to her?" She watched as Piper hurried forward to nudge the bowl toward Jamie.

Francine edged closer and whispered, "Sorry, I didn't think about Piper not knowing."

"I didn't want to worry her."

"You're a good mother." Francine gave a decisive nod. "It will be okay. We'll all get through this, one way or another."

"You're right. And in the meantime, we should enjoy our time together. What kinds of pies did you bring today?"

"Oh, cherry, pumpkin, strawberry-rhubarb, lemon meringue, coconut cream, apple—but don't worry." Francine winked. "I held one apple pie back for you."

"Thank you. For some reason, I'm a little nervous about cooking Thanksgiving dinner this year. It's good to know at least the dessert will be a hit."

"It's always nerve-racking, cooking for your young man."

"Adam isn't my young man," Sunny insisted.

Francine just smiled and moved on ahead in line. Once everyone else had filled their plates, Sunny did the same and went to join the table where the Mat Mates, Francine and a few others were eating together. Piper had already joined them and eaten a good portion of the food on her plate. They kept conversation light, and no one else mentioned Adam's absence. Perhaps Francine had warned them not to talk around Piper.

After the main meal, everyone hit the dessert table, where they had to choose between an amazing assortment of pies, including Francine's, plus a tray of cupcakes decorated with little candy turkeys. Once they'd settled in at their tables, Sunny hit the lights and started the main presentation, the slideshow featuring every one of the residents.

Adam's portraits were even more spectacular projected than they had been on her computer screen, and Sunny found herself transfixed. All around her, the residents laughed and smiled and commented on each of the pictures. The main doors to the hallway opened and closed twice, presumably by someone who needed to run to their apartment and back, but the rest stayed right where they were until the end of the show.

Sunny felt tears gathering in her eyes as she looked at the faces there. Rosemary with her bees. Molly staring at a painting, contemplating where to add the next brushstroke. Alice and Ralph gazing into each other's eyes as they demonstrated the tango in the ballroom dancing class. So much experience. So much life. So much love. She blinked away the tears, ready as always to give the residents a happy face once the show was over. As the last slide popped up, the one wishing everyone a Happy Thanksgiving, the room broke into loud applause.

Sunny walked to the wall switch, but before

she reached it, a familiar figure stepped in front of the screen. Adam! She flipped on the lights, and there he was, at the front of the room. She spotted Phil standing off to the side, along with two men she didn't recognize, one about Phil's height with sandy blond hair, the other an inch or two taller, with dark hair thinning on top. They must have come in during the slideshow.

Adam waved to the residents and picked up the microphone. "Hello, everyone. It looks like we missed an incredible meal. Hope you saved us some leftovers."

"We might be able to scrape together a bite or two," Bonnie called, and everyone laughed.

"I know after all that turkey and then the slideshow, you're probably ready for an afternoon nap, but before you go, I have a couple of gentlemen I would like for you to meet. These are Phil's nephews, Dr. Stephen Ravenwood and Dr. Derrick Ravenwood."

Ravenwood. Why did that name sound so familiar? And did this have anything to do with why Adam and Phil had flown off so suddenly?

"Stephen is a surgeon in Bethel, and Derrick has a dental practice in Juneau. Their father, Oscar, is the man who built the Easy Living Apartments, and they have something to tell you."

The two brothers stepped forward. After a

quick whispered conversation with his brother, the taller one accepted the microphone from Adam and faced the group. "Hi. As Adam said, I'm Derrick and our father was Oscar Ravenwood. Um, this all happened so fast that I don't have any sort of a speech prepared, so I'll just tell you what happened. As Adam said, our father's company built this place. That's what he did. He built dozens of buildings all over the state, and at the time of our parents' death, they owned ten of them. We knew that the Easy Living Apartments existed, of course, but we didn't realize exactly what kind of place this was until quite recently."

The other brother, Stephen, stepped up and pulled the microphone from his brother so he could talk. "Okay, this is kind of getting into the weeds, but for this to make sense, you need to understand that although we knew we had an uncle, we'd never met Phil until he called a week ago. The three of us got together on a video call and got to know each other a little bit, which was really nice. He mentioned he lived in Palmer, but we didn't realize then that he lived here, in this building."

"Right." Derrick resumed the story. "So three days ago, Phil and Adam flew to Juneau to talk with me. They explained all about the grant, and how you had all done so much to try to keep this place together and functioning. I started to realize what a special community this is. Now that we've seen that slideshow and all of your faces, we're even more convinced. We're really proud that our parents started this place, and if Stephen and I had known how special it was..." His voice cracked, and he paused.

Steven took the microphone and finished the thought. "We never would have put it up for sale with the rest of the properties. But backing up, once Adam and Uncle Phil had met with Derrick, the three of them flew to Bethel to meet with me and my wife, Alex." He waved to a woman standing near the door who Sunny hadn't noticed before. She waved back. "And together we came up with a plan to fix this. Western Real Estate Investment will need to agree, but Adam is confident he can make that happen." He offered the microphone to his brother.

"Do you want to finish this?" Derrick asked Stephen.

"No." The younger brother smirked. "I think you can handle it from here."

Derrick grinned and took the microphone. "We're almost to the end anyway." He turned to the audience. "To honor the memory of our parents, we would like to repurchase this building from Western and donate it to the residents here."

There was a moment of stunned silence. And then one person started to clap, and another joined in, and soon everyone in the room was cheering.

It went on for some time, but eventually the room quieted. Alice stood up. "But how is this going to work? You're donating to the current residents, or—"

"I'll let Adam answer that," Derrick said. "Meanwhile, would you mind if we helped ourselves to a little of that food? We didn't get a chance to eat before catching our flight."

"Of course." Several of the residents hopped up and escorted their trio of new guests to the buffet table while Adam encouraged Phil to join him in front of the screen.

"Phil and I talked this over, along with Derrick, Stephen and Alex. We propose setting up a charitable trust to hold the title, with board members serving a fixed term and elected by the residents."

Phil took the mic. "And to get us started, I'd like to nominate Alice Adler to be the first chair of the board."

Bea jumped up. "I second the nomination."

"Now just a minute. This can't be official.

You haven't even set up the trust yet," Alice sputtered.

Adam laughed. "Then how about we nominate Alice as the interim chair, and chair of the temporary committee to oversee the process of getting the paperwork done and running things until we can set up an official election to choose a board?"

"I so move," Phil declared.

"Second!" Bea shouted.

"All in favor, say aye." Sunny noticed Adam scanning the room of eager residents until he found her, and their eyes locked.

"Aye!" Everyone shouted, almost in unison, but Adam didn't respond, his attention still focused on her. She wiped away a tear she hadn't realized was there and smiled at him. Phil gave him a nudge.

"Oh, sorry," Adam murmured. "All opposed, say nay."

Complete silence. After a few beats, Adam gave a little bow to Alice. "Well then, as acting manager, I declare Alice Adler duly elected."

"Thank you." Alice stepped forward. Adam handed her the microphone and moved away, circling around the tables until he came to where Sunny was standing. He stopped in front of her, his eyes never leaving hers.

"You did it," she whispered. "You saved Easy Living."

Adam shook his head. "It wasn't me. Phil and his nephews are the ones who pulled it off. I just went along for the ride."

"I suspect you did a lot more than that," Sunny protested.

It was all still sinking in. "So, we're okay now? We can move forward and know the place will stay the same and everyone will be able to afford to stay?"

"Yes. With the building paid for, the rental income will easily cover maintenance and repairs, along with all the usual operating expenses, just like it did under Oscar's ownership."

Unable to wait one more second, she threw her arms around him. "Thank you," she whispered.

At the front of the room, Alice spoke into the microphone "My first act as chair, I'd like to call a vote while we're all here together. I know we've all enjoyed this lovely meal, and that amazing slideshow—" A sudden round of applause and cheering interrupted her, and everyone looked over toward Sunny and Adam.

She and Adam still had their arms around each other. Laughter broke out and a new round of applause sounded.

Sunny released Adam and turned to wave at the group, her cheeks burning.

Alice chuckled as she waited for the noise to die down. "Yes, exactly. And so, I'd like to thank Sunny Galloway for all her hard work and would like a quick advisory vote. Once the property has been transferred, do we want Sunny to continue on in her role as activities director?"

"Yes!"

"Absolutely."

"You bet!" people shouted from all over the room.

"Could I get a motion?" Alice prompted.

"I move that the Easy Living Apartments residents recommend to the new board that they engage the services of Sunny Galloway as activities director under the same terms and conditions as her existing contract!" Linda called.

"Second!" about twelve people yelled.

"I have a motion and a second. All in favor?"

"Aye!" the crowd roared.

"Opposed?" After a brief silence, Alice smiled. "The motion carries. And secondly, Adam, I know tomorrow is supposed to be your last day with us, but would you be willing to stay on for a little longer, just to help shepherd us through this transition?"

"Sure, assuming I can convince my boss," Adam answered.

"I think that can be arranged."

The voice came from the back of the room.

Sunny turned to see an unfamiliar couple seated at one of the tables near the door, the woman holding a small dog on her lap. Margaret, who was sitting at the same table, stood and motioned for them to stand as well.

Adam shaded his eyes against the glare of the overhead light. "Dad? Mom?"

"Surprise!" his mother called. "Since you couldn't come to us, we found a flight and came to you!"

Margaret waved to the room. "Everyone, I'd like you to welcome Ken and Beverly Lloyd, who, if you didn't catch that exchange, are Adam's parents from Boise, Idaho. In fact, it turns out Ken grew up in the next town over from my hometown. He's CEO of Western Real Estate Investments and from the way he was grinning through all of these announcements, I think he's quite happy with how everything turned out."

Applause greeted the couple, and the two of them smiled and waved their thanks. Once the noise had died away, Ken spoke, his voice carrying easily across the room. Obviously, he was a man accustomed to addressing large gatherings. "Thank you for the warm welcome. My wife and I are happy indeed. Congratulations, ladies and gentlemen. Adam had been telling us what a remarkable community this is, but I have to say I really didn't understand just how remarkable until I saw that slideshow. My hat is off to the Ravenwoods for their generous gift, and I'd like to assure them and you that Western Real Estate Investments will gladly work with them to smooth the process and get this transfer done as quickly as possible."

As a hearty burst of applause filled the room, someone shouted, "This calls for another round of pie. We've got some extra thanksgiving to do!"

CHAPTER SEVENTEEN

THE NEXT MORNING, Sunny was in her office double-checking the recipe for a class later that day that Francine had agreed to teach on making perfect pie crust. After all the compliments Francine's pies had received yesterday, Sunny expected a full class. It was great, doing her job without the constant fear that it was all about to come crashing down around her. Her position here was safe. She and Piper could remain in the family fold here at Easy Living.

Everything was back to normal. Or it would be, once Adam finished getting all the i's dotted and t's crossed and moved on to his next project.

Except Sunny wasn't sure what normal was anymore. Now that she'd spent all this time with Adam, the thought of going on without him felt strange. Empty. He fit in so well. The seniors, all delighted with their portraits, kept asking her if they could order prints from Adam. She would have to follow up with him, but from what he'd told her before about the way he worked most projects, she doubted he would be able to fit in a bunch of extra photography tasks.

"Good morning," a cheerful voice sang out. Sunny turned to find Adam's mom, Beverly, at the door, carrying a bakery box. Her little dog danced in place at the end of a leash. "Care to join me for a cup of coffee? I brought scones."

"Would those happen to be cranberry almond scones from the Salmonberry Bakery?"

"They would, indeed. Bonnie said they were your favorite."

"Bonnie's right. Let's go mooch some coffee from the office. Hold down the fort, Bob." The dog opened one eye in acknowledgment before going back to sleep.

As they walked together, Sunny asked, "How did you happen to find the bakery? Did the Mat Mates wrangle you into one of their early-morning yoga sessions?"

"They did." Beverly laughed. "All six of those ladies are old enough to be my mother, but they put me to shame. And it's not as though this is my first rodeo. I do yoga regularly. But those ladies are amazing."

"Yes, they are." In so many ways.

When they arrived, Adam was sitting at the desk where Tilly used to sit. The office behind him was empty. Beverly held up her bakery box. "I will trade scones for coffee."

"Deal. I was just about to make a pot." Adam moved to the coffee machine. "Where's Dad?"

"Oh, one of the men yesterday, Ralph I think, said he had plans to go flight-seeing in a small plane this morning and invited us along. I decided I'd rather do yoga," Beverly said, rubbing her hip, "although I might regret that when the soreness kicks in. Those Mat Mates are something."

Adam smiled fondly. "You two seemed to have settled right in."

"Yes. This is a great place. I wondered why this project was taking you so much longer than usual, but I'm beginning to understand." She looked over at Sunny with a little smile that Sunny couldn't quite read.

She turned to Adam instead. "Why are you working at this desk?"

"Monique has moved into the main office. She's off now with the plumber, fixing a drip in Phil's shower."

He poured a cup of coffee and handed it to his mother, and then another for Sunny, before taking one for himself.

"Alice told me to say she'd be along soon," Beverly told him as she opened the box and set it on the desk. "When I left her and the other

Mat Mates at the bakery, they were deep in planning."

"You should have seen the craft fair they put on." Adam selected a scone and passed the box to Sunny. "I'm pretty sure if the residents here were in charge, the problems of the world would be fixed before Christmas."

Alice came striding into the office, her eyebrows raised in mock disapproval. "A coffee break already? I'm going to have to knock this staff into shape."

"Hey, some of us have already put in a couple hours work this morning," Adam retorted.

"All is forgiven if you'll pour me a cup. In fact—" Alice exchanged glances with Beverly, which Adam missed since he'd gone to the coffee machine "—I wanted to talk with you about that. I kind of hate to do this because your father is being so decent about selling the Easy Living Apartments back for the same price Western paid, even though you've invested all this time and effort, but you and the residents get along so well, I feel it's only fair to give you the choice. I know you've hired Monique for the management job, and she seems nice enough, but she's still in her probationary period and we've gotten used to working with you. If you're interested in staying, we'd love to have you as our permanent manager."

Sunny's breath hitched. Was it possible? Was there any chance that Adam would stay here, in Alaska, instead of moving on to his next assignment for Western? He'd worked so hard with the goal to head up the company that she couldn't imagine he would settle for something so prosaic as an apartment manager position, but some part of her hoped that maybe, just maybe, after spending so much time with her and Piper, his priorities might have changed.

"I'm sure we can't match what you're earning now," Alice continued, "but—"

"Thank you, Alice." Adam set her cup on his desk and turned to look her in the eye. "I'm honored, truly, that you feel that way. My time here has meant a lot to me, as well, but no. That position isn't for me. I think you'll really like working with Monique, but of course you're in charge now, and if you don't, you can select another candidate. But it won't be me. I'm sorry."

And in an instant, Sunny's fantasy was gone. And of course, it was for the best. Adam should do whatever made him happy. She wanted that for him. She really did.

"I understand." Alice didn't sound surprised. She picked up the coffee he had poured for her. "But I had to ask." She looked over at Beverly, and Sunny could have sworn they exchanged little shrugs of disappointment. But that couldn't be right. Adam's mom had to be rooting for him to become head of the company once his stepfather retired.

Sunny was finding it hard to hold on to her smile, but she managed. "Excuse me. I have to go prepare for Francine's baking class. She's promised to divulge the secret of flaky pastry to anyone who shows up, so I'm sure we'll have a crowd. Thank you for the tasty scone, Beverly."

"But you haven't eaten it yet," Beverly pointed out.

"I'll save it for later." Sunny wrapped it in a napkin and left, escaping to her office where, for once, she closed the door, leaning against it from the inside. How could she feel so devastated? She'd known Adam was leaving right after Thanksgiving almost from the first. But somehow, she'd put off thinking about it, maybe secretly hoping somehow things would work out this time. But she should've known better, and after hearing Adam turn down the opportunity to stay, she couldn't deny it any longer. Adam was leaving.

She would just have to learn to live with it.

IT WAS THANKSGIVING morning at Sunny's house. The turkey was in the oven, Francine's apple pie was on top of the refrigerator, where it wouldn't accidentally get bumped, and Piper was attempting to follow along on a video showing how to fold napkins to look like turkey tails. So far, they were mostly looking like abstract art, but her last attempt was at least standing, if not completely symmetrical. Sunny looked around the room. Hopefully Adam's parents wouldn't mind the paper tablecloth, since it had become a tradition. Sunny spotted a Lego under a chair that they had somehow missed in their house cleaning frenzy and picked it up. She wanted everything to be perfect. Because once Adam was gone, nothing would ever be quite perfect again.

But that was tomorrow's worry. Today, she and Piper should just enjoy the day. Thanksgiving. That's really what it was all about, and with the security of knowing Easy Living would live on and that her job there would continue, Sunny had a lot to be thankful for. To wish for anything more would be greedy.

She was headed to Piper's room to put away the block when the doorbell rang. Bob raised his head and let out a woof, but apparently deciding Piper and Sunny had this in hand, decided not to get up off his bed.

"They're here," Piper announced as she skipped over to answer the door. She'd taken an immediate liking to Adam's parents as soon as she'd met them and quickly bonded with Beverly's dog. She threw open the door. "Happy Thanksgiving!"

"Happy Thanksgiving to you!" Beverly took a step into the house, set Trixie on the floor and gave Piper a hug all in one fluid motion. After Sunny tossed the Lego into Piper's bedroom and came to the door, she got a hug, too.

"Mom, can you move along so that we can all get in?" Adam requested. He was standing in the doorway, holding a huge red gift bag with a green velvet ribbon that almost covered his face. His computer bag hung from his shoulder. Did he plan to work today? Maybe he was getting a jump on his next assignment, since he'd agreed to remain in Palmer long enough to oversee the handover.

"Of course." Beverly released Sunny and moved into the living room. Once his mother was out of the way, Adam followed her in, with his father right behind him. Ken shut the door, while Beverly took the bag from her son and set it aside. Piper eyed the bag speculatively.

"Here, let me take your coats," Sunny said.

"Phil's not here yet?" Adam asked as he unzipped his jacket.

"He's spending Thanksgiving with his nephews at their cabin in Girdwood," Sunny answered.

"I'm glad. It's nice that he's reconciled with his family."

Once they'd shed their outerwear, Piper gave Adam and Ken hugs, too. After the briefest hesitation, Sunny followed suit. Bob even ambled over to sniff noses with Trixie and wag his tail in greeting. "Make yourselves at home. There's hot cider on the stove, if anyone would like some. I'll be right back."

Sunny carried the extra coats to her bedroom. When she returned, Adam and his father were carrying mugs, and Beverly was perched on the edge of the couch, holding the bag Adam had carried in. "We found this at the craft co-op yesterday, and I couldn't resist." She handed it to Sunny.

"For me?"

"You and Piper."

"Ooh." Piper crowded closer, and together, she and Sunny opened the bag to release the wonderful scent of evergreen. Inside was an enormous wreath, made of various types of greenery and trimmed with baubles, ribbons and a wooden cutout of a moose, wearing a hand-painted Nordic sweater.

"It's beautiful," Sunny said. "Thank you so much."

"Adam mentioned that you have a tradition of

hanging your wreath on the door on Thanksgiving evening, so we thought you might like it."

"We love it! Don't we, Piper?"

Piper nodded enthusiastically. "It's so pretty."

"I think we might use it in the house instead of on the door, though. Partly because it smells so good, and partly because my neighbor hung a fresh wreath on his door last year and a moose ate it."

Beverly burst into delighted laughter. "A moose ate his wreath! Oh, wouldn't that be a sight to see. Especially this wreath with a wooden moose on it. Adam, if you could snap a photo of that, everyone would want one."

"For sure," Adam agreed. "I've already got one of a moose looking through the front window at Easy Living, eyeing the ficus tree near the door like it's a salad bar."

"Oh, I didn't see that one in the slideshow."

"Adam had a million wonderful photos," Sunny told them, "and I wish I could have used them all in the presentation, but he insisted I had to keep it under forty-five minutes."

"I'm glad to see you've taken up photography again," his mother told him. "All work and no play—"

"—earns Jack a promotion." Ken finished her sentence, but he was laughing.

Beverly elbowed him in the side. "Shush.

You know very well people are more productive when they live balanced lives."

"It's true." Ken smiled at his wife and turned to Sunny. "I was a complete workaholic before I met Beverly. But after we were married, I started building scenery for Beverly's community theater productions and coaching Adam's baseball team, and I found that all those extra work hours weren't as necessary as I'd always assumed. I learned to delegate."

Adam made a little sound like a strangled cough, and Sunny got the idea that in recent years, he'd been the recipient of a lot of those delegated work hours.

Piper scooted closer to Beverly. "I'm a photographer, too. Ms. Francine gave me a camera, and Mr. Adam taught me how to use it. Do you want to see my pictures?"

"I would love that," Beverly replied, and allowed Piper to lead her to the kitchen bar. Piper opened Sunny's laptop and pulled up her photos. A timer went off in the kitchen.

"That's my reminder to baste the turkey." Sunny reached into a drawer, pulled out a remote control and offered it to Ken. "Adam says you two always watch football on Thanksgiving, so feel free to find the game."

"As long as you turn it off at dinnertime," Beverly called.

"Thank you." Ken grinned and took the remote from Sunny's hand. "We'll just see how the Broncos are faring." Trixie, noticing the remote, jumped into Ken's lap, which Sunny gathered was her usual spot for television viewing.

The turkey was coming along nicely. After Beverly finished admiring each and every one of Piper's photos, she helped Sunny peel potatoes and then showed her how to make the cranberry-orange relish.

Meanwhile, Piper went back to the napkins. During a commercial break, Ken deposited the dog on the floor and wandered over to the table. "What are you working on?"

"I'm trying to make the napkins stand up like the ones in this video," she explained, "but they keep falling over."

"They're not stiff enough. What you need is an iron and starch."

"We have an iron and an ironing board. We were using them to make the leaves." Piper pointed toward the suncatchers in the window. "Mommy, do we have any starch?"

"In the cabinet over the dryer. I'll get it for you in a minute."

"I'll help her," Ken offered. "I know my way around an ironing board."

"He's much better at ironing than I am,"

Beverly told Sunny. "One advantage to marrying an old bachelor."

Ken chuckled and found the laundry room. A few minutes later, armed with crisply ironed napkins, he and Piper were able to fold and fan them into beautiful shapes on each plate.

Ken returned to the couch beside Adam, and they watched the game and talked. Once or twice, Ken brought up something about the next project Adam would be taking on, but Sunny noticed Adam would answer quickly and move to another subject, which was a little out of character for him. But maybe he just didn't want to spend his holiday thinking about work.

Once the turkey was out of the oven, Sunny moved it to the platter, covered it with foil to stand for a bit and collected the drippings from the pan. "I'm a little hit-and-miss on gravy," she confessed to Beverly. "Sometimes it's been really good, and sometimes it's all lumps."

"Adam," Beverly called. "It's gravy time." She turned to Sunny. "My son makes the best gravy. I don't know how he does it."

Adam laughed as he came into the kitchen. "The reason you don't know is because you've turned down every offer I've made to teach you. That way, I'll have to keep doing it."

Beverly winked at Sunny and in a stage whisper said, "He's on to me."

Adam stationed himself in front of the saucepan Sunny had put on the stove. "Okay, I'll need turkey drippings, a wooden spoon, butter, flour, salt and pepper, and thyme, if you have it."

"I do." Sunny collected the ingredients and nodded toward the utensils in a crock on her countertop. "Where did you learn to make gravy?"

"My college roommate was from Louisiana, and he was an incredible cook. He never would give me his family's recipe for gumbo or crawfish étouffée, but he did teach me how to make roux, which is the base of any good gravy."

The roux-making process seemed to go on for a long time, but while Adam did that, Ken mashed the potatoes while Beverly and Sunny moved the other foods to the table. Then Sunny removed the foil from the turkey and Piper arranged fresh parsley around it on the platter. Once Adam had finished the gravy, he poured it into a gravy boat and carried the turkey platter to its place of honor on the table, right next to Piper's centerpiece. Sunny slid Francine's pie into the oven to heat while they ate.

As they gathered at the table, Piper ran to her room and returned with her camera and several felt-tip markers.

"What's this for?" Ken asked her when she handed him a green marker.

"We draw what we're thankful for on the tablecloth next to our plates," Piper explained. "It's what we always do at Thanksgiving. And then we take a picture and put it in our Thanksgiving scrapbook." She pointed to her camera. "This year, I'm taking the picture."

"What a nice idea," Beverly commented.

"I'm not much of an artist," Ken warned.

"That's okay. It's just for fun," Piper told him.

They were all quiet for a minute or two, each working on their own drawing. When she looked up, Sunny had to smile. Every one of them had drawn a picture of a group of people. Ken's were five stick figures in a row, two men, two women and a little girl. Piper had also drawn the same five people, but in her drawing the child was holding a camera, taking a picture of the other four, plus two dogs. Adam's five were all gathered with their arms around each other like a chorus line. Sunny had put them all around a table with a turkey in the middle, and in Beverly's drawing, they were standing next to a wreath along with a moose who was in the process of taking a bite.

Ken chuckled. "Looks like we're all in agreement. Thanksgiving is all about the people you spend it with."

"And pets," Beverly said, pointing at the dogs in Piper's drawing.

"Everybody, smile." Piper focused her camera on the table and the people around it and clicked a few pictures.

"I'd love a copy of that," Beverly requested. "Can you email it to me, please, when you send those other pictures?"

"Sure. Once I download it, I'll send it to you." Apparently, Piper and Beverly had already come to an arrangement. Piper set her camera on the bookshelf in the living room and hurried to the table.

Beverly smiled at her and turned to Sunny. "Would it be all right if I said the grace?"

"Of course." Sunny grasped Adam's and Piper's hands, and everyone else followed suit.

Beverly gave thanks for the food, the company, and that they could all be together that Thanksgiving. At Sunny's request, Ken carved the turkey.

Adam's gravy was outstanding.

"I'm so impressed," Sunny told him. "I thought I was doing the same things I saw you do, but yours is so much better."

"I'll show you how, if you want," he offered.

Beverly held her hand partly in front of her

mouth. "Don't let him do that. If you find out his secrets, you won't have an excuse to make him do it."

Sunny managed a smile, but Beverly's joke was a reminder that Adam would never again make gravy at her house. In a matter of days, he would be leaving, moving on to his next assignment, and there was no reason to think she would ever see him again. To her horror, she could feel tears welling up in her eyes. Fortunately, Piper chose that moment to go into a story about visiting the nursing home with Francine and Thor. By the time Piper had finished talking, Sunny had composed herself.

After the main course, Sunny sent Piper to get the ice cream from the freezer in the garage while she cut the pie. Trixie trotted off after Piper while Sunny took the pie from the oven and Adam collected small plates from the cabinet. As he set them next to her, he whispered, "Thank you for having all of us today. I know you weren't counting on my parents—"

"I'm so glad they came. Your parents are great," she said sincerely. "You're really lucky, you know."

"I do know. And I am thankful." But the look that crossed his face seemed pensive.

Before Sunny could ask what that was all about, Piper came back with the ice cream.

She leaned around Adam to peek at the pie. "Cut me a biiiiig piece, please."

"After all that turkey and dressing you ate? Wouldn't you pop?" Sunny asked with a laugh.

Piper shook her head. "I've got room left."

"Well, I only have a little room left, but I can't resist apple pie, so make mine a small piece, please," Beverly said from her place at the table.

"I'll have what she's not," Ken called, and everyone laughed.

Once they had finished Francine's incredible apple pie, Ken cleared his throat. "I have a little news to share. This won't be official until next month, but I intend to announce my retirement from CEO at the December board meeting. Depending on how the board wants to handle it, I'll probably stay on for another few months to help smooth the way for my successor." He looked at Adam with a proud smile on his face, and Sunny realized he was about to make Adam's dream come true.

But Adam was shaking his head. He opened his mouth to say something, but Ken continued. "When I talk with the board, I'll be making my recommendation for my replacement. I'll give them my top two candidates for promotion from within. Fallon will be one of them. She's done outstanding work, and she has supporters on the board. But I'm convinced once the whole board has examined both records of accomplishment, they'd give the job to the hardest-working member of the Western team. That's you, son."

Adam smiled, but it was a sad smile. "Thank you. It means the world to me that you feel like I could even begin to fill your shoes, but—"

"But what?" Ken frowned. "You're ready. I know the idea of the head job can seem overwhelming, but don't sell yourself short. You know this business and the company inside and out. You've been preparing yourself for this for years."

"I have," Adam agreed. "And if this had all taken place a few months ago, I would have been thrilled. But during my time here in Alaska, I've learned a few things. There are places that suit people, that feel like home. And Alaska feels that way to me."

"Are you taking the manager's job then, after all?" Beverly asked, her voice eager. "So you can stay?"

Ken swiveled toward his wife. "What manager's job?"

Piper seemed to sense the tension in the room. She slid out of her chair and came to stand close beside her mother. Sunny put a comforting arm around her, and Piper leaned into her shoulder.

"Alice offered Adam the job of managing the apartments once the transfer is complete," Beverly explained to Ken.

Ken snorted. "Apartment manager? When he could be CEO?"

Beverly shot her husband a look of impatience. "Maybe he doesn't want to be CEO. Have you not noticed the past three days how relaxed and happy Adam seems here?"

"Well, yeah, because he's found a successful solution to the dilemma of how to balance the needs of the people in Easy Living and our investors. And because he's looking forward to the challenge of his next assignment."

Beverly shook her head. "No, that would be what you were looking forward to. Not Adam."

"Uh, excuse me." Adam chuckled. "Mom, I appreciate what you're trying to do, but I'm right here in the room and I can speak for myself."

Beverly made a little bow and gave a flourish with her hand. "By all means. Go ahead."

"Thank you." He turned his gaze to Ken. "Dad, you've done so much for me, and I can never express how grateful I am that you came into my life. I know you've hoped I would be the one to take over as CEO when you retire, and I'm sorry to disappoint you. But I've come to realize I can't base my life on not disappointing you."

Ken seemed dismayed. "I never meant—"

"I know you didn't. It wasn't that you pushed me into this profession. It was my decision. I admire you. I wanted to follow in your footsteps. But I've concluded that it's time I branch out and make a new path of my own." Adam held Ken's gaze, unblinking. "I don't want to be an apartment manager or a CEO. I intend to set up a photography studio, here in Palmer."

He was staying! Sunny's heart seemed to leap in her chest. Adam was staying in Alaska. Staying here, in Palmer. Did that mean—

"Photography?" Ken frowned. "Are you absolutely sure? I know you enjoy it, but a hobby is one thing. Making a living—"

Ken stopped talking when Adam got up, crossed the room to his computer bag and pulled something out. He returned to the table and handed Ken a folder before sitting.

"What's this?"

"A business plan." Adam waited while Ken opened the folder and skimmed the first page. "I'm not that teenager anymore, with a camera and a vague dream of making a living taking pictures. As you can see, I've identified multiple income streams for photography. I plan to specialize in portraits, but I'll also do wedding photography and art photography."

"Hmm." Ken flipped to the next page, and then the next, nodding as he read the figures. "How big is Palmer? Six, seven thousand? Is that really a large enough population to support a photography studio?" Ken looked up at Adam. "If you're really going to do this, you'd be better off in Anchorage."

"No." Adam leaned over his shoulder to point at something on the page. "The type of portraits I want to do will mostly be off-site, either at the subject's home or outdoors. I'll go to them. It won't matter where my studio is."

"But the population base in Alaska—"

"I'm not worried about the population base." Adam turned to smile at Sunny and Piper. "The people I'm interested in are right here."

A little gasp came from Beverly's direction, but Sunny kept her eyes on Adam. He was gazing at her with a look so tender, it melted her heart. Before she could react, he'd moved to her side of the table and dropped to the floor on one knee. "I don't know if this is the best time or the worst time for this, but as long as we're laying all our cards on the table…"

He took Sunny's hand, and he looked into her eyes. Beside her, Piper trembled with excitement. "Sunny Galloway, I love you. I love your optimism, your kindness and your loyalty. And I love your daughter." He gave Piper a wink and reached into his pocket to pull out a diamond ring. "Will you marry me?"

"But— I— When did…?" Sunny suddenly couldn't speak, the lump in her throat holding back the words, even as tears fell from her eyes. Adam wanted to spend his life here. With her and Piper. She squeezed his hand, swallowed and was finally able to find her voice. "Yes! I would love to marry you!"

Adam slipped the ring on her finger. "I found this at a jewelry store in Juneau when I was down there. The jeweler said they have a branch in Anchorage, so we can exchange it if you don't like it."

Sunny gazed at the ring, a sparkling diamond in the center surrounded by six points made of tiny oval diamonds and sapphires. "I love it! And I love you! So much!"

Piper leaned closer to examine the ring. "It's a snowflake, like the ones we caught on our tongues at the first snowfall, when we all made wishes."

"That's exactly what I thought of when I saw it," Adam told her. "That day, I wished that I could spend all my days like that, with you and your mother." He kissed the back of Sunny's hand. "And now my wish will come true."

"Aww." Sunny sniffed. Beverly handed Piper a napkin, and she passed it to Sunny so she could wipe her cheeks. "I wished for the same thing."

"Me, too!" Piper chimed in.

"I knew it," Beverly said. "I knew he was in love." She aimed a victorious smile at Ken.

He shrugged and smiled back. "You were right. But then, you usually are." He put an arm around Beverly's shoulders and squeezed.

"Dad." Adam still held Sunny's hand as he spoke. "I am sorry. I know I've upset your plans."

"I'll be okay, and so will the company," Ken assured him. "All I've ever wanted is your happiness. And it's clear that you've chosen a partner who will make you very happy. If being a photographer in Alaska is what you truly want to do, then I support you."

"Thank you."

Piper jumped up and down. "Group hug!"

And suddenly all five of them were standing and hugging. Beverly was laughing, Trixie was barking, and even Bob got up from his bed and wandered over to see what all the fuss was about.

"Oh!" Piper's eyes went wide. "You should

have told me you were going to propose to my mom. I would have taken a picture!"

Adam laughed. "Let's get one now, then, of all of us. Together."

CHAPTER EIGHTEEN

SUNNY HAD BARELY stepped into the building the next morning and taken off her gloves before the first person noticed her new ring.

By midmorning she had been congratulated by pretty much everyone. When questioned, she'd assured her well-wishers that, no, she wouldn't be relocating to Idaho, and intended to stay at Easy Living for the foreseeable future. Even Phil had stopped by supposedly to report someone's noisy muffler, but the complaint had been half-hearted, and he nodded at the ring with a gruff "Congratulations." Sunny had responded with a hug and profuse thanks for his part in saving Easy Living, which sent Phil fleeing, but with a grin on his face.

Adam, Alice, Ken and the Ravenwood brothers were spending the morning meeting with attorneys about drawing up the necessary transfer papers. How they'd managed to find someone who would see them the day after Thanksgiving was a mystery to Sunny, but she suspected

Alice and her extensive network might have had something to do with it.

The morning had gotten off to a fast start. Now it was time for bingo. Bob had tagged along and was asleep on a rug at Sunny's feet. "G-54!" Piper called out. Since today was a school holiday, she'd come to work with Sunny. The Friday session was more sparsely attended than usual. Beverly had stopped by earlier, only to be swept off with some of the Mat Mates to check out the Black Friday sales downtown. Sunny suspected that's where most of the usual bingo crowd had gone, as well.

"B-15."

"What was that?" one of the residents asked, adjusting his hearing aid.

"B-15," Piper repeated, and paused to wait for the resident to mark his bingo card. Piper had learned so much from the people here, including patience and kindness, just as they dealt with her youthful exuberance. Sunny was once again filled with thankfulness that she and Piper could remain here with this family, even while they made Adam and his parents part of theirs.

Bob raised his head and looked toward the doors. Sunny turned to see Bea gesturing for her to come out. After a glance to make sure all was going smoothly, Sunny slipped into the hallway, where she found Beverly, Trixie and the Mat Mates gathered, all but Alice, of course. Judging from the number of shopping bags at their feet, their morning had been a success.

"We have an idea we want to run by you," Molly said. "What would you think about us putting on a play? Something that involves some of the reading group children, as well as residents as actors?"

"Phil said he would play piano for us if we choose a musical," Rosemary commented.

"Phil said that?" Bea asked.

Rosemary nodded. "I spoke to him about the music I've been hearing from his apartment. It turns out he's a professional musician, and when I mentioned we were thinking of doing a play, he agreed right away."

"Well, wonders never cease," Bea replied.

"A play sounds like a great idea to me," Sunny said.

"We thought about trying to do some version of *A Christmas Carol* this Christmas, but Beverly is already in a play in Boise through December," Bonnie explained. "And since she'll be directing our play, we'll need to wait until Ken has retired and they've moved up here to start rehearsals."

Sunny blinked. She turned to Beverly. "You're moving here?"

Adam would be so pleased.

Beverly put her finger to her lips and winked. "Shh, don't say anything. Ken doesn't know it yet. But I planted the seed last night of perhaps buying a condo or cabin in the area, so we'd have a place to stay when we come up to visit. And since he enjoyed spending time with you and Piper yesterday, it didn't take much convincing. Oh, by the way, would it be all right if we take Piper to Anchorage for the day tomorrow? Linda was telling me about the children's museum there, and it sounds wonderful."

"Piper would love that. Thanks so much."

"Piper is such a sweetheart. We can hardly wait to spend more time with her." Beverly opened one of her bags. "I found this adorable knit hat with fox ears. Do you think she'll like it?"

"She'll love it."

Down the hall, the elevator doors opened. Alice, Ken and Adam stepped out. As soon as Adam spotted Sunny, his face broke into a huge smile. She met him halfway down the hall where he greeted her with a kiss that started off as a short hello, but as her arms went around his neck, turned into something more. After a bit, he pressed his forehead against hers and smiled. "Hi there, fiancée."

"Hi yourself." She sneaked a glance at the beautiful ring on her hand and then kissed him once more before she released him. "How was the meeting?"

"Productive. But I'll let Alice tell you about it." He gestured toward the crowd. Alice and Ken had joined Beverly and the other Mat Mates, and the entire group had been watching the kiss with amused expressions on their faces.

Sunny could feel her cheeks beginning to burn. "I guess I need to remember that when we're here, we most likely have an audience."

"An understanding audience, though. Where's Piper?"

"Calling the bingo numbers inside. It's the last round."

"Good, because we're all meeting with Phil and his nephews for lunch to celebrate."

"Sounds great. We should be done with bingo in a few minutes, and Molly's drawing class doesn't start until two."

Sunny went back into the room just in time to hear someone call, "bingo!" Once the winner had chosen a prize and she had thanked everyone for participating, the group broke up.

"We're going out to lunch," Sunny told Piper.

"For pizza?"

"I'm not sure. We're going with Adam and his parents, and the Mat Mates. We'll be meeting Phil and his nephews there."

"Goodie. I hope it's pizza. Mr. Adam likes pizza."

Sunny laughed. "Almost as much as you do."

When she and Piper stepped outside, Ken was the first to notice them. "Piper! Come here. Beverly was just telling me we're taking you to the museum in Anchorage tomorrow."

"The one with the dinosaurs?" Piper asked eagerly as she hurried over.

"Yes, the one with dinosaurs, mammoths and meteorites," Beverly confirmed. "Linda was telling me about it. Have you been before?"

"Not for a long time. It's fun! You'll like it." Piper fell in with the group, which was heading toward the elevators. "There's this rock that glows in the dark." Piper continued telling them about the museum as they walked.

Adam reached for Sunny's hand, and they lagged behind the others. "So, Mom and Dad are taking Piper to a museum. Does this mean you and I might have a little time alone together tomorrow?"

"Why, I think it does." She smiled at him. "What did you have in mind?"

"Maybe we should finally go on a real date.

A nice dinner. But without the coloring, although, I did enjoy those place mats." He sent her a smile and she happily matched it. The elevator doors opened, and the group crowded in. Ken started to hold the doors, but Adam signaled for it to go on, that they would take the next one. "And maybe a movie. I guess we'd need to go to Wasilla for that."

They arrived at the elevator and stopped.

"Or, we could call the real estate agent to see if we could check those two buildings you mentioned in your business plan to find out if either of them would be suitable for a photography studio."

"You wouldn't mind spending your Saturday looking at vacant buildings with me?"

"I can't think of anything I'd rather do." She raised up on her toes to brush a kiss across his lips. "Oh, and guess what? Your mother is considering a move up here, at least part-time. I'm not sure if Ken will be on board—"

Adam chuckled. "Don't tell Mom because it's a surprise, but he already has his eye on an acre lot with a view just on the outskirts of town. He wants to build custom." He gave Sunny an appraising glance. "You're okay with that?"

"With what?"

"With them moving here. Not everyone wants their in-laws so close by."

"In-laws." Sunny gave a delighted laugh. "I'm going to have *in-laws*. Piper is going to have grandparents. Oh, Adam, I'm so excited. We're going to be a family."

"Yes, we are. Have you given any thought to when? Do you want a big wedding? Or something simple?"

"Yes, and yes. Something simple, but I want to invite all the residents. How do you feel about a Christmas wedding?"

"Could we really do that? I understand weddings take a long time to plan."

"Well, that's true of most weddings, but not everyone has the resources I do. The Mat Mates have all offered to help. Remember, these are the same people who put on that craft fair."

"Good point. Will Bea use her Clydesdales to bring you to the wedding?"

"I'm sure she will if we ask. I wonder what color her hair will be."

Adam laughed. "I suspect it will be whatever color you choose. She would do most anything for you. All of them would. They love you, Sunny." He leaned over to give her another sweet kiss. "And so do I."

* * * * *

Get 4 FREE REWARDS!

We'll send you 2 FREE Books plus <u>2</u> FREE Mystery Gifts.

FREE
Value Over
$20

Both the **Love Inspired®** and **Love Inspired® Suspense** series feature compelling novels filled with inspirational romance, faith, forgiveness, and hope.

YES! Please send me 2 FREE novels from the Love Inspired or Love Inspired Suspense series and my 2 FREE gifts (gifts are worth about $10 retail). After receiving them, if I don't wish to receive any more books, I can return the shipping statement marked "cancel." If I don't cancel, I will receive 6 brand-new Love Inspired Larger-Print books or Love Inspired Suspense Larger-Print books every month and be billed just $6.24 each in the U.S. or $6.49 each in Canada. That is a savings of at least 17% off the cover price. It's quite a bargain! Shipping and handling is just 50¢ per book in the U.S. and $1.25 per book in Canada.* I understand that accepting the 2 free books and gifts places me under no obligation to buy anything. I can always return a shipment and cancel at any time by calling the number below. The free books and gifts are mine to keep no matter what I decide.

Choose one: ☐ **Love Inspired**
Larger-Print
(122/322 IDN GRDF)

☐ **Love Inspired Suspense**
Larger-Print
(107/307 IDN GRDF)

Name (please print)

Address   Apt. #

City   State/Province   Zip/Postal Code

Email: Please check this box ☐ if you would like to receive newsletters and promotional emails from Harlequin Enterprises ULC and its affiliates. You can unsubscribe anytime.

Mail to the **Harlequin Reader Service:**
IN U.S.A.: P.O. Box 1341, Buffalo, NY 14240-8531
IN CANADA: P.O. Box 603, Fort Erie, Ontario L2A 5X3

Want to try 2 free books from another series? Call 1-800-873-8635 or visit www.ReaderService.com.

LIRLIS22R2

COUNTRY LEGACY COLLECTION

COUNTRY

COUNTRY

COUNTRY

EMMETT
Diana Palmer

COURTED BY THE COWBOY

THE RANCHER AND THE BABY

Cowboys, adventure and romance await you in this new collection! Enjoy superb reading all year long with books by bestselling authors like Diana Palmer, Sasha Summers and Marie Ferrarella!

YES! Please send me the **Country Legacy Collection!** This collection begins with 3 FREE books and 2 FREE gifts in the first shipment. Along with my 3 free books, I'll also get 3 more books from the **Country Legacy Collection**, which I may either return and owe nothing or keep for the low price of $24.60 U.S./$28.12 CDN each plus $2.99 U.S./$7.49 CDN for shipping and handling per shipment*. If I decide to continue, about once a month for 8 months, I will get 6 or 7 more books but will only pay for 4. That means 2 or 3 books in every shipment will be FREE! If I decide to keep the entire collection, I'll have paid for only 32 books because 19 are FREE! I understand that accepting the 3 free books and gifts places me under no obligation to buy anything. I can always return a shipment and cancel at any time. My free books and gifts are mine to keep no matter what I decide.

☐ 275 HCK 1939   ☐ 475 HCK 1939

Name (please print)

Address   Apt. #

City   State/Province   Zip/Postal Code

Mail to the Harlequin Reader Service:
IN U.S.A.: P.O. Box 1341, Buffalo, NY 14240-8571
IN CANADA: P.O. Box 603, Fort Erie, Ontario L2A 5X3

COMING NEXT MONTH FROM

HARLEQUIN
HEARTWARMING

#447 WYOMING CHRISTMAS REUNION
The Blackwells of Eagle Springs • by Melinda Curtis

Horse trainer Nash Blackwell's life-altering accident was...well, just that. He wants to rebuild. The first step is winning back his ex-wife, Helen Blackwell. Can trust once broken be regained?

#448 THE CHRISTMAS WEDDING CRASHERS
Stop the Wedding! • by Amy Vastine

Jonah Drake's grandmother will marry Holly Hayward's great-uncle—unless Holly and Jonah can stop them! The family feud is too unyielding for peace now, even at Christmas. Working together is their only option...but love brings new possibilities.

#449 THE DOC'S HOLIDAY HOMECOMING
Back to Adelaide Creek • by Virginia McCullough

Jeff Stanhope's focus is family. He's the new guardian to a teenager—and trying to mend things with his estranged sister. The last thing he needs is to start falling for her best friend, single mom Olivia Donoghue.

#450 A COWBOY'S CHRISTMAS JOY
Flaming Sky Ranch • by Mary Anne Wilson

Caleb Donovan needs Harmony Gabriel. The event planner can throw his parents a wedding anniversary like no other, though she shows up for the job with her baby girl. Caleb has all the family he needs...but soon he *wants* more.

YOU CAN FIND MORE INFORMATION ON UPCOMING HARLEQUIN TITLES, FREE EXCERPTS AND MORE AT HARLEQUIN.COM.

HWCNM1022

HARLEQUIN
PLUS

Announcing a **BRAND-NEW** multimedia subscription service for romance fans like you!

Read, Watch and Play.

Experience the easiest way to get the romance content you crave.

Start your **FREE 7 DAY TRIAL** at
<u>www.harlequinplus.com/freetrial</u>.